THE MYSTERIOUS MARQUESS

THE BAD HEIR DAY TALES—BOOK TWO

GRACE BURROWES

GRACE BURROWES PUBLISHING

DEDICATION

To the Old Guard of any age

CHAPTER ONE

Lucien Pritchard's favorite chess piece was the rook, formerly referred to as the chariot or the marquess. The rook began the game in the corner of the board, the whole battlefield open to his view. As a war prize, his value exceeded that of even the queen.

Lucien's opponent, one Leopold St. Didier, was in danger of losing his queen's rook to a lowly pawn. The match was of no moment to the other gentlemen gathered in the club's subdued opulence, merely an idle contest between two of the quieter members.

Lucien knew better. "You are distracted," he said when St. Didier moved a bishop rather than implement the obvious defensive strategy.

"You are too polite to suggest I forfeit, and you are right." St. Didier tipped over his king. "I am distracted. I saw the ring."

"I beg your pardon?" Lucien's question was casual, but those four words—*I saw the ring*—filled him with frustration. He returned his army to its opening formation, taking care to move the pieces in rank order and without haste.

"The lion rampant." St. Didier allowed his defeated forces to languish on their squares.

"The lion of England. A ring is a sentimental affectation, St. Didier. When one leaves Albion's shores, little reminders of home take on comforting significance."

"And my lord left these shores nearly ten years ago. What brought you back?"

My lord. *Plagues and afflictions.* "A sailing ship brought me back, and another might soon carry me away again."

"My lord excels at the tactical retreat." St. Didier extended a hand across the chessboard, the polite gesture signaling defeat.

Lucien shook when he'd rather have upended the board. "The lion rampant is probably the most common device in British heraldry." He set about restoring proper order to St. Didier's vanquished pieces.

"But your lion rampant is in the attitude sinister rather than the traditional dexter, and that caught my eye."

Lucien had worn the signet ring only once in recent months, to a gathering hosted by the Dowager Duchess of Huntleigh and attended by her nephew—who happened to be the present duke and Lucien's employer—and that fellow's new bride. St. Didier had been in attendance as well, damn the luck.

"Say what you have to say, St. Didier. Whether a decorative creature faces left or right is hardly of any moment. You did not invite me to this table for the sake of a passing diversion." Though to be fair, St. Didier played well, albeit conservatively.

"You were a decorative creature once," St. Didier replied. "A marquess's heir. One wonders what turned you up so difficult and contrary."

"I am contrary by nature." Lucien wasn't yet thirty, but he abruptly felt as weary as a spavined coach horse. "What does great-auntie want now?"

"She wants you home, where you belong, managing the family's affairs. I am not here on her behalf."

Of all the cousins, in-laws, step-relations, and impersonators thereof at Lynnfield, only one individual interested Lucien significantly.

"Who put you on my trail?" Lucien braced himself for disappointment, and yet, hope stirred as well.

St. Didier's calling was to discreetly locate missing, distant, and otherwise obscure heirs on behalf of titled families in want of same. He knew the arcana of inheritance, legitimacy, and royal patents, and he'd recently rescued the Huntleigh dukedom from the near occasion of escheat.

Leopold St. Didier knew Society's scandals and was himself the scion of a house relieved of its honors for want of a proper heir.

"Lady Penelope asked me to locate you," St. Didier said, picking up the black queen. "She sends her regards."

What the rubbishing hell did that mean? "Please convey my greetings to her ladyship in return."

Lucien waited for whatever came next. A request for funds, word of some elder's failing health, a warning that Auntie was growing dotty. Pen would be that decent, he hoped. He would be decent enough to respond civilly too.

"Her ladyship is troubled by a legal matter," St. Didier said. "You can solve it for her."

Once upon a time, Lucien would have surrendered his life for Penelope's happiness. He would still die to keep her safe and, in a sense, nearly had.

"St. Didier, you try my patience. The hour grows late for a mere majordomo. My solicitors have always known how to reach me."

"Her ladyship dislikes confiding in what she refers to as a boogle of long-winded weasels."

Her ladyship was apparently still outspoken. Good for her. "She sometimes called them a sneak of weasels," Lucien replied and immediately regretted it. "Both terms are correct."

St. Didier wasn't given to smiling, but his dark eyes gleamed with apparent amusement. "The solicitors drafted your betrothal agreements, and you and the lady signed them."

"We were *told* to sign them." *Ordered* to sign them. "Both of us were yet in our minorities, so the agreement was never binding on us." Lucien had consulted independent counsel to confirm that fact before leaving England.

"Just so. You were both underage, and now you have both attained your majorities."

A cold, sad feeling took up residence in the center of Lucien's chest. "Her ladyship is free to do as she pleases." She always had been, did she but know it.

"You will execute a formal repudiation of the betrothal agreement?"

"Of course." The pain in Lucien's chest congealed into sorrow, but cutting the last tie was doubtless for the best.

"Her ladyship thanks you."

Lucien plucked the black queen from St. Didier's grasp and put the piece on its proper square. "She has nothing to thank me for. Send me the relevant documents, and I will append my signature before witnesses."

"As it happens, I have the papers with me now."

Lucien had known this day would come, but he hadn't known it would come under the guise of a friendly game of chess at a quiet club for gentlemen of slightly awkward standing. Younger sons, former MPs voted out after a single term, wealthy gentlemen whose fathers had been in trade... The Marches was a place for those whom Society tolerated rather than accepted.

Signing a repudiation would be one more step away from the past, a step Lucien should have been eager to take.

Should have been... "If you intend to witness my signature," he said, "we still need two more witnesses to appease the formalities. I cannot allow my ancient history to become common knowledge here." A delaying tactic—strategic retreats usually were—also a valid concern. These men knew him as Pritchard, general factotum of the new Duke of Huntleigh, not as a marquess's heir who'd disappeared from Society years ago.

St. Didier paused, withdrawing an empty hand from the breast of his evening coat. "My apologies. Discretion is warranted for the lady's sake if not for yours. You are right again."

"Come around tomorrow," Lucien said, minutely relieved to have order established on the chessboard. "The ducal abode is deadly dull now that Their Graces have taken ship. I am to have tea with the dowager later in the day, but I can attend you any time before noon."

Before polite society was out and about, enjoying the increasingly temperate weather and the increasing stores of gossip to be gathered in the shops and on the bridle paths.

"Tomorrow, then. You are being unexpectedly reasonable."

Pen had anticipated a fight? "I wish her ladyship every happiness. You may tell her as much. Another game would suit."

St. Didier obliged, but the game did not suit Lucien at all. Too many games played with Penelope—chess, backgammon, and even kissing games—crowded onto the field of memory. Lucien won none-theless. He usually won.

Not all the time, though. Pen had been a fiend for the sneak attack. A queen in her hands was the equal of any rook. Did she still play? If she didn't, that would be a shame, but against whom could she aim all that skill and guile?

"Twice defeated," St. Didier said some thirty minutes later. "I must give some thought to my strategies. Shall we enjoy the night air while the rain has let up?"

God, yes. Solitude beckoned. Solitude and the decanters. "You didn't bring your coach?"

"I like to walk. I'm not the inveterate perambulator that Huntleigh is, but neither am I sedentary by nature."

St. Didier was given to prowling, stalking, and noticing, all the while pretending to be just another serious, dark-haired gent blessed with skilled tailors and some means.

When he and Lucien reached the street, mist diffused the lamplight, and the hour—neither late nor early—meant no wheeled traffic rattled along on the cobbles.

A good night for sorrowing. "How is she?" Lucien asked when they were two streets away from the club and the lamps were farther apart.

"Lady Penelope? She's robust, astute, formidable."

Pen was also pretty, but nobody noticed that in the face of her intellect and personality. "Does she laugh?" A younger Lucien had delighted to inspire her laughter.

"I cannot say. Our dealings have been largely by letter. When I did meet with her, she appeared to be thriving. Very certain of her objectives."

Too certain, sometimes. Stubborn, heedless... all the shortcomings she'd ascribed so credibly to Lucien, though he was, in fact, the soul of reason under most circumstances.

"Give her my regards. I'm around the corner here. Good night, St. Didier. Your discretion is appreciated."

"Spoken like a peer, if you don't mind my saying so. Are you sure you don't want to make a short visit to Lynnfield to discuss the situation with her ladyship?"

"I know my own mind, sir." And knew better than to clap eyes on Penelope at any distance less than twenty yards. "Good night, St. Didier."

"Until tomorrow."

They bowed and parted, but a question occurred to Lucien, one he could ask no other. He retraced his steps lest he shout his query into the London darkness.

"I assume Lady Penelope is tending to these legalities at long last because she has marriage in mind," he observed, trying for nonchalance. "Who is the lucky fellow?"

"Hmm? Oh, the lucky fellow. Well, they aren't engaged, of course, given the betrothal agreement with you, but the churchyard speculators allow that her ladyship has been saving her waltzes for Sir Dashiel Ingraham. Not a love match, one notes, but very cordial."

Lucien was grateful for the darkness. "I see." He saw Penelope smiling up into the face of an Adonis who would never be worthy of her and, in fact, wasn't worthy of a baronet's honors either. "Sir Dashiel Ingraham."

"He's home from the wars, considered quite the catch, and the two of them do seem to get on."

Sir Dashiel excelled at getting on. He'd even managed to leave the military without being court-martialed for his crimes.

St. Didier arranged a claret-colored scarf about his neck. "Shall we say ten of the clock tomorrow?"

That scarf—a red flag against otherwise subdued attire—caught Lucien's eye. Penelope was forthright to a fault, not given to subterfuge, much less subtlety. Lucien had loved that about her.

Appreciated that about her, rather, and yet, his chess master's imagination considered it just possible that Pen had got herself into a situation involving Sir Dashiel that wasn't quite what it appeared to be.

Or perhaps it was exactly what it appeared to be: an impending courtship between two adults, who would make a fine, cordial match.

But Sir Dashiel Ingraham... Lucien's soul rebelled at the very thought. Years ago, Penelope had been unwilling to trust the good intentions of a young man she'd considered her best friend. What did Sir Dashiel offer that Lucien had lacked?

"You can send the documents over," he said, "but don't bother coming around. I'll be looking in on Lynnfield, after all. The legalities can wait a few days."

St. Didier offered a slight bow. "Very good, my lord. I am at your service if you'd like a traveling companion." He walked off into the night.

"Don't milord me," Lucien muttered as St. Didier's footsteps faded.

Lucien turned the opposite direction and considered the decision he'd just made. He'd hear nothing but milording at Lynnfield, that and Auntie's lectures and importuning. If he could hear Penelope's laughter, though...

Well, no. Best all around not to hear Penelope's laughter. All that was in the past.

The rain resumed, and Lucien marched for the deserted house he'd lately been calling home.

"Why now?" Tommie groused, laboring slightly in the cool morning air. "Why does the blighter have to come home after all these years? Lynnfield runs fine without him lurking in the library at all hours."

Tommie was being loyal, and Lady Penelope Richard appreciated loyalty. "Lucien is our marquess, Tom. We hoped he'd come home sooner or later." *Hoped* wasn't quite the right word. *Dreaded* might be closer to the mark.

Penelope smiled at the pair of gardeners wrestling a potted peach tree into its designated corner of the garden. The younger of the two tugged his cap. The elder merely nodded.

"You defend him," Tom muttered. "For pity's sake, Penny, slow down. Last I heard, ladies were to move about with languid grace, fluttering their fans and making sheep's eyes at the nearest bachelor. That would be me, by the way, but if you insist on dashing the entire distance to the stable, you'll find yourself quite without my handsome and charming escort."

Tommie was flustered, bless him. The whole Lynnfield miscellany, from the marchioness down to Aunt Purdy, was abuzz with news of Lucien's return, and thus the staff and neighbors were abuzz. Even the pantry mouser had been tearing about the kitchens in an unseemly display when Penelope and Tom had made their escape.

"His lordship won't turn you out," Penelope said, slowing marginally as they passed from the garden onto the path that led to the stable. "He'll not turn anybody out. One word to the solicitors at any point, and we'd all have been banished from the property."

"Not you. Her ladyship wouldn't allow that. She couldn't manage without you. Why can't gentlemen be ladies' companions? We don't get megrims, we are pleasant to look upon, we are endlessly diverting when provided with an appreciative audience, and we are handy when a bit of muscle is needed."

Tom was pleasant to look at—merely pleasant. His features were friendly rather than handsome, and he could be diverting when he wasn't so desperately worried. He would have made a jolly squire, with his blond hair, blue eyes, and solid construction, but he suffered the sad lack of funds that struck many an otherwise worthy fellow from the rolls of the eligibles.

"You will always be welcome to bide at Finbury," Penelope said, though she'd rather he didn't. "The dower cottage sits empty, and you'd enliven the neighborhood considerably."

"Kind of you, Penny." A hint of masculine peevishness conveyed both relief and resentment. "Why does everything smell like shit, pardon my language? The whole shire reeks."

"Because in spring, Thomas, we clean out the byres, sheds, and muck pits and spread the manure on the fields, the better to grow our corn and clover." He ought to know that, but Thomas, raised as a gentleman and more interested in fashion than farming, likely thought eggs grew on trees.

"I take it you've forgiven his lordship for jilting you?" Thomas asked as the path wound across a corner of the park.

"The marquess did not jilt me."

"Suppose he hasn't. You're still technically betrothed to him, aren't you? Does a betrothal expire? Is it like taking the king's shilling? You are free to turn your back on the whole business after a time certain?"

The morning was lovely, the dew sparkling on the grass, the birds in full chorus, and the trees showing the luminous green that spoke of leaves not entirely unfurled. A good morning for a solitary gallop, but there had been Thomas, lurking in the kitchen hallway, as if he, too, needed to avoid breakfast *en famille*.

"The solicitors will sort out any lingering legalities," Penelope said. "I'd appreciate it if you didn't mention old business to Sir Dashiel."

Thomas stopped to pick a daffodil and slip the stem through the buttonhole on the lapel of his riding jacket.

"I'll be silent as Uncle Malcolm, and I will tell the rest of the elders to do likewise. I'd like to give our marquess a piece of my mind, though. Leaving you all but at the altar, no word, no apology. Lucien has a nerve strutting back here like he owns the place."

He did own the place, in point of fact. "I bear the marquess no malice, Tommy. We were too young for marriage anyway." By Penelope's standards. By Society's standards, they'd been plenty old enough.

"Were you secretly relieved when Lucien bolted? You can tell me, Many Penny. Were you grateful for room to breathe before you took on the Lady Lynnfield folderol? You hadn't had even one proper Season at that point, if I recall. The marquess was rushing his fences, but that's what university boys do. I speak from experience."

Thomas had lasted two years at university before being sent down the final time for drunkenness. The real offense had been lewd behavior, a euphemism for taking a bet to pelt along the banks of the River Cherwell *sans vêtements.*

Tom had won the bet, likely the last income he'd enjoyed since taking up residence at Lynnfield, and the last time he'd exerted himself at speed anywhere save a dessert buffet.

"You needn't ride with me," Penelope said, ignoring Tom's attempts to pry into the past. "I'm only out for a hack around the orchards."

The cherry trees were blooming, a sight to cheer up any morose soul, not that Penelope was feeling morose.

"You didn't answer my question. You were glad to see Lucien go, weren't you? I certainly was. He's too dour by half. All that chess and reading, and the French and Latin and Italian. I don't think he realized what language he spoke half the time. One worried for his reason, and then to disappear... Not the done thing, Penny dearest. Even you must admit as much. An impecunious old baron might get away with that nonsense, but not a marquess who has no heir. Then to remain gone for years and to lark about a continent at war. The Deity gave us a brainbox. Somebody should have reminded Lord Lynnfield of that salient fact."

Tom's precarious status at Lynnfield would inspire him to needle, pontificate, and fret without ceasing. His worry was legitimate. Lynnfield was home to more mooching aunties, unrelated "cousins," and long-term visitors than Windsor Castle.

But Penelope needed peace, and for once, she intended to get what she needed. "I have a job for you, Tom. I can't entrust it to anybody else."

They emerged from a hedgerow to behold the stable, a stately building shaped like a two-story U. The same gray granite quarried for the manor was in evidence here. Grooms were watering horses before turning them out for a morning at grass. A chestnut mare with a golden foal mincing at her side cropped grass under the shade of a gauzy maple.

I will miss this, if Lucien sends us all away. The thought struck from nowhere, borne on piercingly bright beams of spring sunshine and redolent of pastoral contentment.

"What's this errand, Penny? Will it take me to Town? I could use an excuse to nip up to London if Lucien intends to make a plague of himself here."

"We'd best accustom ourselves to calling him Lord Lynnfield. Might you trot over to the Ingrahams' and let Dashiel know the news? He should hear it from us, though I'm sure word has already made the rounds in the village."

"Suppose you're right. You don't want to tell him yourself?"

"That would make the whole business too important. Lucien is Lord Lynnfield. That he's looking in on the family seat is only to be expected. He won't realize this means every menu will have to be revised, the bouquets changed more frequently, the library dusted more regularly. If those tasks are to be tended to, I'll need to meet with the housekeeper, butler, and gardeners. We're to have a distinguished guest for an unspecified period, and arrangements must be made"

"Righty-ho. Hasn't anything to do with you, other than counting out the fresh linens and candles. A triviality wrapped in a nothingness tied up with complete indifference. Wouldn't want Dash to worry. You are shrewder than you look, my girl."

I am not a girl. I am not yours. "Thank you, Tommie. I knew I could count on you."

He strode off, bellowing for a groom to fetch his horse, though the horse was not, in fact, his.

Ten minutes later, Penelope settled onto her mare, thanked the groom, and guided her mount from the stable yard at a walk. Lucien had left on a brisk and brilliant morning like this, cantering over the hill without a backward glance.

Had he bothered to look behind him, he'd have seen Penelope, standing alone at the orchard gate, silently wishing him Godspeed at the same time she'd longed to call him back. Whatever else had been true, she hadn't been ready for marriage, especially to Lucien.

She could admit that now, to herself at least.

For half an hour, Penelope put her mare through her paces, and as always, Ursuline was game. They hopped a few stiles for form's sake, then cooled out on the bridle path that ran between the mill and the cherry orchard.

When Penelope reached her destination, she dismounted with a sense of having found a small store of peace. The blossoms were a canopy of white, the air graced with hints of almond, rose, and vanilla. She let the mare steal a few mouthfuls of grass—bad manners, that—and perched on the low stone wall encircling the orchard.

Penelope closed her eyes, the tranquility of the surrounds sinking into her mind and body. If she married Dashiel—*if* she married him, very much *if*—her solitary hacking days would be over. Dash had earned his Town bronze, and he'd cut a swath as an officer, but in a wife, he'd expect the traditional version of decorous behavior. That predictable hypocrisy should not annoy Penelope, but it most assuredly did. Too much like dear Henry, God rest his strutting soul.

"You still come here."

Penelope opened her eyes. The voice was both familiar and different. Deeper than she recalled Lucien's voice being, the hint of an accent all but gone. Not French, as most people thought, though Lucien was fluent in French, but the Welsh that vined through and around his whole ancestry.

She rose and turned, keeping the low wall between them. Lucien stood, bareheaded, two yards off. The sight of him gladdened her heart at the same time it nudged at long-dormant rage.

"Do you still hide among the trees, Lucien?"

His expression subtly shuttered, not that Lucien had ever been an open book. "You were preoccupied and did not notice me in the shade. You are looking well, my lady."

The honorific was bracing. She'd been Pen to him as far back as she could recall. "As are you, my lord." He looked older, of course. Leaner, wearier, and *bigger*. Lucien had shot up to six feet by the time he'd turned fifteen and had added a bit more in the subsequent years, but he'd remained wiry and lanky in his youth. Since then, he'd put on muscle, particularly in the chest and shoulders, though his thighs had always been...

Penelope pretended to fiddle with her skirts, though she wore a plain, country riding habit. No great billows of fabric swirled about her boots. No clever hooks or loops were needed to make walking possible.

Lucien prowled close enough that Penelope could see the golden flecks in his blue eyes. His dark hair was longer than he'd worn it as a younger man and had acquired reddish highlights. He gazed down at her, a serious, exquisitely attired stranger who bore a resemblance to an old and much-missed friend.

The impression was unnerving, which inspired Penelope to marshal her composure. How dare he intrude on one of her rare moments of solitude? How dare he ambush her when she'd desperately needed privacy and peace?

"Are we to be awkward with each other, my lady?" His question was utterly neutral.

"We are to be cordial," Penelope said, looking for some sign that this remote, lordly creature had at one time been her Lucien. The marquess she beheld was not a happy man. She could deduce that much, and she steeled her heart against the questions raised by such a conclusion.

"One is relieved to hear it." He let out a single shrill whistle, and a leggy black gelding trotted up from the direction of the mill. "Lady Penelope, may I make known to you Lorenzo the Magnificent. If you have contemplated the splendors of nature sufficiently for the nonce, I can give you a leg up."

She wanted to give him a black eye—and to ask what troubled him. "Are you offering to escort me back to the stable yard like some neighbor who just happened to cross my path by the trout pond?"

Lucien occupied himself taking up his horse's girth two holes. "I thought we might ride back to the manor together."

He was apparently still a bad liar, a small consolation. "They've missed you, my lord. The marchioness has already had the marquess's suite aired. The prodigal son did not receive as sincere a welcome as you will."

He ceased fussing with his saddle. "That bothers you?"

In a subtle, easily denied way, he was inviting her to *talk*, and in that direction lay perils without number.

"If you leave the past alone, Lucien, I will do likewise. I was barely out of the schoolroom when last we saw each other, and we are all but strangers now."

He studied her for an interminable moment, and she studied him back. He'd not only aged, he'd *matured*, and Lucien had never been frivolous by nature. A stubborn youth had become an implacable man, despite all the fine tailoring and politesse.

"I regret causing you any sorrow, my lady, if, in fact, I did."

Penelope perceived for the first time that they might, perhaps, somehow, have caused *each other* sorrow. That suspicion made no sense, but Lucien was guarding sadness behind his vast reserves of dignity. She'd have bet the whole cherry crop that his remorse was genuine.

"Likewise, my lord. No more need be said on the matter." She tugged her mare forward, used the wall as a mounting block, got herself into the saddle after only minimal awkwardness, and took up the reins.

Lucien swung onto his gelding, and Penelope set a placid pace for the manor. She needed time to think, to adjust, to recover. The blighter hadn't been expected for hours, and yet, here he was, looking all lordly and impressive.

For just a moment, when she'd first beheld him on the far side of the wall, she'd been tempted to yank off her glove and slap his lordly face. He had all but jilted her, he hadn't left her a word of explanation, and now he was back with the barest scintilla of an apology.

And he had the nerve to be attractive too. Not quite handsome—he was too sharp-featured for that—but attractive.

She'd wanted to slap him, hard.

She'd also wanted to hug the breath right out of him, and that bothered her all the way back to the stable. Ursuline had not even been led away before the marquess's arrival precipitated general jollification. Amid much shaking of hands and backslapping among the assembled males, Penelope slipped into the shadows and left his lordship to enjoy his triumphant return without her.

Let him be reminded of what abandonment felt like, even if only to a minor degree.

CHAPTER TWO

"Who were all those people I was introduced to at luncheon?" St. Didier asked as Lucien wandered beside the bookcases lining the library's longest inside wall.

St. Didier had met about half the current crop, by Lucien's reckoning. "Friends and relatives. Mind your valuables around Aunt Purdy. Despite her harmless appearance, she is an adept and compulsive thief, though the goods are always returned. The marchioness did not sell off my books. I am inordinately gratified to see that her threats were hollow."

The philosophers still had pride of place in the first bookcase, Greek, then Roman, then Church, followed by the poets in historical order. Biographies gathered dust beside histories, and unbound plays going yellow about the edges shared shelves with translations.

Charles Jarvis's attempt to render *The Ingenious Gentleman Don Quixote of La Mancha* in English had prompted Lucien to learn Spanish.

"More friends than relatives," St. Didier remarked, taking down a volume at random. "I had occasion to familiarize myself with your ancestry. Why do so many of your forebearers have the surname Richard?"

"Because *ap Rhisiart*, or *ap Richard* becomes Pritchard when you're a Welshman trying to curry favor with your English cousins, or Richard, Richardson, Ricard, even Picard if you find yourself in France. Those relatives you met at luncheon are here because they had nowhere else to go. Somebody moved my translation of *Don Quixote*."

St. Didier sniffed the open pages of his selection. "Don Quixote was like that, always moving about. Do you support all these friends and relatives?"

"The estate does. You'll meet a few more at dinner." Most of them were not much changed. Aunt Purdy was still small, dithery, and given to wearing a yellow bandeau in her white hair. Uncle Malcolm hadn't spoken a word when he'd laid eyes on Lucien, albeit nobody had heard him speak for decades. Malcolm's white hair was longer, and his eyebrows were as fierce as ever.

He had bowed and shaken hands at length, conveying as much welcome with his silence as Aunt Purdy had with all her fluttering. Cousin Tommie hadn't been in evidence, but then, he wasn't much in evidence even when present, as best Lucien recalled.

"More at dinner?" St. Didier snapped the book closed. "Do you collect eccentric relations? Lady Penelope is sensible in the extreme, but she seems to be the exception."

Penelope was exceptional in many regards, or she had been. The woman Lucien had met that morning in the orchard resembled the Penelope of his youth in only general particulars. Russet hair, now confined in a chignon rather than flying about in all directions. A sturdy physique had grown slender through the waist and been all primmed up in a military-style riding habit. Even her voice had lost the melodious quality of the native Welsh speaker and clipped itself like English privet into precise angles and controlled volumes.

The young Pen had been sensible when it suited her, outlandish when that suited her better. She'd worn men's hats and been a better shot than the gamekeeper, though she'd never aimed a weapon at a living creature.

To a younger Lucien, she'd been fascinating, wonderful, and terrifying by turns, but that girl was no longer biding at Lynnfield, which should have been a relief.

"At supper," Lucien said, "you will meet Aunts Phoebe and Wren, and Cousin Lark, who styles herself their companion. Do not stand up with any of them at the spring assembly, because they will dance and drink you under the table. They dwell in the dower house by choice—the aviary in family parlance—but won't miss supper at the manor tonight. Uncle Theodore will escort them over. He bides with Malcolm and Purdy in the family wing and has a legendarily hard head."

St. Didier reshelved his book—*Lord Chesterfield's Letters to His Son*—among the philosophers. "None of these people show up on the official genealogy by which you inherited the title."

That St. Didier had gone a-snooping to such a degree was to be expected. Polite society paid him handsomely to snoop and sniff about, provided he was at all times discreet. That he could recall a family tree he'd likely seen once, months ago, was unnerving.

"The people biding at Lynnfield showed up on the doorstep," Lucien retorted, "in search of shelter and sustenance. What is family for, if not to take us in when we've nowhere else to go? They might be step-relations, in-laws, or informally associated with the titled branch, but they are family."

St. Didier frowned at the translations. "I am not in a position to comment on the various species of family, much less their purpose, having so little of my own. You have a large and interesting collection of books to go with your collection of relatives. When will I get to meet the marchioness?"

"Before supper. Auntie is keeping her powder dry. Letting me develop a false sense of calm. We gather for conversation in the music room prior to the evening meal, and she holds court for half an hour. Tonight, we will dress, though by the time I left, dressing for dinner even on Sunday was becoming a rule more honored in the breach than the observance."

"*Hamlet*," St. Didier said, perusing the plays. "When will you sign the documents that rescind your betrothal to Lady Penelope?"

The single word *never* popped into Lucien's mind. He nudged it away as he would a half-grown canine who had yet to acquire manners. *Down, boy.*

"As it happens, the lady and I encountered each other this morning. The subject did not come up. When I am satisfied that Lady Penelope is making a sensible choice, I will accommodate her request."

St. Didier selected a book on famous chess strategies. "She's of age, my lord, and knows her own mind. You have no authority over her, and she can take the matter to the courts if you prove obstinate."

"She's also unhappy," Lucien said, though prior to this conversation, he had not applied that label to her ladyship. Serious, mature, reserved... no true pejoratives, unless compared to the younger Penelope.

Who had been vital, intense, passionate, by turns hilarious and profound.

"You fear she'll leap into marriage simply to win free of Lynnfield?" St. Didier asked, sniffing the chess monograph.

"A woman could make a greater mistake." So could a man. "I'd like to discuss the situation with her. Our first encounter did not lend itself to the topic. I'm not refusing her request, but neither will I execute the documents without establishing the lady's motives for presenting them to me now."

St. Didier took a visual inventory of the library, probably a habit with him to study and memorize surroundings.

"I hope you aren't given to dueling, my lord. I can serve as a creditable second, but the practice is foolish and has landed more than one family in misery and penury."

The comment, while casual, suggested at least one of St. Didier's titled ancestors had counted among the fools.

"I have been home less than a day, St. Didier. I exchanged barely a hundred words with my former intended, and those were the merest platitudes. I have yet to make my bow before my aunt, and I am tired. Let the matter rest, please."

Lucien infused his request with a touch of lord-of-the-manor and a touch of sincerity. He was tired—exhausted—and not only because they'd taken rooms at the village posting inn well after midnight.

"Lady Penelope is tired too," St. Didier said. "One sees it in her eyes, hears it in her silences. She's been running the place in your absence, would be my guess, while letting the marchioness pretend to hold the reins. You had best offer the lady your thanks for that bit of heroism before you pull any dog-in-the-manger behaviors with the betrothal."

"I'll thank you not to imply that I've been negligent, St. Didier. I kept my own hand on the reins."

St. Didier tucked his book under his arm. "You kept in touch with the solicitors and bankers. You did not sort out menus or plan entertainments. You did not settle squabbles among the vast horde of elders. You did not hire and sack staff or listen to the gardeners maunder on about smut and beetles. You were kicking your heels in Italy, growing rich trading in art while transforming your employer into a gentleman. You owe Lady Penelope her freedom, and while I am not keen on serving as a second, I am handy with both a pistol and a sword. Until supper, my lord."

St. Didier left without bowing, suggesting that he, the perpetually detached observer of a Society that no longer welcomed him, had meant every word.

"I meant every word too," Lucien muttered to the empty room. "Pen's unhappy, and she was unhappy before she caught sight of me today." So very unhappy that she'd been on the point of tears in the orchard, and that, too, was a change.

The younger Penelope had disdained tears. Who had given the lady reason to cry, and why had she sought the orchard—their favorite retreat once upon a time—to hide her tears?

"Good of you to pass along the news in person," Sir Dashiel Ingraham said, clapping Tommie on the back. "We aren't all as gifted with your delicate sense of consideration, old chap. I hope the roast met with your approval?"

Tommie had found the roast a bit tough, by Lynnfield standards, but the company at luncheon had been excellent: the baronet; his pretty youngest sister, Tabitha; the vicar; and his twin daughters. Sir Dashiel had insisted that Tommie stay for the meal to balance the numbers and add some refinement to *the usual bucolic blather*.

The marquess wasn't expected at Lynnfield until later in the day. Otherwise, Tommie would have demurred. Would not do to snub the great man upon his return home after years abroad. Besides, one wanted to form one's own impression on such an occasion, Uncle Theodore being an unreliable reporter, at best.

Tommie accepted his riding gloves and spurs from his host. "You deserved to know that the shire's ranking title is deigning to put in an appearance at the family seat. Can't have his lordship ambushing you in the churchyard."

Sir Dashiel patted Tommie's back yet again. "As a fellow who's acquired some experience of the world, you grasp these subtleties. In the military, unless we were in parade dress, our sense of decorum endured regular beatings, and the lordlings were often the most in want of dignity. But then, Lynnfield never served, so I must not attribute to him an officer's sense of mischief."

No, his lordship had not bought his colors. Tommie had often wondered what exactly the marquess had been about, traveling around the Continent in a time of war when the man had no heir. Lynnfield wasn't the sort to volunteer explanations, and he was a bit off in the attic. Too much education was the problem. That, and the natural Welsh tendency toward peculiarity.

"The marquess was overdue for an appearance," Tommie said, bracing himself on the sideboard to buckle on a spur. "Been least in

sight for years. The old girl was nearly out of patience with him."
Tommie had the gratifying sense that Penny was none too happy
with his lordship either, though her reasons might differ from the
marchioness's.

"Between us," Sir Dashiel said, "the man has much to answer for.
That assemblage of oddities at the manor doesn't exactly raise the
tone of the neighborhood, does it?"

Tommie apparently did not number among those oddities, at
least in the baronet's estimation. Let it be said, Sir Dashiel was a man
of discernment.

"They're a harmless lot," Tommie replied, though such a weak
defense of the elders felt disloyal. "I rather enjoy them, for the most
part." Uncle Malcolm's company was restful, and Uncle Theodore
had a key to the wine cellars that came in handy when the molly-
grubs threatened.

"You are too kind," Sir Dashiel said as Tommie affixed his second
spur to a boot. "I do believe the vicar's younger daughter was making
sheep's eyes at you over luncheon, my friend. The ladies know the
genuine article from the yokel edition."

"Miss Hannah is barely out of the schoolroom." She had, though,
smiled shyly at Tommie any number of times—as had Miss Tabitha
when her fingers had brushed Tommie's while passing the peas. Such
a different sort of meal from the usual melee at the Hall. One could
engage the whole table in polite chat, enjoy the food such as it was,
and take one's time.

Quiet, pleasant, free of the sort of jokes in bad taste that Uncle
Theo let loose to amuse and annoy the ladies. The food was better at
the Hall, though, as was the wine.

"You had best give a good account of yourself at the assembly,"
Sir Dashiel said, winking. "The ladies of the shire will go into a
collective decline if you sit out so much as one dance. They know I'm
spoken for, so you have become the object of all their maidenly aspirations. A thankless post, I know, but you must bear up manfully."

Sir Dashiel had the looks to go with bonhomie. He was enviably brawny, both tall and muscular, and his wheat-blond hair had a natural wave. In later life, he might develop a prosperous paunch, but for the nonce, he maintained a soldier's physique and took a keen interest in his acres.

Next to Sir Dashiel, Tommie felt short, dull, and invisible, despite standing five foot nine in his booted feet and dressing in the first stare of rural fashion. One would envy the baronet bitterly, except that the baronet was such a cordial gent, one should like him.

"If it weren't for the assemblies," Tommie said, "we'd have no entertainment hereabouts at all. One hopes the waltz will finally be permitted."

"The marquess must have a word with the organizing committee. The youth of the shire will worship at his feet if he can give them but four waltzes a year. Suggest that to him, why don't you? I would delight in the occasional waltz with my intended, though she'll likely be my wife before the summer assembly rolls around. That's in confidence, mind you, Thomas. A few formalities remain to be addressed."

Another wink. Tommie's personal opinion of winking was that it gave one a criminal air, but Sir Dashiel's winks were by way of just-between-us confidences.

"I leave Penny's personal affairs to Penny," Tommie said. "She would not appreciate meddling, and how the marchioness will manage without her defies my imagination." How would any of them manage without her? Who would return the trinkets Purdy stole? Who would interpret Malcolm's silences? Who would keep the marchioness flattered and happy?

Sir Dashiel laid a hand on Tommie's shoulder. "That's an opportunity for you, isn't it, old boy? The marchioness will soon be bereft of her familiar, and don't think I will allow my wife to spend her days running back and forth to the Hall. Lord Lynnfield can manage his own household, and Penelope will be kept busy managing mine."

Odd, that Penny never mentioned any sort of understanding with Sir Dashiel, never alluded to being spoken for. Then too, a man in love should have referred to managing *our household*, but Sir Dashiel had hereditary honors to pass along. He clearly viewed himself as having more in common with the aristos and their dynastic unions than he did the squires and their homespun courtships. Then too, he was the owner of several thousand productive acres, a war hero, and nobody's fool.

Some fellows had all the luck.

"You don't think Lynnfield's return will upset Penelope, do you?" Sir Dashiel asked, passing Tommie his hat. "Their acquaintance goes back years, though I was always a bit foggy on the details. She doesn't mention him."

Sir Dashiel, catch of the shire, hail fellow well met, and all-around paragon-at-large, was fishing. Tommie was torn between the respect he might garner for bearing relevant truths and the liking he could earn by currying a bit of harmless favor.

Truth lost, not for the first time. "If Penny is at all bothered by the marquess's return, it's because she'd rather he'd stayed in Italy. Lynn-field is an odd duck, to retreat into euphemism. He picks up languages like most fellows try on hats, and he can play chess for days on end. I mean day and night, six games going at once, doesn't eat or sleep until he drops from exhaustion after thirty successive victories. His memory is prodigious, and he tends to laugh at jokes nobody else gets. Not easy company, though time might have improved him."

Sir Dashiel grimaced. "Or made him worse. I'd better get my happiest-man-in-the-world speech rehearsed, hadn't I? Penelope doesn't suffer fools, much less madmen. I don't suppose you know her ladyship's ring size?"

"Ask Aunt Purdy. She's good with those details."

"Purdy is the little one with flowers on her bonnets?"

"That's Aunt Phoebe. Calpurnia is the shortest, and her bonnets tend to riot with ribbons. She's particularly partial to the yellow hue of the daffodil."

Sir Dashiel looked as if he was about to wink again. "How very *Welsh*, but then, we English must have our roses, mustn't we, and the

Scots love their thistle and heather? You're sure Penelope doesn't harbor some sort of misguided youthful tendresse for the marquess?"

Tommie had been at university in the years before the marquess's departure and had taken little notice of matters much beyond the next exam or the barmaid's ankles.

"I cannot speak for Penny," Tommie said, "but I can tell you that in nearly ten years of absence, the marquess never wrote to her, she never wrote to him, and she has never spoken admiringly about him to me. To her, his arrival means more work for the maids, footmen, and kitchen staff and thus more work for Penelope. Nothing more."

"Dear me. You posit the situation of a maiden in need of rescuing, and I am just the fellow to oblige her. You really should come calling more often, Thomas. I mean that."

Absurd flattery, but carrying a hint of sincerity too. "I must be off. The Hall will be all aflutter in anticipation of the marquess's arrival, and one wants to lend a calming influence where possible. Thank you for an excellent meal, and my regards to your dear sister."

Sir Dashiel shook hands—firm, manly grip, sincere blue eyes— and remained on the steps of his manor house, looking genial and hearty. One could hate him without too much effort, except that Sir Dashiel *was* genial and hearty, and the denizens of the Hall *were* an odd lot.

Tommie had told only the one lie, after all. Penny and Lucien had been quite thick all those years ago. If Sir Dashiel was foggy on that detail, to allow him to remain in ignorance was simply the kindness one friend extended to another.

CHAPTER THREE

"Oh, d...ear." Penelope had nearly cursed. The inspiration for her profanity stood by the library's French doors, the same place his ghost had stood for nearly a decade. "I didn't realize the library was occupied, my lord. You will excuse me."

"I will not." Lucien abandoned the shaft of golden afternoon sunlight he'd been standing in and advanced on her. "Somebody has moved my *Don Quixote*, and I will ransack this entire library to find it. I did good work with that project, and it's nowhere to be found. Tell me the footmen didn't use those pages for the spill jar, please. If Aunt Purdy nicked it, she will un-nick it before supper or enjoy the pleasure of dwelling in the gatehouse."

Penelope endured again the sense of disorientation that Lucien's appearance in the orchard had caused. His voice was the same, but different. Deeper, not as lilting. His movements were just as quicksilver-y, but had acquired a prowling quality too. He'd crossed the library without making a sound, and while his impatience was endlessly familiar, the hint of a threat backing it up was new.

Woe betide whoever had purloined the knight of the sad figure.

"I will locate my lord's manuscript after the maids have given the place a thorough dusting." If the marquess had been searching for his treasure, he'd done so without disturbing a single book. "Nobody would dare make tinder of anything written in your hand, my lord." As for Aunt Purdy, she stashed her *finds* in the dower house lumber rooms, where they safely collected dust until Penelope retrieved them.

"Stop 'my lording' me."

Penelope was tired, busy, and vexed. She made for the door.

"Please," Lucien called after her. "Stop 'my lording' me, please. I haven't used the title in years, and plain Pritchard grew on me as a form of address."

Giving orders had also apparently grown on him. The young Lucien had been a polite, diffident soul, despite his lofty title, and not at all interested in telling other people what to do.

"You are not plain Pritchard," Penelope said, rounding on him. "You are Lucien, Marquess of Lynnfield. Why do I have the sense you would rather *be* plain Pritchard?"

His lips kicked up at one corner, and he slanted her a mischievous look. "Pritchard saw a lot of places where a marquess would not be safe or welcome. Beautiful, interesting places, and he met the fascinating people who dwelled in such locations."

His tone was wistful, which should have been Penelope's cue to stalk off and make another pass through the kitchen, where Cook's nerves were doubtless again in need of calming.

"What were you doing, my lord, all those years away? The family speculates, and you might be better served by appeasing their curiosity."

Penelope had wondered, too, of course, for the first two or three years, but then she'd acquired some discipline to go with her dignity and put Lucien, Marquess of Misplaced Hopes, from her heart and mind. Mostly.

"I was on the king's business, growing up, seeing the few great capitals Napoleon wasn't busily sacking. The Russians get credit for destroying Moscow. Do not tangle with an angry Russian if you can avoid it. Some brilliant chess players, though, and from all walks of life."

Her annoyance with him gained a second wind. "I ask you about ten years of your life, and you are maundering on about chess three sentences later. Very well, have your mysterious past. If you are done with the library for the nonce, I'll send in the maids for a quick tidying up. We usually leave the thorough annual cleaning until evening fires are less of a necessity."

"When did you become the head housekeeper, Pen?"

Nobody else called her that. Pen, Penmanship, Penultimate, Penumbra... Lucien's vocabulary had no end, and he'd made a game of modifying her name to suit the moment. The family had other names for her Lady Many Penny, Penny, or—when they wanted some special favor—Lady Penelope.

"I am not the head housekeeper any more than you are plain Pritchard, but your aunt, in case you haven't noticed, is getting on. Her memory is not what it once was. The staff and family require attention, and I'm able to provide it. I'll see you at supper."

She would go directly to the kitchen, where the pandemonium was sure to distract her from the look in Lucien's eyes. Was he *disappointed* to find her directing maids and devising menus? Somebody had to do it, else food arrived to the table cold, cutlery was never polished and rugs never beaten.

Penelope was within six feet of the door before realizing that privacy with Lucien was likely to be in short supply, and now was the time to approach him about rescinding the betrothal agreement. She turned, intent on her topic, only to find that Lucien was two paces behind her.

"I didn't hear you following me."

"You are much preoccupied with domestic matters," he said. "The solicitors gave me accounts, Pen, and their reports focused on harvests, expenses, and Aunt's health. I should have known that you were maintaining order in the house itself, and I thank you for it. You didn't, and don't, owe me or any of us that."

What an odd, infuriating thing to say. "We don't owe each other anything."

He regarded her the same way he used to look at a chessboard when the game defied his preferred strategy. That look presaged intense concentration and a formidable will in service to an even greater intellect.

"We were friends once," he said. "Companions in adventure and misery. My fondest memories of Lynnfield largely involve you and your mad schemes. You owe me nothing—you are right about that— but I offer you a gentleman's regard and whatever version of friend- ship is appropriate in your eyes, given the passing years."

Penelope wanted to shove him in the chest, hard. She'd some- times caused him to stumble with that maneuver, when she'd caught him unawares.

A lady was above schoolyard fisticuffs. "We can be cordial, my lord. We shall be cordial. If I've taken a hand in the running of the household, I did so because I like to be busy, and the marchioness asked it of me." *Not because I missed you and wanted to keep your home in good order for when you returned.*

Was he attempting some sort of sideways apology with this little speech? Penelope gave him the same sort of study he was turning on her, and that was a mistake.

Behind Lucien's calm, blue-eyed regard lurked more of those emotions Penelope had put aside years ago. Lucien was alone in that vast mind of his, still, again. He was homesick while standing in the very library he'd made his private fiefdom by the age of ten.

"I'm glad you've come home." Penelope wished the words back to no avail, because they were only slightly true. She also resented his return, as she'd resented his departure. Friends didn't abandon friends without a word, and Lucien had been right about that part.

They had been companions more than friends and possibly even the juvenile version of inchoate lovers. More than possibly.

Damn him to blazes, anyway.

"I am glad to be here," Lucien said slowly. "Much to my surprise. I've asked Mrs. Cormac to attend me tomorrow after breakfast. Would you like to be present for that interview?"

The titled head of the household did not meet with the house-keeper. "You should confer with Mr. Kerry first, my lord. The butler is senior to the housekeeper." *And male.* Mrs. Cormac would no more enjoy taking orders from the marquess than the footmen would like taking orders from the housekeeper.

"I met with Kerry after lunch and asked if I might convey my thanks for past years of loyal service to Mrs. Cormac in person. He allowed as how gratitude communicated directly would be permitted."

Lucien was applying chess strategies to managing the household. That was new. "I'll leave you to converse with Mrs. Cormac private-ly," Penelope said, making another charge for the door. A *ladylike* charge. "Until supper, my lord."

She didn't pause for a curtsey, and Lucien made no further effort to stop her, nor did he bow. The lack of punctilio on both their parts bothered Penelope all the way up to her bedroom. She should have confronted him about the betrothal legalities, should have explained to him that companions in adventure who go off without a word of farewell are not entitled to trust or friendship upon their return.

Penelope stalked up the steps, trying unsuccessfully to rekindle the fury that had kept her such good company in Lucien's absence. Possibly, a younger Lucien hadn't known how to say good-bye. He'd been little more than a youth when he'd left, and corresponding from the Continent had been all but impossible while hostilities raged.

Perhaps he hadn't felt entitled to write...

By the time she reached her apartment, her ire had muted to an old useless sense of bewilderment. Lucien's mind was impossible to navigate. He was in some ways a prodigy, in others a dunce. Penelope had liked that, liked having the common sense that Lucien lacked, the everyday skills he'd never been taught.

He'd delighted in learning how to set a snare and marveled at Pen's skill with a fishing rod.

"I should take him fishing." She said the words aloud in the safety of her dressing closet, even as she knew them for foolishness. Sir Dashiel was protective of her good name, ridiculously so given that he had no claim on her. He would nonetheless take a dim view of any outings with the marquess that could be considered private.

Besides, Lucien was an adult. He could take himself fishing eight days a week if he chose to.

Penelope retrieved a manuscript wrapped in oilskin from the bottom drawer of her wardrobe and took it to the footman dozing in his chair at the end of the corridor.

"Young Kerry, might you take this to his lordship's apartment and leave it on the escritoire in his sitting room?"

Young Kerry, who resembled his uncle in every particular, except that Young Kerry had a full head of flame-red hair, accepted the parcel and bowed.

"Of course, milady. On his lordship's escritoire. If you'd like, I can wait while you pen him a note so he knows who it's from?"

"He'll know. Away with you. Cook will need every hand to get the feast properly laid, and you will want to finish your nap before battle is joined."

He grinned and strode off, and Penelope took the maids' stairs down to the kitchen. She really should have confronted Lucien about the betrothal.

Time and past to get that detail out of the way.

"Are you normally mute over the chessboard?" St. Didier asked, putting his queen away first. "A good game takes concentration, but your lordship seems both intensely focused on the board and off in another world."

Lucien was at war with himself. The small, safe corner of his mind where he kept All Things Penelope had expanded to take over any and all adjacent territories.

"Uncle Malcolm plays excellent chess without speaking a word. I was merely developing an understanding of my opponent. You are good at devising and testing strategies," Lucien said. "Not as interested in executing them. Murray has the same sort of mind, but he fortunately had Wellington to tend to the execution of his military plans."

St. Didier peered at him. "General Sir George Murray?"

Lucien began returning his pawns to their barracks, but he'd bungled, and St. Didier would not be thrown off the scent.

"One could hardly be on the Continent and not hear of his exploits. He was as angry with the Spanish and Portuguese at times as he was determined to best the French, but he kept his eye on the main objective through many vicissitudes."

"You've met him?"

Never lie unnecessarily. One of very few commandments uniformly adhered to in Lucien's former profession.

"Our paths crossed. One tended to prefer the company of the British army to that of its French opponents. Another game?"

"No, thank you. Who was the tulip at supper? We were not introduced, and somehow, the oversight does not leave me feeling slighted."

Lucien put away the major pieces in rank order. "Cousin Tommie, and he actually is a cousin, or second cousin at some remove. He had the bad luck to be orphaned and the worse luck to be orphaned by parents with more social standing than coin. The estate was taken for debts, and Tommie has been at loose ends. He's educated and not as frivolous as he appears, but lazy." Or he had been. Lucien's measure of the man was years out of date.

St. Didier sipped his brandy. "Angry at the world? He's getting a bit long in the tooth for that posture. Put him in charge of your art business."

Lucien's art business was supposed to be a hobby, a reason for a slightly eccentric peer to hare about the Continent. The enterprise had grown, though, with many Continental families looking to turn assets into coin and Lucien having an eye for what would appeal to English tastes.

"Tommie can manage in French, and he could probably make himself understood in Italian, thanks to his grounding in Latin, but other than that, he's not exactly a polyglot."

Tommie did have social polish, though. He dressed the part, and he was going to waste at Lynnfield.

"If you wait to hand the business over to an exact replica of you, my lord, you are doomed to disappointment. The House of Lords needs every rational mind it can command, and yours falls among that number."

Penelope could manage the art business. She might lack a grasp of vernacular Dutch, and she was surely not well acquainted with Russian, but if she decided to take on the art dealing, she'd make a proper job of it.

"There you go again," St. Didier said, pouring another half inch of brandy into Lucien's glass and then into his own. "Off blowing up castles in Spain."

Lucien had blown up only the one, and that had been mostly a home for bats. "Something is amiss with Lady Penelope."

The fire burned softly, and the clock ticked while the brandy dulled the sharp edges and geometric fence lines in Lucien's mind. The best hours for thinking were at the beginning and end of the day, though Lucien hadn't meant to include St. Didier in his musings.

"She's overtaxed with duty," St. Didier said, nosing his drink, "and under-rewarded with pleasure. One sympathizes." He took a sip, the gesture conveying a hint of self-mockery.

The level of the brandy in the decanter was considerably lower than it had been three games ago. St. Didier had almost won the first game, and Lucien had kept his focus on the chessboard thereafter.

St. Didier had been attempting to ply him with drink. Interesting.

"Her ladyship is *lonely*," Lucien said, seizing on the word as an exact fit for his theories. "The restlessness, the bustling about, the being everywhere at once. She was like that as a girl, until she settled in. Happened again when her brother Henry went off to university. When he bought his colors, I doubt she slept for a month."

Lucien set his glass aside. Mention of the late earl was not for the fuddle-headed.

"I gather the young earl did not survive the war?"

"French snipers. Another pointless death. Lieutenant Lord Carweneth was leading the advance patrol, scouting for someplace to camp that had water but wasn't too exposed. Maps were useless in that area, and then he ran into bad luck. Very bad luck." Not quite an accurate retelling, but close enough for present company.

"Let us hope," St. Didier said slowly, "that having concluded more or less a century of war, with every petty despot and half the monarchies in Europe, that we English can learn to enjoy the blessings of peace."

Lucien raised his glass and pretended to sip. In the absence of war, England was falling apart. Bread riots, draconian oppression of any dissident voice, the rule of law contorted for the benefit of the wealthy few. Defeating Napoleon had exposed the conflicts long brewing within British society all the more clearly, and those could not be solved by force of arms.

Temporarily contained, put off, and repressed, certainly, and look how those measures had ended for the French.

"Does her ladyship blame you for her brother's death?" St. Didier asked.

"I was nowhere near the fighting, ever." Not true, of course. "I have no heir, St. Didier. I took precautions."

"The usual precaution is to marry and have lots of sons. You were betrothed at the time you went a-Maying under Napoleon's nose."

Back to this. St. Didier was nothing if not tenacious. "When I went *traveling*, I was not yet of age to marry without my guardians' consent. Marriage should be undertaken as an independent choice. I was entitled to see something of the world before settling down."

St. Didier's frown conveyed pity. "Perhaps Lady Penelope, your betrothed, is angry with you for abandoning her. An outlandish theory, I know, but you say something is amiss with her, and all but jilting the woman might qualify as the source of her upset."

The lateness of the hour, the brandy, and the long day conspired to defeat Lucien's natural reticence. "I left her a note."

"One note in ten years? Perhaps the rumors about your mental unsoundness are true."

"I'm not unsound. I'm Welsh and as brilliant as much of my race is prone to being. I was raised among a troupe of eccentric relations, taught by tutors who valued learning over intellectual conventions, and allowed to think for myself." Then too, Lucien had left eight years, seven months, and nineteen days ago, not ten years.

"Yourself suspects something is amiss with Lady Penelope. Myself agrees. She does strike me as a woman scorned."

"Spooked, certainly. This handmaiden-at-large role suggests she has made herself as necessary as possible." But the plan had gone awry, and now Sir Dashiel could offer to rescue her from the surfeit of duty she'd taken on at the Hall. "I did leave her a note."

Small, simple words, but over the years they'd come to justify every path that turned Lucien away from home and every risk he should never have taken. "I asked her to come away with me," he went on more softly. "I made all the arrangements. We would travel as cousins, which we are albeit third cousins at least, and I had a lady's companion ready to travel with us."

"Travel where?"

"Southern Italy was safe at the time. Greece was quiet. The Outer Hebrides would have suited me. I needed to get away. We were being forced to the altar for the convenience of our elders, and I thought we could kidnap each other instead."

"The usual term is 'elope.'"

Lucien rose and returned his glass to the sideboard, the contents untouched. "Exactly what I wanted to avoid. Penelope at seventeen was fiercely contrary. Her older brother barely bothered with her, her wealth was a burden—or so she claimed—and marriage was a trap. Sir Dashiel and his ilk were swarming about her even then. She was full of passionate arguments, and more than half the time she even made sense."

"You adored her."

I still do. "I was young, St. Didier. She was younger. We deserved to decide for ourselves whether we married, and quitting Lynnfield seemed the only way to gain us that freedom." To give Pen a semblance of a choice about her own future.

"So you moved your pieces into position, planned your escape, invited the lady to join your little adventure, and she—wisely, I might add—declined the great and clod-pated honor you were, or possibly were not, doing her."

Lucien hadn't aired this ancient history with anybody. His former employer, His Grace of Huntleigh, probably guessed most of it, but the duke was a kindhearted creature and good at ignoring another person's foolishness.

"She was to meet me in the orchard, but I waited an hour past the appointed time. Penelope was punctual even then, and her absence spoke clearly. In hindsight, I can see that my plan was ill-advised."

"Some might say mad."

Some who had never been nineteen, forbidden to serve in the military, passionately in love, and frustrated beyond all telling.

"Penelope apparently found it so, and yet, she is out of charity with me now. I let her know in a postscript that the solicitors would have my direction should she choose to bide at Lynnfield and that she could write to me using them as a poste restante. She never wrote."

St. Didier rose and stretched, then brought his glass to the sideboard as well. "You are trying to find logic in a woman's moods. That is surely the sign of a man who has parted from his good sense."

"Women are rational, St. Didier. Terrifyingly so at times. I did leave Penelope a choice and a simple means of communicating with me, but our every word and glance now are fraught with resentment on her part and bewilderment on mine."

"So you, in your time-honored fashion, are worrying the problems of why and what-happened and how-did-this-occur. Sign the documents rescinding the betrothal, and her regard for you might improve. Documents have come to mean a great deal in this modern world of ours. More than a man's word or his whole course of conduct."

St. Didier was alluding delicately to the letters patent that had controlled his family's title and the lands that went with them. Letters that specified a male entail on all the honors and thus left St. Didier to earn his living by his wits.

Letters patent. Betrothal agreements. Solicitors' reports. Documents. Missives. Epistles...

"Penelope never got my note." The only possible explanation for her grudging civility. "She cannot have read that note. Pen is fairminded to a fault, and I played fair. If she never got the note, she's playing fair now too. If she never read my note, then by her lights, I left like a thief at dawn and gave her no way to contact me."

An enormous weight lifted from Lucien's mind and heart. He sank into a wing chair near the hearth, relief knocking the pins from under all previous assumptions. The game made sense to him now, though victory was far from assured.

"Notes don't just grow legs and steal away, Lynnfield."

"They blow away in the breeze, they become a toy for the cat, they are set aside by servants looking for a particular vase. They are snatched up for tinder when a fire must be lighted." None of those scenarios was likely—the note had been tucked into Penelope's tackle box, where she'd been sure to see it—but the general theory was still sound.

Penelope had never read the most sincere, passionate words Lucien had ever written.

"What will you do about this revelation?" St. Didier asked. "Assuming you are correct?"

"I am correct. I know I am correct."

"You will have some difficulty convincing that lady that a note written years ago that she never read changes everything."

A chess player knew differently. One move could and often did change the whole game. "I will write another note. Thank you for your company this evening, St. Didier. I'm off to see to my correspondence."

CHAPTER FOUR

The conservatory in spring was a quiet place, and Penelope sought its refuge under the banner of transplanting morning glory seedlings into the pots they'd occupy on the back balcony. By high summer, the balustrade would be awash in cascading blooms, but for now the job involved dirt, a little delicate greenery, and patience.

"You are also the undergardener now?" Lucien put the question pleasantly, but one look at him, and Penelope knew he was ready to join battle. His eyes had acquired the same quiet sparkle when he'd devised a new defense to some venerable chess opening, or puzzled out a rebuttal to a theory of Stoic philosophy.

"I needed the peace and quiet. The morning glories needed larger pots." In truth, she'd craved the scent and sight of growing plants, but any sortie out of doors would have been observed and remarked upon.

Lucien surveyed the table, littered with dirt, trays of freshly sprouted plants, and empty clay pots. "I can help."

Oh right. By wrecking her peace. *Again.* "I can manage, my lord."

"Two can manage more quickly, and then you can get on with inspecting the broom closets or whatever else Auntie demands of you." He peeled off his morning coat, slipped off his sleeve buttons, and folded back his cuffs.

A gentleman would never appear in such dishabille before a lady, but Pen had seen Lucien wearing only a pair of sopping-wet drawers, and he'd seen her in a damp shift. Years ago. They had not been children, but they'd been as innocent as two former children could be.

"Lynnfield has good dirt," Lucien said, drawing a tray to his side of the table. "Uncle insisted that good dirt was the reason the Conqueror crossed the Channel. Kent is one great expanse of good dirt, and where we haven't put the soil in cultivation, we still have good woods."

He set to work as if he'd been transplanting seedlings every spring for years, though he hadn't. What he had done was develop the ability to fall in step with Penelope at whatever task she'd been involved in. If she was darning a stocking, he'd pick up her embroidery hoop and finish a violet while maundering on about languages that had no definite article. If she'd been memorizing a poem, he'd quiz her stanza by stanza.

"Mighty oaks from little acorns grow," Lucien muttered, prying a pale seedling from the tray.

He had good hands. Largish, in keeping with his height, also competent. He had the same ability with musical instruments that he had with languages, and the first time Penelope had realized that Lucien was no longer a boy, he'd been holding a silver flute. He'd held that flute with the hands of a man rather than a youth.

She searched her recollections for a bit of Chaucer to toss back at him in response to the quote about mighty oaks. *Love is blind* sallied forth from memory.

She mashed a seedling too firmly into the dirt and inadvertently tore off a leaf. "Weren't you supposed to meet with Mrs. Cormac this morning?"

"Mission accomplished. She has her niece in mind for the post of under-housekeeper, but I have forbidden her to retire for at least another twenty years."

Had Lucien just made a joke? His sense of humor had always been subtle. "Mrs. Cormac would be well past her three score and ten years by then, my lord, assuming she lives so long."

He tucked his seedling into its dirt bed off center in the pot. Penelope appropriated his first completed effort and redid the business properly.

"It occurs to me," Lucien said, "that you have taken to thievery, my lady."

Penelope slid the tray of seedlings closer to her side of the table. "You have me confused with the Board of Excise, my lord." The Board of Stamps and Taxes was no less rapacious. Aunt Purdy was merely a zealous and stealthy borrower of other people's goods.

"You have stolen all the available jobs from people here at Lynn-field who need something useful to do with their time. What would you think of putting Tommie in charge of my art business?"

While Penelope dug her fingers through rich, dark soil and gently handled new plants, she was aware that Lucien's conversation was serving some purpose known only to him. He was setting up the board and putting pieces in play. That comment about stealing jobs was so like him—insightful, but apropos of nothing in particular.

Trying to chivvy him away was pointless. He would not leave until he was good and ready to, of all the ironies.

"Tommie is bored," Penelope replied. "He does the pretty in the churchyard, attends all the hunt meets, and stands up dutifully at every assembly, but he would benefit from gainful employment suitable to a gentleman's son. He might even know a little something about art, but I can't see him bestirring himself to any effort greater than turning pages at our next musicale."

"The finer points of art can be learned. The part about making commerce appear genteel might fit his capabilities. How rusty is his French?"

"Very."

"I can send him to Paris to brush up, then. Only Parisian French will do for the cits and spares. Why isn't Aunt Phoebe assisting to repot these"—he peered at the tray of seedlings—"plants?"

"These are the morning glories that will festoon the back terrace balcony by midsummer. If we don't start them indoors, they won't begin blooming until summer's half over."

"Lark, Phoebe, and Wren could be given responsibility for the gardens. Lark has a flare for organization."

She had a flare for ordering footmen to move the furniture around just before company was expected and extra duties were already pressing upon them. But then, the gardeners did not have extra duties when company was expected, and Aunt Phoebe did arrange lovely bouquets.

"I can speak to the flock about taking an interest in the gardens. The marchioness isn't much of a horticulturalist, though Aunt Phoebe knows her blooms and herbs."

"You speak to the flock, and I will have a word with Mr. Osian about some new ideas for his gardens. Lynnfield will be the better for it. You ignored my note, Pen. Am I in your bad books?"

The note he'd had delivered to her before breakfast, asking for a quick word in the library. "I unearthed *Don Quixote* and had him returned to you. You need not thank me."

"I do thank you for safeguarding my translation, because you did, didn't you?"

"He was in a safe place, true enough. I left him there lest anything untoward happen to him."

Lucien retrieved the pot Penelope had fixed and tucked a second seedling into the soil near the rim. "Seems a bit too much dirt for one poor little fellow all on his lonesome. I wasn't referring to the note you ignored this morning. I was referring to the note you ignored the day I left Lynnfield."

Penelope's hands went still. Lucien had begun his attack, and he wasn't being subtle about the opening salvo.

"*What note?*"

He studied her across the table, his gaze unreadable. "Precisely.

What note? The note begging you to come away with me, explaining that we could travel without fear of scandal. The note conveying that my future was yours to command, but Lynnfield was doing too good a job of commanding both of us, and I needed to leave."

Lucien was a bad liar, and he found dishonesty morally distasteful. Lies were complications in his lexicon, though he was capable of a euphemism in the name of tact. Sometimes.

"I received no note, Lucien. Where did you leave it?"

"In plain sight in the fishing cottage, half tucked into your tackle box. I addressed it to you and sealed it. I used the old code and spouted off at some length. I knew you would put that box back in your dressing closet without fail—you are a tidy soul—and thus my note was certain to find you."

Penelope finished the pot she was working on and crossed to the basin and towel sitting on an unused birdbath.

"What difference could this note possibly make now? If you even wrote it. Why tell me this?" She scrubbed at her hands, knowing the dirt under her fingernails would require a penknife to dislodge.

"I tell you this because you were left with the impression that I, like your parents, your brother, your governess, and probably everybody else who mattered to you, simply disappeared. This is not so. I sought to disappear *with you*, not *from you*."

Lucien remained at work as he spoke, patting soil into place and turning the pot this way and that. He was putting two seedlings into every pot, too, which Mr. Osian, martinet in charge of the gardens, would disapprove of.

"One seedling per pot, Lucien." Penelope rubbed her hands dry until they were pink.

"Two, for company, and because the one might not survive, so we're saved having to replant if we start with two. Mr. Osian can complain to me if he takes issue with my gardening. You took issue with my departure. I also informed you in that note you never read of a means of corresponding with me. I refuse to believe that you withheld even the occasional friendly word out of spite."

"You expected me to *leave Lynnfield* with you?"

"You did not want to be herded up the church aisle by a lot of solicitors and guardians who had no care for your happiness. You said so."

She had said so. Loudly, but only to Lucien. "I didn't mean..."

He paused between pots, his hands dirty, his physique impressive, his expression patient. "Yes?"

"I was seventeen when you left. Opinionated, unhappy, worried for Henry, furious with him... I said a lot of things."

Lucien took up another seedling, easing it gently from the tray. "If it's any consolation, I agreed with you. A lady should choose a spouse for herself, and for that matter, so should a gentleman. We have few enough choices in life, and that one ought not to be left in the hands of lawyers and meddling relations. My solution was to turn our backs on the lot of them."

Logical, also daft. "To elope?"

"Not in the marital sense. I had a companion lined up for you, and we would travel as cousins, which a generation or three back, we are. I was interested in Italy at the time, but Greece also appealed."

They had pored over Gibbon's *Decline and Fall of the Roman Empire* by the hour. "Then you sought to avoid marrying me, but you would not leave me here to contend without you?"

"Something like that." He tucked the seedling into the dirt, then found it a companion. "In any case, I had a plan, one that might have worked for a time, but you never learned of it, and you never received your invitation to join me in adventure. I thought you should know the facts."

Penelope could hear Sir Dashiel scoffing in her head. *Not facts, my dear, fanciful claims from a man who at best can be described as fanciful himself.* Though Lucien wasn't fanciful in the unbalanced sense Sir Dashiel implied. Cerebral, logical, and an intellectual magpie, by turns focused and flighty...

"What did you think when I failed to join you in your travels?" Penelope asked slowly.

"I thought you'd chosen the safety of a known environment over the perils of journeying with me. In hindsight, I applauded your common sense. Your logic was splendid. You could not be forced to the altar if I wasn't on hand to be forced along with you. When I took note of that salient fact, I found other places to be."

Penelope dried her hands and refolded the towel. She wanted to march out of the conservatory in high dudgeon, she wanted to swat Lucien with the towel, and she wanted—most of all—to believe him.

"You blame *me* for your absence all these years?"

"Of course not." Another pair of seedlings were gently patted into place. "I am explaining the reasoning I applied to a bewildering time in my life. I became useful on the Continent, then I found a settled post in Italy. St. Didier explained to me, however, that just as betrothal to me entrapped you once before, it might well be entrapping you again, and I had to see for myself how you're faring."

He set the clay pot aside, dusted his hands, and strolled to the washbasin. "I missed you terribly, Penelope, but lectured myself about a gentleman abiding by a lady's choices. I see now that, once again, you had no real choice, and I apologize for that. I never meant to abandon you."

Pretty words and possibly even true. "What difference does any of this make now?" Even while Penelope tried for a dispassionate tone, she reeled with what-ifs and why-in-the-worlds.

When Lucien had made use of soap and water, he wiped his hands slowly and thoroughly, and repositioned the towel exactly as Penelope had folded it.

"I want the truth between us, Pendragon. You believed I abandoned you. I believed you rejected me. We were both in error. You did not wrong, disappoint, or betray me, and I am vastly relieved to know it."

He took up her hand, cold now, kissed her palm, and closed her fingers into a fist, then collected his coat and walked out into the morning sunshine.

"Saddle the bay," Sir Dashiel said, striding into the stable yard. The morning was well enough advanced that the grass would be dry, and the situation at Lynnfield wanted reconnoitering. He had considered inviting Penelope to hack out with him, but was honestly out of charity with her.

To get word of the marquess's arrival from Tommie the Twit and then to spend an interminable meal attempting to pry details from the fellow had been beyond vexing. The past—Sir Dashiel's, the marquess's, the marquess's *and* Penelope's—mattered little, provided sleeping dogs were allowed to lie. The war was over, so to speak, and reasonable people let bygones be bygones. The future, however, was another matter.

Ten minutes later, a groom led out a dark, leggy gelding, no white on the creature save for a star on his forehead.

"He's still carrying extra weight," Sir Dashiel said, eyeing the horse's barrel. "Limit his grass if you have to use a grazing muzzle to do it."

"If you say so, Sir Dashiel." The groom, a wizened, scruffy gnome, looped the reins over the gelding's head and led him to the mounting block. "Thor's dam were born to the plow, though, and blood will tell."

Pay wages one day late, and the staff turned up disrespectful from boot-boy to butler. "You question a former officer's assessment of a horse's condition?"

The gnome—Dashiel forgot his name, if he ever knew it—patted the horse's shoulder. "No, sir. Just sayin' Thor's an easy keeper, like most plow stock tend to be. A good quality in a beast, usually, but he'll have to miss more than a few days' grass before you see some ribs."

"His sire was one of the finest hunters ever to leap a stile. Thor can do a better job of living up to his patrimony."

The groom stepped back, and the horse stood still to be mounted.

Dashiel took up the reins, nudged the gelding with a spur, and departed for the Lynnfield property line. Thor was not a flashy equine, but he'd do for a social call, if the day held that, and he'd stand patiently. Dashiel's hunters could not stand still for two minutes without having galloped off five miles of the fidgets first.

"Give me an eager hunter, and I'm a happy man," Dashiel muttered, topping the rise that bordered Lynnfield land. Penelope was an accomplished rider, but she did not follow the hounds. Just as well, because Dashiel would forbid that activity once they were married.

"Speak of the devil," he said, bringing Thor down to the walk. "Or the angel, as the case may be."

Her ladyship's horse was a flat streak galloping across the pasture below, heading straight for the stone wall bordering the grassy acres. Horse and rider cleared the obstacle in perfect rhythm. Penelope turned her mare to sweep up the hill, the horse slowing when no fences were in sight.

Dashiel aimed his mount down the slope and intercepted his intended and her winded horse.

"What a lovely picture you make, my dear," he said, tipping his hat. "Roses in your cheeks, a sparkle in your eye. Good morning." Penelope looked a bit untidy, truth be told. The wind had snatched a few tendrils from her chignon, and the toe of her boot was dusty.

"Sir Dashiel, good day, and that's Thor, isn't it? Greetings, Thor."

The horse's ears flicked at the mention of his name.

"Thor is in want of exercise," Dashiel said, bringing his gelding alongside the mare, "and your mount needs to cool out. Shall we share the path for a bit?" And where was her groom, for pity's sake? No hint of scandal had attached to their courtship, and Dashiel was determined that none would.

Though to be fair, Penelope was on Lynnfield land, and Dashiel had known her for years.

"I planned to admire the view from the crest and then wander home," Penelope said. "The view can wait for another day."

"Why not join me for luncheon? Tommie honored us with his presence yesterday. Saved us from the ladies outnumbering the gents. Vicar and his beauties were on hand, and the meal was quite congenial."

"Then you heard our news," Penelope said. "The marquess is back, and we've been all at sixes and sevens. You'd think Cook had never prepared a roast before."

Roasts had become increasingly rare at Raven's Roost, alas, and yesterday's offering had been no credit to the kitchen.

"How is our marquess?" Lord Lynnfield had been a daft boy, educated at home rather than benefitting from public school's civilizing influence. He'd gone to university, where he'd doubtless taught Latin to the dons and philosophy to the trees.

"Until yesterday," Penelope said, "I hadn't seen Lucien for years, Dash. I have no idea how he is or who he is. He looks well, still serious, still keeps himself to himself."

A detached, less-than-specific report. Too detached?

"He hasn't explained his sudden compulsion to travel on a Continent at war all those years ago?" The horses ambled down the track side by side, and Dashiel knew the gratification of an objective achieved. Who better to report on Lord Lynnfield's situation than the woman who ran that man's household?

"His lordship has explained himself to some extent, and I grasp his reasoning. But for university, his world was Lynnfield from birth onward. For a young man with a voracious intellect, such limitations chafed."

Penelope defended the idiot. To buy a commission and serve honorably in the military was how young men *saw the world*. Lynnfield could plead the imperiled succession of his title—fair enough—but the conventional price for eschewing military service was confinement to English shores.

Not that Lord Lynnfield had ever grasped, much less abided by, convention.

"I can't help but worry that his lordship was up to no good on the

Continent," Sir Dashiel said. "What need has a marquess to plunder what little art Napoleon didn't steal? Seems a bit dodgy to me."

"Mind your tongue, Dash. Lucien had no need to plunder anything. His lordship is quite well fixed, and I'm sure he took every precaution to ensure his safety. Lucien can defy expectations, but he's not a fool."

More praise for a man who'd been a poor neighbor, at best. "One heard you and he were betrothed at one time. Do you still bear him some lingering fondness?" Tommie was apparently ignorant of the legal details. Fortunately, the marchioness had been more forthcoming. "I would not begrudge you some tender feelings toward a friend of your childhood, my dear."

Penelope pulled her mare up at the foot of the hill. "*Begrudge* me, Dash?"

She did this. Periodically tested him with minor displays of independence. Little ladylike fits of pique. He'd find her skittishness adorable were matters not growing so dire.

"A turn of phrase, Penelope, nothing more. Lord Lynnfield has always been an enigma to me. When most gentlemen were eager to lay down their lives to keep king and country safe from the Corsican menace, Lynnfield went sightseeing. When I spend every waking hour ensuring Raven's Roost prospers, my lofty neighbor can't be bothered to drop around home even every other year. He abandons all responsibility—*he abandoned you*—and you defend him. I am in thrall to duty, and you don't bother to tell me when the great man returns. Forgive me a little puzzlement."

She urged the mare forward. "Lucien gave us very little warning of his plans, Dash. I have been busy, and I will be busy for the next little while. The elders get up to mischief at the least provocation, and Lucien's return is a very great provocation indeed."

"Then I had best invite you and the conquering hero, along with his dear auntie, to Sunday supper, hadn't I?" Perhaps a ham would do. The hams were still in decent supply and good quality.

"We should invite you first, Dash. If anybody knows the protocol, you do."

Penelope was in error. The marquess was to call first on the vicar, then on the neighbors in descending order of social standing. The neighbors were then free to reciprocate, and *then* invitations to social gatherings at Lynnfield could be issued.

But if the marquess must ignore the niceties, Dashiel would accommodate him. "Very well. I consider myself invited to Lynnfield. Sunday will do nicely, and I will bring Tabby. She grows restless when some of her friends are being presented in Town, and she's expected to bide another year in the shires. She will make a complete cake of herself before his lordship, but tell him not to get ideas regarding my darling sister."

"Dash, you are being quite forward."

Faint heart never won fair maid—or her fortune—and Lord Lynnfield was a complication Dashiel could not afford to ignore. No telling what his lordship knew of the campaign across Spain, thought he knew, or might recollect at the wrong moment.

"The Pritchards and the Ingrahams are old friends," Dashiel said. "Nobody need stand on excessive ceremony. I'm frankly curious about the marquess, and Tabby needs a bit of a social coup to lift her spirits. Shall we say two of the clock?"

Penelope fussed with her reins and smoothed her habit over her boot. "Very well. Two of the clock Sunday. Be prepared to talk about something other than planting and who is going up to Town. Warn Tabby that if she assays her French, the marquess will reply in that language for the duration of the meal."

"That leaves discussing the spring assembly in the King's English. I shall do my best."

"Go give Tabby the news. She'll fret over what to wear, but Sunday finery will more than suffice."

Dashiel was being dismissed three-quarters of a mile from the Lynnfield stable yard, but perhaps that was for the best. He'd gathered what intelligence he needed, the news was mostly positive, and better not to be seen alone with her ladyship.

"I will bid you a lovely day, my dear, and count the hours until Sunday afternoon." He saluted with his crop, wheeled Thor in a sloppy about-face, and cantered off up the hill. At the crest, he slowed the horse to glance back the way he'd come.

Penelope was nowhere to be seen, suggesting she'd spoken the truth. She was busy, and Penelope toiled like Lynnfield's self-appointed head drudge on a typical day. If a woman was determined to exhaust herself, she should do so in service to her husband and children, not for a pack of half-witted dotards.

Dashiel put Thor through his paces and found the horse in good condition, for all that he'd come off of winter unfashionably well fed. An hour later, Dashiel turned his mount over to the same groom and was halfway to the house before he realized what had bothered him about Penelope's report on affairs at Lynnfield.

She'd never denied harboring feelings for the marquess, and she'd repeatedly referred to his lordship as *Lucien*.

Blast and damnation, the Marquess of Lynnfield might well become a problem after all.

How typical.

CHAPTER FIVE

Uncle Malcolm and Uncle Theo played cribbage by the parlor windows. Aunt Purdy plied her needle in a wing chair near the fire, and Cousin Lark wandered through a Beethoven slow movement at the keyboard. Tommie read a fashion magazine while doing justice to the brandy.

To Penelope's eye, the tableau offered another typical evening in the family parlor except for Lucien at the desk in the corner, his attention on some budget or ledger that required frequent use of the abacus.

"You should at least pretend to read, Penelope," the marchioness said, quietly enough that Lark's music would hide her words from the rest of the room. "Lucien won't move until he's satisfied that his numbers tally to the farthing."

"They might be Aunt Phoebe's numbers. Lucien asked her to put her mind to enlivening the plantings at the front of the manor and along the drive. She disappeared back to the dower house with Aunt Wren in tow."

The marchioness's knitting needles slowed. "Enliven the plantings? Those flower beds haven't changed since Capability Brown was a sapling. Salvia, daisies, climbing roses... very pretty, very *reliable*. I don't suppose you've given any thought to the grounds at Raven's Roost? Sir Dashiel is a conscientious farmer, for all he doesn't put much stock in his estate's presentation."

Presentation, as her ladyship referred to it, cost money. "What has Sir Dashiel to do with anything?" And when had her ladyship developed the habit of introducing him into any and every casual discussion?

"You rode out to meet him this morning, Penny. I was young once. I do understand." She smiled at her knitting and rearranged the yarn on her needle. "You and Sir Dashiel will suit. Have no fear in that regard. He's a man of the land, a former officer. Others have loftier titles, true, but he's a dependable, known quantity, and you have never been impressed with Town life."

An earl's daughter could look much higher than a mere baronet, but her ladyship had a point. Sir Dashiel was loyal to his acres, well liked, and... and what? Handsome? The neighborhood Adonis, to hear the marchioness tell it.

His looks hardly mattered. He'd served on the Peninsula for less than two years, and the baronetcy had been his grandfather's accomplishment for some bit of daring during the American war.

When had everybody, Sir Dashiel included, begun assuming he and Penelope would make a match?

"Dashiel has grown presuming to the point of arrogance," she said. "Somebody told him about that old betrothal between Lucien and me, and he brought it up today when he interrupted my ride."

The marchioness started on a new row. She had aged well, blond hair turning flaxen, figure still handsome. Like Penelope, she had funds of her own. Unlike Penelope, she longed for Town and a livelier social life. She'd make the trip to London in a few weeks, when the Season was in full swing, buy out the shops, reap a harvest of gossip, then return to Kent exhausted and in much better spirits for having enjoyed her preferred diversions.

The abacus clicked with an irregular rhythm, Uncle Malcolm

threw a fresh square of peat on the fire, and Lark launched into a lively scherzo.

What do I want? What did Lucien want? Why come home now? Why come home at all? And yet, Penelope admitted that his arrival was timely.

Sir Dashiel had insinuated himself into the role of suitor, and Penelope had allowed him to. She hadn't precisely encouraged him, but neither had she objected. She, too, had begun, all unaware, to assume that she'd eventually give Dashiel leave to pay his addresses.

Gracious saints.

"You've invited Sir Dashiel to Sunday supper," the marchioness observed. "You must be sure Vicar joins us next week. We will parade all the local beauties under Lucien's nose, though Tabby Ingraham isn't out yet. In my day, we didn't let that bother us. A girl looked over the prospects from the first possible moment."

"Sir Dashiel mostly invited himself, and he's usually the first to insist on observing protocol."

"The highest sticklers can often be found canoodling behind the privet hedge. Mark me on this. Ride out with Sir Dashiel if you please, but if he suggests you dismount to admire the view, expect mischief to follow. Delightful mischief, viewed in a certain light."

Penelope had experienced Sir Dashiel's brand of mischief—a kiss to the cheek, lips brushing her knuckles, a hand lingering on hers when she took his arm.

Nonsense, all of it. She could not dismiss Lucien's little gesture in the conservatory—a kiss to her palm—quite as easily. She and Lucien had kissed before, years ago, and assured each other they were conducting experiments in the name of curiosity, then they'd laughed about the results.

Lucien's conclusion, offered with dancing eyes, had been: The business might benefit from practice. He'd been a rascal, in his subtle, bookish way. The whole undertaking had been awkward, sweet, and tempting from Penelope's perspective.

Uncle Malcolm put the cards and cribbage board away. Uncle Theo was refilling his glass at the sideboard.

"I do believe I have read enough for the nonce," Penelope said, rising. "Uncle Malcolm, would you light me up to my room?"

Malcolm slid the cards and the cribbage board into the drawer assigned to their keeping and nodded. He lit a carrying candle from the candelabrum on the desk and gestured to the door. He often saw Penny to her apartment, his company restful and undemanding. The small gallantry also spared Malcolm from watching Theo make his nightly slide into inebriation, though Uncle Theo's version of excess was simply to grow quieter and quieter until he nodded off.

Lucien did not so much as look up from his ciphering as Penelope offered her good-nights. The house was chilly, though all the sconces were lit for a change in deference to Lucien's return.

"Are you glad to have Lucien back?" Penelope asked as she and Malcolm climbed the main staircase.

Malcolm nodded and cocked his head. *Are you?*

"I am as well. Lucien livens things up. He's given me some things to think about." He'd planned their elopement, for pity's sake. Both of them too young to marry without the consent of guardians, and Lucien hadn't even intended that they marry. Not immediately, perhaps not ever. "He and I are still engaged, technically."

Malcolm offered no reply, but then, his world was circumscribed by which birds, blooms, and butterflies were in the area and whether Aunt Purdy had helped herself to his field glasses again. He read in several languages and had a deft hand with a botanical sketch.

"Malcolm, are you happy?"

Penelope wasn't in the habit of interrogating him—Malcolm was a private, dignified fellow—but of all the elders, she considered him the closest to an ally.

Malcolm stopped outside the door of Lucien's apartment and tapped on the carving. A nature scene of a cascading cataract, the pool at its base—the lynn, in older parlance—and the trees and beasts gathered about the water. The lion and the lamb, a biblical allusion, along with bears, wolves, and various birds and livestock.

Malcolm glossed a finger over the nightingale high up in an oak and then touched that finger to Penelope's forehead. He nodded and smiled, then offered Penelope his arm again.

What was that about? "Sometimes, Malcolm, I wish you would just give me a few words. Purdy says you talked as a child, and you went silent only when you left Wales as a youth. I would love to hear your voice, even if you insisted on keeping to Welsh. Without Lucien on hand, mine has grown rusty."

One's native tongue should never grow rusty, and yet, the elders were nearly scandalized to be overheard in Welsh. Penelope suspected that Phoebe, Wren, and Lark remained in the dower house in part for greater privacy so they need not watch their language, as it were.

Uncle Malcolm stopped again, this time outside of his own chambers. Penelope had rarely been invited inside and knew not to touch or move anything without Malcolm's permission. She waited in the corridor until Malcolm emerged from his sitting room, a book in his hands. He held the book to his chest for a moment, then offered it to her.

"The *Salmau Cân*. Malcolm, are you lending this to me?"

Malcolm nodded bashfully and touched the tip of his index finger to his lips.

The book was a psalter translated into metric Welsh. "I'm to say the verses?"

Malcolm made a sweeping, operatic gesture with his right arm.

"Or sing them, in Welsh, of course. Thank you, Malcolm. I will take the best care of this loan. You are so thoughtful."

He bowed and disappeared again, a silent elf of tallish human proportions.

"Good night, Uncle," Penelope murmured, taking the psalter, which looked like it well might be two centuries old, to the nearest alcove. She sat beneath the sconces, candlelight flickering over the pages.

"*Yr Arglwydd yw fy Mugail; ni bydd eisiau arnaf...*" She was still reading when the nearest sconce began to sputter. She rose stiffly and made her way to her rooms. How often had Malcolm thumbed through these pages, and did he ever sing the verses to himself? So much silence for one man, and yet, he appeared happy and content.

Penelope was still musing on that conundrum when she opened the door to her sitting room and found Lucien asleep on the sofa, wrapped in her favorite old merino shawl.

Lucien was aware of Penelope's presence before he opened his eyes—before he was fully awake, in fact. She brought the scent of roses with her, old-fashioned and sweet. Even her shawl bore a lingering hint of her fragrance.

"Lucien, what on earth are you doing here?"

He sat up. She had a book—she'd been pretending to read some herbal in the family parlor—and she looked prickly, tired, and dear.

"I was waiting for you, and now my patience has been rewarded. Sit with me, please?"

Ten years ago, she would have settled beside him without hesitation and certainly without asking his permission.

She took the wing chair near the hearth. "I should open the door, except that would let out all the heat."

Lucien rose and draped the shawl around her shoulders. He'd lit the fire before he'd dozed off, though a footman should have come by and seen to that amenity.

"We are old friends," he said. "Old somethings, at any rate, and relatives. Please don't let decorum come between us now, Pen."

She gathered the shawl around her, toed off her slippers, and tucked up her feet. "Not decorum, Lucien, propriety. We are no longer children."

"Neither are we strangers. I saw Sir Dashiel intercept you on horseback this morning. Is he a problem?"

Pen arranged her skirts over her toes, a degree of modesty she'd never have bothered with earlier in life.

"You think because you claim to have left me a note all those years ago that I am in charity with you, Lucien. I am trying to be, but adjusting my perspective will take time. You were still gone, and I still had no idea where or why. Eventually, the solicitors let us know that you were racketing about the Continent and sending home *objets d'art* and the occasional painting. The note condoling me on Henry's death was something, I suppose."

"The earl died defending his country, and you deserve to be proud of him." Lucien could tell her that much, because any man who died in uniform was presumed to have ended his days as a hero. Henry had, in fact, expired without getting off a shot, ambushed on a dusty farm lane along with most of the men in his patrol.

"Henry was an idiot," Penelope said, perhaps the first negative word she'd ever uttered about her older brother. "No heir, barely of age himself, but by then, I was betrothed to you and thus off his hands, wasn't I?"

"Henry wanted to be off Lynnfield's hands, Pen. Young men are acolytes of pride and pigheadedness, and he wasn't simply a young man, he was a peer. Earl of Carweneth. Young peers are doubly clueless. Witness, my scheme to spirit you away to freedom."

She peered at him in the gloom. "That was your plan, wasn't it? To gain freedom for us both. Bold creature."

Her tone held a hint of relenting, perhaps even affection, but Lucien's present task did not involve dwelling on the past.

"Tell me about Sir Dashiel."

"What is there to tell? You've known him longer than I have. Conscientious about his acres, served loyally in uniform, baronet, attentive to his younger sister, and..."

"Pen?"

"And not bad looking, though I suspect he deems himself handsomer than he is."

"You could never abide a weak chin."

She hid a smile under the guise of rearranging her shawl. "Dashiel might have convinced himself that he and I have an understanding."

Ballocks to that. "*Do* you have an understanding?"

"Why should it matter to you?"

While dozing, Lucien had pondered this conversation, and he'd been prepared for that salvo. "Who do you suppose will negotiate your settlements, Pen, if you favor Sir Dashiel with your hand?" Which, by the by, she could not legally do as long as she was betrothed to Lucien.

"Oh." More tucking and fussing and scooting about. "I can't foresee that any negotiations will be needed in the immediate future."

Not good enough. "He watched you," Lucien said, rising and poking some air into the fire. "When you rode out. I was in the orchard, where I'd been told I could find Mr. Osian, and I saw Ingraham perched up on the ridge, surveilling you as you enjoyed a solitary gallop."

"Surveilling?"

Wrong word. Too military. Savoring too strongly of espionage. "He waited until you'd cleared as many fences as you pleased, then intercepted you."

"Dash is polite, in the usual course. He could hardly have galloped down the slope and challenged me to a race."

How many times had Lucien raced her, on foot, on horseback, through a book? "You should be aware that Sir Dashiel's reputation in the military was less than pristine."

Penelope ceased her fussing and adopted the guileless expression Lucien positively hated. "Did he kill people, Lucien? Shoot them dead on the battlefield just like every soldier to take the king's shilling? Just like Henry doubtless did?"

Lucien replaced the poker in the hearth stand and sat cross-legged on the rug facing Penelope's chair. "Ingraham lasted less than two years in uniform—for the duration of a single campaign and two winter quarters, as it happened—because he was suspected of blackmailing his fellow officers. He got himself attached to the quartermaster's outfit and hid stores in the tents of anybody who crossed him. A word in the ear of the military police, and those enemies were facing a court-martial."

Penelope scowled at the fire. "Have you any proof of these accusations?"

"Somebody turned the tables on Captain Sir Dashiel Ingraham and secreted French lace under his pillow, or perhaps they found the lace Sir Dashiel had put there himself. The military police, who were beginning to smell foul play, were only too happy to report what they'd found."

"*French* lace?"

"The wives of several senior officers identified it as such. He was sent home with all possible haste, and nobody regretted his departure." Except possibly the French, who had at the very least traded lace for edible rations.

"Dash thinks himself clever, and he's not stupid, but he's..."

Lucien waited, though if Penelope took to defending a traitor...

"French lace is bad, isn't it?" Penelope asked, worrying a nail. "Worse than pilfering an extra blanket from the supply wagon."

"Much worse. The French were meagerly provisioned and expected to forage for their sustenance. Parts of Spain are desert, other parts mountainous, and foraging is difficult. Napoleon's rank and file would barter boots, brandy, *anything* for bread before you could say *vive l'empereur.*"

Penelope muttered something about privet hedges. "I have no understanding with Sir Dashiel."

Relief washed over Lucien, followed immediately by caution. "But?"

"But I might have been contemplating one in the abstract. You used to study a chess problem, then put it away and work on your translations. In some antechamber of your mind, you were still working on the chess problem, and when you woke up the next morning, you'd have a solution."

"An understanding with Sir Dashiel was forming in your mental antechamber?" Not good. Not good at all. Not quite disastrous either.

"By default, I suppose. At first, I resented being stashed away in the shires with her ladyship, but I've seen enough of Town to know I belong in the country. I've learned how to be useful here, how to go on, and I would miss the fresh air and greenery. A village market is a very different article from what happens in London, and a village assembly is very different from its Mayfair cousin."

Blessedly so. "Sir Dashiel could offer you a secure future among people you know and care for." Lucien avoided the word *love* out of habit. "He is the closest to an eligible in the surrounds, and he is interested. That doesn't obligate you to reciprocate, Pen. Why not hire a companion and retreat to Finbury? It's all of fifteen miles distant." Not quite easy visiting distance, but not the Antipodes either.

"Finbury? I hadn't thought of that. The tenants have been there forever, but I do own it."

She was too young to play the spinster, and she'd be bored witless at Finbury, which was a modest manor with a few well-run tenancies to its name. Self-supporting, though isolated by Kentish standards.

"Have you seen Finbury lately?" Lucien asked. "We could jaunt over there and look in on the place."

Penelope studied him from her perch in the wing chair, the limited light making her look very like her younger self in a severe mood, of which there had been many.

"We should not be having the discussion at this hour under these circumstances, my lord, but I don't seem to be insisting on the proprieties with you, do I?"

"One rejoices to agree with a lady. I have yet to hear an answer to my original question, though. Is Sir Dashiel a problem?"

"You did ask that question. You also issued the order, 'Tell me about Sir Dashiel.'"

"My apologies." Never argue with a lady, especially when she was right and had a nearly faultless memory for conversations.

"Sir Dashiel likely has formed expectations," Penelope said, "that are at least premature and, at the worst, problematic. Let me ponder the situation, because I don't want you humiliating him with any marquess-of-the-manor highhandedness. Nothing is so tedious as ill will between neighbors, and Sir Dashiel is very aware that you outrank him by miles."

"You outrank him, Pen." Half her appeal to Ingraham doubtless lay in the fact that she was an earl's daughter. Her fortune was the other half. That Penelope was also whip-smart, independent of mind and spirit, pretty, and possessed of a good sense of humor was all likely outside Sir Dashiel's notice.

Well, not the pretty part. He'd appreciate her good looks, the rotter.

"My honors are of the courtesy variety," she said. "Sir Dashiel can pass his baronetcy on to his son. You really should go, Lucien."

Yes, he really should. The conversation had produced insights rather than solutions, but before a fellow could devise a solution, he had to learn the problem's metes and bounds.

Lucien rose from the floor, not as easily as he once would have. "I apologize for intruding into your private apartment, but I couldn't find another opportunity to broach a difficult topic with you confidentially. If you see any need for me to intervene with Sir Dashiel, I am at your service. Otherwise, I leave the puzzle for you to solve in your own fashion."

"You don't like him, do you?"

"I don't respect him." Or trust him, or like him, or think him worthy to kiss Penelope's muddy hems.

"You haven't told me the whole of it, have you, Lucien? You heard things, rattling around on the Continent. You crossed paths with officers on leave and so forth."

"I did, but I will not slander a man with rumor when I have facts to present instead." Nor would he recite proof of that man's perfidy unnecessarily. The war was over. Lucien took up the poker again and banked the fire, then replaced the screen and offered Penelope his hand. "Off to bed with you."

She took his hand, and when she rose, she kept her fingers linked with his. "When you were traveling, you thought about me and about my refusal to come with you, and you came up with reasons why that was for the best, didn't you?"

"Endlessly."

"Until you convinced yourself the whole plan was foolish and you were actually relieved that I didn't go with you."

"I could never quite achieve relief, in fact, but I did try." With Penelope, only the truth would do.

"In the same fashion, I have tried to convince myself that Sir Dashiel is an acceptable suitor. I nearly succeeded. Something he said today, about not begrudging me my sentimental attachments, stayed with me. The marchioness favors such a match. She sings Dashiel's praises at every turn, but I am too willing to believe that he was ungentlemanly in uniform. My instinct has been at war with pragmatic arguments."

Lucien held very still. "Always a formidable battle."

"My reinforcements arrived in time. Good night, Lucien. I'm glad you're home, mostly." She kissed his cheek and slipped off to the bedroom, closing the door gently in her wake.

Lucien sank into the wing chair, still warm from Penelope's heat, and pondered a victory snatched from the jaws of defeat.

She could have married him. She very nearly did marry him. She still might marry him, in a weak moment in the middle of a weak year.

As Penelope moved quietly in the next room, Lucien pictured her unbraiding her hair and brushing it out. Masses of silky chestnut tresses that caught firelight and turned it to sunshine.

Focus, man. You've been solving the wrong problem.

He mentally probed around the edges of his hypothesis, turned it over and inside out. Tried thinking about it in French and then Welsh and came to the same conclusion from every direction.

The right problem was not how to stop Penelope from marrying Sir Dashiel, but rather, how to persuade her to marry Lucien. His conclusion had the feel of a theorem proved, *quod erat demonstrandum*. Correct, complete, and satisfying.

Curiously thrilling too.

When no more shadows flickered beneath Penelope's door, Lucien rose and took himself into the chilly corridor.

He had the sense he'd just lit upon a revelation dazzling to him but obvious to any passerby. He was prone to such moments, but no matter.

Penelope was in no way bound to Sir Dashiel—let there be rejoicing in the land—and Lucien was free to court her. He was so lost in thought that he almost missed Uncle Malcolm standing quietly in the shadows. Such was Malcolm's self-possession that even in a nightcap and dressing gown, he presented an imposing figure.

"I'm preparing to court her," Lucien said when Uncle looked ready to embark on the silent version of a stern lecture. "She hasn't given me permission to pay my addresses yet, but I'm preparing a siege that will make Wellington's efforts in Spain pale by comparison."

Uncle Malcolm shook a finger in Lucien's face, then grinned, smacked him hard on the shoulder, and withdrew into his apartment.

"Right," Lucien murmured to the closed door. "Make a proper job of it, or there will be dire consequences. Let the wooing begin."

He was hopeful that Penelope would know when and how to give Sir Dashiel his well-deserved congé and was even more hopeful that she'd do just that when the moment was right.

CHAPTER SIX

Penelope rose to the cheerful din of springtime birdsong and to a puzzling sense of relief. Lucien was home—that was part of the relief —but there was...

Ah. She had resolved to disabuse Sir Dashiel of any wayward matrimonial notions. The situation had weighed on her more than she'd admitted, but Lucien had given her a nudge in the direction of clear thinking. That Sir Dashiel had sold his commission just as Wellington was making some headway across Spain had puzzled everybody, but the baronet had come home to the requisite hero's welcome all the same. Dashiel had heirs—a cousin or three in Surrey —and his sisters were settled with the exception of Tabby.

Pilfering, of all the foolishness. Helping himself to the general stores and causing mischief like some churchyard gossip. There were worse crimes, but such behavior was unworthy of any officer. As for the French lace, the less said the better. An effective countermeasure by some fellow officer who'd had enough of wasted resources and false accusations.

Penelope rebraided her hair, chose a sensible day dress, then chose one a bit less sensible, then stuffed them both back into her wardrobe and donned her riding habit. She took her first cup of tea on her bedroom balcony, swaddled in her shawl and pleasant memories.

Lucien, sitting on the floor like a tailor's apprentice, as if he wasn't sixty-eighth in line for the throne. Lucien, asking, with that particular detachment he adopted when a question mattered, if Sir Dashiel was a problem. Lucien, tending the fire like an underfootman. Lucien, asleep on her sofa, wrapped in her shawl.

"How I have missed him." Missed him as she'd miss a best friend, a confidant, a boon companion, because he'd been all of that. She'd forgotten, though, that Lucien also had a protective streak.

Is Sir Dashiel a problem?

He might well have become one. Penelope would find a way to dissuade the neighborhood baronet from making a cake of himself, though the matter wanted thought.

The new day, however, called for a good gallop. She spread butter and jam on a thick piece of toast and made for the stable, where she found Lucien perched on the mounting block. The moment was prosaic—gentleman lounging in the stable yard on a gorgeous spring morning—but her heart leaped all the same, and that was as disconcerting as it was inevitable.

He was home. He had not abandoned her. He'd looked for a way to free them *both* from Lynnfield's demands. Foolish young man. Brave, daring foolish young man, and now he was home, not as young and no sort of fool.

"Penelope, good day." He rose and bowed over her hand. "I could not face breakfast with the elders. I'm out of practice."

"They aren't as lively as they used to be. Theo's habitually sore head makes him as quiet at breakfast as Malcolm. The flock usually breaks their fast in the dower house, and Tommie likes to read the paper."

"What of Aunt Purdy?" Lucien posed the question in Welsh, and to hear Welsh again, and from him, was luscious.

Penelope answered in the same language. "Aunt Purdy reads the Society pages while Tommie reads the financial pages, then they switch. The marchioness and I generally discuss the schedule for the day or week and any looming events."

Grooms led horses in from a night at pasture, stopping by the water trough some yards away. Morning sun glistened on verdant grass, and the last of the daffodils along the stable's north-facing wall bobbed gently.

Another morning at Lynnfield, but special too.

"Purdy reads the financial pages?" Lucien asked, sending a glance toward Lynnfield's stately façade. "That's new."

"She hordes fripperies because she had to leave so much behind in Wales, or that's Theo's theory. The financial pages interest her. She invests her widow's mite here and there and has done quite well. Her less attractive behaviors haven't been as frequent since her funds began increasing."

Lucien was bareheaded, and Penelope spied his top hat on the ladies' mounting block. She retrieved his millinery and positioned it on his head.

Before she stepped back, Lucien put a hand on her sleeve. "You started Purdy on the investing, didn't you, Pen? You used to pore over the financial pages."

She still read them when everybody else had finished with them. "I have funds, and I like to know how those funds are faring, so yes, I made some suggestions. The solicitors obliged, and the results have been encouraging. Purdy still borrows a pocket watch or brooch from time to time, but not nearly as often as she used to."

"Thank you. Purdy's larceny gave me nightmares. If she stole from the wrong party, she could end up being hauled before the assizes, and that would never do."

The horses were led out, Penelope's chestnut mare and a dark bay gelding.

"Good morning, Lorenzo," Penelope said, stroking the bay's nose. "How is he settling in?"

Lucien took up the girth a hole. "He's a well-traveled beast, though lately he's been biding in Town. Some ruralizing will suit him. His Magnificence is rising eight and blessed with a very good opinion of himself, which is mostly justified. He will purr if you offer him an apple."

"This is Ursuline," Penelope said, gesturing to the mare. "Nobody wanted her because she wasn't quite built for the plow, and she's tall to be a lady's mount."

"Tall and solid. Is she sensible?"

"Very, and honest to a fence. We suit." She scratched the mare's chest, which occasioned some undignified lip-wiggling from the horse. "I've known her to enjoy oranges, pears, and grapes."

"She has your appetite for fresh fruit. Up you go." Lucien passed Lorenzo's reins to the groom and led Ursuline to the taller mounting block. "I know a young lady whose favorite friends are a pair of carved wooden bears. She sleeps with them under her pillow and calls them her Ursulas, though they are properly referred to as Ursa Major and Minor. Her pet dragon, also carved of wood, stands watch on the bedside table each night."

What did it mean, that after all these years, Lucien recalled Penelope's love for fresh fruit? "Would this imaginative young lady be your daughter, my lord?"

He tugged on Ursuline's girth and apparently found it sufficiently snug. "I have no children, Pen. My travels did not lend themselves to those sorts of attachments."

And yet, he knew the child's bedtime routine. "Who is she?"

"My former employer's cousin of some sort. Let's be on our way, and I'll tell you the whole story."

A fair offer. Penelope settled into the saddle and took up the reins. Lucien arranged her skirts, a courtesy a gentleman was expected to perform while the lady controlled her mount. He had a word with Jeffers, the groom on duty, and swung into the saddle.

"Lead on, my lady. I want to renew my acquaintance with the

whole estate, but one morning is insufficient for that undertaking. I am at your command."

"Let's start at the top of the ridge. I will never tire of that view."

They walked their horses from the stable yard, the mare and gelding clip-clopping side by side onto the lane that led to the home farm.

"How is it a peer of the realm was in another man's employ?"

"Do you want the polite version or the less flattering tale?"

The serious note in his question bothered her. "I want the truth."

"What follows is a confidence, Pen, but you have long held my confidences. The honest label for much of what I got up to is 'spying.' The word is ugly, and the reality can be too. The military likes to pretend that spying is cheating. That wars are won by good, honest slaughter of one's fellow man, by marching the enlisted men to death for the sake of Merry Olde, or blowing up siege walls that have stood for centuries. That's honorable warfare for you. A sanguinary challenge for true men. Skulking about behind enemy lines, capturing the enemy's dispatches, and cozening his generals' servants in their weak moments is not done."

"Except it is?"

"No officer worth his rank wants to be responsible for avoidable bloodshed, and all the marching and arming and victualing is damned expensive. Wellington relied on reconnaissance officers whose work consisted of observing territory and reporting back to headquarters. The Spanish did a magnificent job of intercepting French dispatches for us. For the truly dirty jobs, His Grace relied on spies."

The morning, among the prettiest Kent had to offer, lost some of its shine as the track turned up a wooded incline.

"Some of those jobs fell to you, though you are a peer and left England without an heir." Why on earth take such risks? Lucien wasn't fanciful, nor was he irresponsible.

"I left England when I was thinking none too clearly. The art collecting began without any particular intention on my part, then a colonel on leave took me aside and explained that I was well placed to be of assistance to the crown on a particularly delicate matter."

Why would Lucien, whose thinking was prodigiously clear and quick...? *Oh dear.* "You missed Lynnfield."

He brushed a glance over her. "I missed *you*, more than I thought possible. I labored under some mistaken impressions, and—lest we forget—I was young and pigheaded. Enough said on that topic. Nobody would suspect a man in my circumstances, a peer of the realm, a hobbyist polyglot overly attached to his chessboard, to be on the king's business. I was safe enough most of the time."

Penelope's Welsh was rusty, but she had an excellent command of common sense. Clearly, Lucien had risked his life, repeatedly, and without the protection of an officer's uniform.

"This is why you didn't come home? You were defeating Napoleon, one pawn, one rook, one dusty portrait or silver tea service at a time?"

They left the trees near the crest of the long ridge that bordered the western edge of Lynnfield proper. The track continued at an angle to the ridge, ascending more gradually.

"In that business, Pen, you adopt a role and try to become it. I went into the game thinking I'd try my hand, translate some purloined dispatches, get the French general's groom drunk, and have some stories to tell in my dotage, assuming I survived to enjoy a dotage. But the stakes are so high and the prizes to be won enormous. Battles averted or won versus battles ending in a rout. Weeks of supplies for the French stolen, weeks of our supplies carried off by brigands. A war within a war and not a shot fired. One is seduced into thinking one matters."

"You did matter. You do matter." Ye gods, if she'd lost him *and* Henry... Penelope turned her face to the sun and sent up a prayer of gratitude that Lucien had come home. Not that he'd come home to her and Lynnfield, or that he'd come home hale and handsome, but rather, that he'd come home *at all*.

"I ended up in Italy, and because I spoke the language well, and not many Britons do, I spent much of the war there. I was safer in Italy than I'd been in France and Spain—though if anybody asks, I was never in France while hostilities raged—and I took up employment as the majordomo to an English sculptor."

"Not His Grace of Huntleigh? You were a duke's *butler*? Lucien, that would be humorous if it wasn't so outlandish."

"He wasn't His Grace of Huntleigh when our paths crossed. He was a tired, grouchy, talented artist whose staff was stealing him blind. He knew it and didn't care, and that drove me nigh to Bedlam. He was so enthralled with his marble and alabaster and clay... Somebody had to take him in hand, and the exercise brought much-needed balance and order to my life as well."

"His Grace is on his wedding journey, isn't he?"

"He is, and his advice to me was that I should do exactly as I had advised him to do and go the hell home."

In Welsh, the profanity wasn't as harsh. "You've been in England for months, and you didn't think to come to Lynnfield?"

"I passed through the neighborhood, saw that all was prospering, and returned to my duties in London. I did not venture onto the estate itself for fear of seeing familiar faces, but by God, this view is wondrous, and I have longed to see it again."

The conversation had been lovely too. Honest, a bit rambling and unexpected, but personal. When was the last time Penelope had had a personal discussion with anybody? Her exchanges with Malcolm halfway qualified, which was a compliment to Malcolm and a pathetic comment on her social life.

"Are you home to stay, Lucien?" *Please say yes.*

"I am, much to my surprise. I expected to look in on matters here, sort out a few issues, and... I don't know what I thought I would do with myself. I was so homesick and so determined not to admit it, but here you are, and when I'm with you, I have no dignity. Only embarrassing quantities of honesty. How about you preserve me from further mortification and tell me how you've managed all these years and how you're planning to put an end to Sir Dashiel's matrimonial campaign?"

"I haven't worked that out yet," Penelope said, "but something will come to me that preserves his pride and my reputation. In all those years away, Lucien, wasn't there anybody special?"

He brought his horse to a halt at the very top of the hill and gazed not at the glorious patchwork of pastures, fields, and forests spread out beneath them, but at Penelope.

"There was you, Pentimento. There was always and only you."

"Your ladyship, good day." Leopold St. Didier bowed to Rhian, Marchioness of Lynnfield, in an abundance of caution.

Lynnfield Manor was one of the least formal peerage establishments he'd come across, and the older generation could be shockingly casual. Marchionesses as a species were nonetheless due considerable deference, even at the first meal of the day.

"Mr. St. Didier, do have a seat." Her ladyship presided over the head of the table, the room's sole occupant. "The household is quite at sixes and sevens, but you may depend on the breakfast parlor for peace and quiet until well after nine of the clock. Are you missing London?"

He settled at her right hand. "No, actually, and yet, one feels one should not be away from the place too long."

"Precisely. The beating heart of good society, the universal nexus of art and culture, the best place to shop. How does anybody stay away?"

St. Didier poured himself a cup of steaming China black. "The unrelenting stench of coal smoke and, worse, the noise, the wretched poverty, and human misery?"

"Serious conversation at the breakfast table is bad form, young man. I knew your mama. She would scold you roundly for such observations, and yet, you do have a point. One doesn't long for

London, exactly. One longs for Mayfair and its surrounds. Fill your plate, and we will establish our mutual acquaintances."

She liked giving orders, did her ladyship. St. Didier disliked taking orders, but he'd learned to tolerate them of necessity. Besides, he was hungry. Fresh country air and all that. He served himself some omelet and a few slices of ham and took a generous bowl of orange sections as well.

"How is it you knew my mother?"

"Her godmother was Lady Paloma Essington until Lady Paloma became Lady Barnstable. Her ladyship and I attended the same select academy for two interminable years, and the connection was formed. Being a godmother is somewhat like being a grandmother, without the tedious family gatherings. Lola and I spoiled our godchildren competitively. Why aren't you married, Mr. St. Didier?"

St. Didier tucked into his eggs. "I am flattered to believe you'd ask me that, whether I was the head gardener or a royal duke."

"Spring turns an old lady's thoughts to matchmaking. Lucien is home, and as soon as Mayfair grasps that he's back in Britain, a stampede of heiresses and originals will renew their acquaintances with me. Good of him to reappear while I still have my wits about me."

Nobody could accuse the marchioness of subtlety. "His lordship is young yet, and he'll need some time to take up the reins here. He's been in London since autumn, from what I understand, and in spring, a young man's thoughts can turn to preserving his bachelorhood."

The marchioness sipped her tea, the gesture conveying disapproval. "His lordship was off traveling for years, sir. *Years.* Lucien is my great-nephew, not my son. My late husband and I did not see any of our children survive to start their schooling, much less arrive to adulthood. Lucien might be similarly cursed. He needs to get on with his responsibilities and to blazes with skulking about on the crown's business. Undignified business, at that. At least he bought some lovely art while he was up to no good."

St. Didier hid his shock behind the complicated process of

selecting an orange slice. "Skulking about on the crown's business, my lady?" One suspected, of course, but one did not mention such suspicions. Not at the breakfast table and not at the club two hours past midnight when only close friends were at hand.

Not that St. Didier had close friends or frequented clubs in the small hours.

"Oh, don't take that tone with me, Mr. St. Didier. I hear all the gossip. All of it, and when half of Mayfair had sons, nephews, and grandsons in uniform, letters supplemented the talk. Lucien was positively identified in Bordeau when he was supposedly writing to me from Berlin. I could go on, but suffice it to say I do not appreciate Fat George putting the Lynnfield succession at risk, but that's precisely the sort of game Prinny plays. All lark's tongue in aspic on the surface and a lot of deviltry beneath. He would love to get his pudgy hands on Lynnfield, and then we'd all have to remove to Finbury and impose on Penelope."

"I have never been served lark's tongue, in aspic or otherwise, and I hope to die in that state of grace. More tea, your ladyship?"

"You are changing the subject. Somebody put the manners on you, but there are times, young man, when manners are an obstruction. I've said the same thing to Sir Dashiel, who thinks his gentlemanly airs will impress our Penelope. The fellow has her on some sort of pedestal, I fear, and Penny will miss her chance if she's not a bit more forthcoming."

From spying to matchmaking. Who said country life was dull? "I am not well acquainted with Sir Dashiel, but he seems to enjoy a good opinion of himself."

"Penny thinks well enough of him too. She sees him for what he is—uppish gentry with some military pretensions."

St. Didier mentally winced on behalf of Sir Dashiel's dignity. "Why isn't he Captain Sir Dashiel? Most fellows are proud to brandish their military past on occasion."

Her ladyship set down her tea cup. "One doesn't pry, Mr. St.

Didier." She said this in all seriousness. "Penelope's brother died in uniform, and I can see Sir Dashiel being delicate enough to drop the use of his rank rather than remind Penny of a sad loss. He's that considerate."

Sir Dashiel was not considerate. St. Didier had observed the man on a previous outing to Lynnfield, and whatever adjectives might be applied to Sir Dashiel—priggish, scheming, self-important, over-bearing—he was not considerate unless *appearing* considerate served some end of his own.

"Will you take Tabitha Ingraham up to Town with you?" St. Didier asked.

"Next year," her ladyship replied. "Those oranges look good. Suppose you fetch me a few slices, there's a good fellow."

St. Didier followed orders again, taking a few more slices for himself too. For this late in the season, the quality was excellent.

"Does Lady Penelope return Sir Dashiel's esteem?" he asked, resuming his place at the table. "She appears to be a very capable sort." More of a potential marchioness than a potential wife to a baronet.

"Penelope likes to stay busy, and heaven knows, this old pile has provided her with opportunities for bustling about. Lucien is home now, though, so Penelope need not remain bound by any responsibili-ties here. She's not getting any younger, and when Lucien takes a wife, Lynnfield will have less room for an unmarried heiress without portfolio."

St. Didier chose an orange slice and was rewarded with an abso-lutely scrumptious burst of gustatory sunshine. By contrast, the day beyond the window, which had started with such promise, was turning a bit dodgy. The breeze had picked up, making the daffodils around the fountain bob, and clouds were scudding in from the east.

"Then I gather you favor a match with Sir Dashiel for Lady Pene-lope?" Lady Penelope would have Sir Dashiel sorted in very short order, but she'd be wasted on that exercise.

Then too, she was still technically betrothed to the marquess, wasn't she?

"Penelope has known Sir Dashiel for ages, and they get on quite well. They make an attractive pair on the dance floor, and no bride wants to go far from familiar surrounds when she sets up her own household. Besides, Penelope has no other options in terms of suitors, unless she's willing to do the Town whirl again. She honestly did not *take* when she made her previous attempts. She'd best accept what's on offer from Sir Dashiel, if she knows what's good for her."

St. Didier tried to enjoy his oranges, but the turn of the conversation bothered him.

Exceedingly.

Lady Penelope Richard had inherited the entire personal wealth of a family that knew it was down to a sole heir and had planned accordingly. She had at least ten child-bearing years left, likely more, and she was the daughter of an earl.

Any other marchioness would consider that Sir Dashiel's aspirations aimed far too high for his station, Byronic curls and baronetcy notwithstanding.

As the orange slices met their fate, St. Didier mentally began the arrangements necessary to return to Town on the morrow. Lady Penelope was still his client after a fashion, and thus he was entitled to make a few inquiries on her behalf.

Her ladyship had at least one other option when it came to suitors. An option that should be obvious and appealing to the marchioness.

Lucien, Marquess of Lynnfield, looked at Lady Penelope as if she were a chess riddle, a Canova goddess, and a treasured friend, all rolled into one magnificent woman. His lordship was arse over ears for the lady, and if she didn't return his regard, St. Didier would be very much surprised.

He had not been surprised in ages. He was puzzled, though, by the marchioness's insistence that Lady Penelope make a match with Sir Dashiel. Damn puzzled.

"If your ladyship will excuse me, I must prepare for my journey back to Town and get off a few letters before I take my leave of Lynnfield tomorrow." He rose and decamped, swiping a whole orange from the bowl on the sideboard as he headed out the door.

CHAPTER SEVEN

Lucien had not planned to share his ride with anybody, much less make disclosures to Penelope that would give Wellington nightmares. But then, His Grace was said to confide in the ladies, to talk to them of personal matters rather than to his fellow officers or peers, and the ladies respected the duke's confidences.

More to the point, the war was over, thank all the gods in all the pantheons. As if to prove that fact, there sat Penelope on her mare, looking gloriously vital in the morning sun and more dear than home and hearth.

"There was me?" she asked, brushing back a stray tendril of hair. "What does that mean, Lucien? You were off lurking in castles, or wherever a purveyor of fine art and wicked secrets lurks, and I was here, mediating arguments between Purdy and Wren over a purloined ring."

"You were here," Lucien said, tapping his temple. "And here." His heart. "I tried forgetting you, but then somebody would mangle a quote, and I'd hear your voice correcting them. I tried ignoring you, but then a young girl would brush past me, with exactly the same sense of suppressed hurry you brought with you so often, and you would haunt me again. Would you have come with me, if you'd found my note?"

Penelope sat atop the chestnut mare, the perfect equestrienne on a perfect morning—but for a few clouds gathering to the east—and yet, she was also his precious Pen. Quick-witted, practical, kind, and honest.

"I'm not sure, Lucien. I might have talked you out of going. I might have understood why you left. We will never know. Isn't it enough that I'm glad you're back?" She urged the mare forward, and Lucien nudged Lorenzo onward too.

She was glad he was back. That was something, but not nearly enough. Lucien decided on strategic retreat. "How have you occupied yourself in my absence?"

She rode along the crest of the ridge, into the morning breeze teasing at her chignon. "I read the whole library, first. Then I took up the study of Russian for the sake of novelty, but I haven't your capacity for independent scholarship with languages, and nobody was on hand to help with pronunciation. The marchioness trotted me up to Town for a few Seasons. London bored me witless. The fittings alone... Do you know how difficult it is to stand on a stool for two hours without moving while women pretending to be French randomly stick you with pins?"

"Nevertheless, you put up with it." Put up with it and pretended to enjoy it, but Penelope was a poor liar, one of many qualities Lucien esteemed about her.

"The marchioness sets such great store by the whole whirl, Lucien. She has friends in Town, old friends who've known her since girlhood. I know what it is to miss a friend."

As the sun passed behind a stray cloud, Lucien asked the pathetic, callow question. "You missed me?"

Her smile was pure mischief. "I hated you, or tried to. Abandoning Lynnfield with no explanation, no warning. All the people who said you weren't quite mentally stable dined out on the mode of your leave-taking. I hated *them* in earnest. In hindsight, though, I knew you were unhappy here. You were always studying the maps, corresponding with university professors on the Continent, staring off at the horizon and looking glum. When I ceased being wroth with you, I wanted you to be happy, but it doesn't sound as if you were."

He'd been a proper wreck for the first two years. "I was useful. I suspect you were useful too."

She turned her mare down the Lynnfield side of the hill, onto a path that led to the lake. "I wasn't born here. I am just another item in the estate collection of rummage-sale relatives. Usefulness was a comfort, especially after Henry died. Then too, the marchioness isn't exactly lazy, but she does like to issue little decrees and tell others what to do."

Lucien had found Auntie curiously reticent since his return. Brusquely welcoming, also distracted. "She can hire a companion to order about if you are tired of humoring her. I do think a jaunt to Finbury is overdue, Pen. You own that place, and the solicitors won't bother to look in on it often enough."

They passed back into the trees, the air noticeably cooler despite the lower elevation. "You've seen it recently, I suppose. What aren't you telling me, Lucien?"

What a spymaster she would have made, with her ability to connect hints and clues and come up with insights.

"Did you give permission for your tenants to create a water meadow where the river crosses the northern acreage?"

"No. I can see why they'd want to—better hay, earlier hay, a safe-guard against drought—but the miller would object to having the water diverted from time to time."

"As will the downstream farmers in dry seasons. You are the land-lord. All maintenance and improvements fall exclusively within your purview, and a water meadow is an improvement."

Penelope made a face. "You won't tell me to write a stern letter to the solicitors and go back to my needlepoint, will you?"

"You'd beat me with my own hat if I made the attempt." She'd hated needlepoint as a girl.

She eyed his top hat. "That's Bond Street work, my lord. I'd beat you with the nearest handy birch rod. Let's race to the lake, shall we? The weather seems to be turning on us, and we aren't likely to have as much time in the saddle as I'd wished."

"From the gate at the bottom of the hill."

Lorenzo had been living the life of a Town horse, while Ursuline was leggy, fit, and game. Despite the gelding's best efforts, the mare had him by a length.

"Walk to the cottage," Penelope panted when they pulled up on the track that circled the lake. "Your horse wants conditioning, my lord."

"My lady wants graciousness in victory," Lucien retorted. Pen had also lost a few hairpins somewhere after the first quarter mile, and a long, coppery curl had come loose at her nape over the second stile.

"Allow me my small pleasures," she said, patting her horse. "Ursuline loves a good gallop, and so do I."

I love you. Lucien mentally chopped the words into tiny pieces and threw them into the lake, though they were true.

Always had been, always would be.

"We should have raced the other direction," Lucien said. "Looks like a shower headed this way." Or possibly the harbinger of an entire stormy day. No predicting spring weather in Kent, though Welsh weather was even more mercurial.

"Do you know what I miss most about Wales?" Penelope said, showing no sign of turning her mare around. "The rainbows. We have them here, but not as vivid, not as many. Once upon a time, I saw three different rainbows from the top of the hill behind our dower house."

That dower house was Prinny's now. "My summers with my mother's parents were magical and not only because they told me all the stories, taught me all the songs, and kept up my Welsh. The land in Wales isn't sedate like dear old Kent. The air isn't soft."

A rumble of thunder sounded from the east. "We'll get soaked, Lucien." Penelope didn't seem particularly bothered by the prospect.

"Not if we wait it out in the cottage."

The lake cottage, a four-bedroom dwelling Lucien had been advised to keep in reserve lest more relatives come straggling up the drive, sat back some twenty yards from the shore with a lovely view facing out over the water, a small barn, and a modest walled garden.

"They'll worry at the manor if we don't come home," Penelope said.

"They will not. You and I have been out in downpours before, Pendragon, and then there was the time we were nearly caught in a blinding snowstorm. Most of that lot won't even be aware that we've ridden out, and the stable knows better than to sound the alarm."

The cottage came into view around a bend in the shore. A venerable willow in the chartreuse glory of new foliage dipped a few fronds into the water, until a stiff gust sent ripples chopping across the lake and branches tossing on the wind.

"Lorenzo hasn't another hard run in him just yet," Lucien said, which was true. "The cottage boasts a chess set, as I recall."

"And a roof," Penelope said. "The roof decides me. Trot on, girl." Ursuline obliged smartly, as did Lorenzo, and within two minutes, they'd reached the little stable yard beside the barn.

"I'll get a fire started," Penelope said, extricating herself from the saddle without any assistance. "You tend to the horses. Just take off bridles, loosen girths, and—"

A spatter of hail whipped down.

"Go," Lucien said, swinging a leg over the pommel and leaping down. "Go, start us a fire. Find the chess set."

He would have jogged the horses into the barn aisle, the better to avoid a drenching, but Penelope put a hand on his arm, looked him right in the eye, and kissed him on the mouth, then grinned like an imp. She lifted her hems and pelted along the path to the back porch of the cottage, while Lucien stood in the frigid rain and watched her go.

The two horses regarded him as if he'd lost his wits, and yet, he didn't look away until Penelope found the key above the lintel and slipped into the house.

Nefoedd, helpwch fi os gwelwch yn dda. "Heaven help me," he translated for the benefit of the horses. "I cannot allow her to keep kissing me like that."

Lucien saw to the horses, by which time a sleety mess had started in earnest. He made his way to the house, bareheaded and without haste, the better to marshal his resolve where Penelope and her runaway kisses were concerned.

"I correct myself: Penelope can kiss me all she likes. It's the scampering off afterward that we must address," he muttered, giving the door a hard stare. "A chance to kiss her back would be sporting and—"

The door opened. Penelope grabbed him by the sleeve and pulled him over the threshold.

As it turned out, kissing her back served very well indeed.

Penelope had loved Lucien the boy, who'd befriended her when most young fellows would have turned up their noses at a homesick female of any age, much less one somewhat their junior. She had been Lucien the youth's boon companion and become infatuated with Lucien the young man.

Lucien the adult male, home from the war, half mystery, half long-lost love, was a fascinating blend of his various predecessors and compelling in his own right.

He'd been a slender youth, tallish, and quick rather than substantial. The man glaring at the cottage's back door window was trim, also wrapped in muscle. His quickness of mind and body was accompanied by a sense of power he'd lacked earlier in life.

And he is mine.

She accepted that truth with equal parts relief and rejoicing. Lucien was hers, he was home, and the moment called for boldness.

Penelope yanked open the door and pulled Lucien inside, and then she indulged in an unrestrained bout of kissing. Somewhere between fusing her mouth to his and lashing an arm around his waist, she shoved the door at his back closed.

He hauled her close, lifted her off her feet enough to reverse their positions, and caged Penelope against the door with his body.

"No disappearing," he muttered. "You don't get to leave me standing in a puddle of bewilderment and unrequited passion this time."

What was he...? Oh. "Those were test kisses. I was giving you a chance to hare off." *Again.*

The kitchen was gloomy and chilly, but Lucien's gaze could have lit signal fires at twenty paces. "I am finished with haring off. Done, through. *Fini. Gorffenedig. Fertig und vorbei. Finito.* Do you understand?"

"You are home to stay in French, Welsh, German, and Italian. Good, because if you do disappear on me again, note or no note, I will be similarly finished with you, sir." Penelope delivered that ultimatum unrehearsed, but the words had come from her heart.

If Lucien abandoned her again, she would not answer for the consequences.

"Understood." His gaze became, if anything, more fierce. "You should also understand that you need not deploy kisses to keep me at Lynnfield, Pen. Kiss me because you want to, not because you abhor the thought of running the place in my absence again."

Must he be so irresistible when making his proclamations? "You were gone, but I had Lynnfield in your place. Don't blame me for guarding what was left to guard."

He made a sound, part exasperation, part surrender, then leaned closer. "My heart is yours to guard. Always has been. Always will be."

Not a proclamation, a declaration, and Penelope would have

been happy to stand in a puddle of joy, except that Lucien had resumed kissing her. His approach was nearly reserved, so gently did he press his lips to the corner of her mouth, and Penelope somehow bore it.

She withstood the pleasure of Lucien's arms coming around her securely and enfolding her in strength and warmth. She endured the way he cradled the back of her head in his palm and urged her closer, and she accorded herself saintly restraint for not attempting to wrap a leg around his hip, though her riding habit would have doomed that undertaking in any case.

"I like this," she murmured as Lucien pressed lazy kisses to her brow. "You were never this patient in your youth."

"I was never this determined."

She closed her eyes and tried to think, such as any command of her mental powers yet remained to her. Lucien had been prodigiously stubborn as a boy. He'd lived on bread and water for a fortnight rather than apologize to his tutor for declaring that six extant royal princes were a burden on the national exchequer.

Penelope had slipped him the odd meat pie and some fruit tarts, of course.

The tutor had given notice before it was all over, and Penelope suspected that had been Lucien's objective.

"You were very determined," she said, patting Lucien's bum.

"You made me look lackadaisical by comparison. Kiss me."

She pinched him. "Don't give me orders, Lucien. That hasn't changed."

"Please kiss me, or I will take matters into my own..."

She kissed him, slowly and sweetly, and only then realized how snugly he'd been holding her. His embrace relaxed, and the gloomy old kitchen became magical. Rain pattered down, the wind moaned around a corner of the house, and as the fire in the hearth gradually overcame the chill, Penelope's sense of urgency faded into wonder.

"You won't do anything impetuous, will you?" she asked during their next intermission.

"Go down on bended knee? The floor is cold and in need of sweeping, but the notion has a certain appeal."

"Impetuous," Penelope said, easing back and taking Lucien's hand, "like disappearing into London to visit the jewelers' shops. Sending an express off to your pet duke about impending nuptials. Confiding in St. Didier."

Lucien led her to the fireplace, shrugged out of his riding jacket, and laid it on the raised hearth. "Would it bother you if I let St. Didier know that I'm courting you?"

Courting. Well, yes. "Has he become your friend?"

Lucien sat on his folded coat and tugged on Penelope's hand. When she'd taken the place beside him, he looped an arm around her shoulders.

"I suspect St. Didier is your friend, Pen. He threatened to all but thrash me if I toyed with your affections, and he was in deadly earnest."

"He's always in earnest. I like that about him. No silliness or pomposity. He's also discreet. I suppose you might intimate to him that he need not thrash you after all." The fire was warm at Penelope's back, and Lucien was warm as well. *May the rain last all day, please.*

"Penelope, I am courting you. You need not fear that I'll decide to resume spying or take up another butler's post. I was so homesick for so long... Then I reasoned that Lynnfield was muddling on well enough without me, and Huntleigh needed some assistance, though he was plain Finn Cathcart to the world. I will not gallop off without an explanation, and I will not decide that I'd rather court Tabby Ingraham, or whoever the local reigning belle is."

"I believe you."

Lucien bent his head to murmur near her ear. "But?"

Penelope sat back enough to meet Lucien's gaze. "Sir Dashiel must not learn of our courtship too soon or from anybody but me. His pride will be wounded regardless, but we have no call to be callous.

He will be Lynnfield's neighbor for all the rest of his days. One wants good relations with one's neighbors."

"You aren't simply looking around for delaying tactics, are you, Pen?"

"No." Not truly. "Perhaps a little. You've only just come home."

Lucien sat up, though his arm remained around Penelope's shoulders. "I owe you years of patience, Pen-and-Sword. Take all the time you please. Rearrange all the furniture in your mental attics until you are comfortable with the notion of marrying me—or you have decided we would not suit. I left without explanation, as far as you are concerned, and now I'm back, alluding to a note you never saw and sentiments I never declared. I was off doing God knows what, God knows where... Regaining your trust will take time."

"I should argue with you. Tell you that my trust and my heart have always been yours. Add a few Welsh endearments." She would not be lying, exactly, at least not about her heart, but as for her trust...

"But you are too honest for placatory platitudes," Lucien said, "and I treasure you for that. Haste isn't usually my style either, if we've reached the blunt-speaking part. Perhaps your hesitation is justified."

"Justified how?"

"Do you know what my mother's last words to me were?" He took Penelope's hand in both of his.

Lucien never spoke of his parents. "What did she say?"

"'I love you. Always remember that I love you.' She died shortly thereafter, though she was a young woman. If I feel a sense of urgency about courting you, perhaps I am driven by old ghosts."

Penelope laid her head on Lucien's shoulder. "I'm sorry, Lucien. She was devoted to your father, I'm told."

"Too devoted? Papa's death devastated us both, then Mama was gone too. I had so many questions, but then it was decided I was to be sent to Great-Uncle Thomas, and when I was allowed to visit Wales, I could not bring myself to pester my grandparents with a boy's questions."

And all he'd have earned in response to those questions was more words. So much about Lucien was illuminated by this quiet conversation. His fascination with the empirical quality of natural science, his love of all things rational and cerebral, even his keen ear for the spoken word.

His unfailing kindness to another orphan.

"Lucien, you aren't rescuing me, are you? Taking pity on the spinster antidote third cousin before she succumbs to the charms of the bumpkin next door?"

Lucien gave her a one-armed hug. "Call Sir Dashiel a bumpkin to his face, and he will expire of injured pride. I am not rescuing you, though you did rescue Lynnfield in my absence. I am not taking anything like pity on you, though you might be said to be taking pity on me. I'm eccentric, you know, and I was too stupid to avoid the Continent in time of war. When polite society learns that I was a peer's butler, they will declare me entirely *non compos mentis*, and what they've said about the Lynnfield elders does not bear repeating."

And in London, Lucien would have collected *all* the gossip, one way or another. "The gossips haven't been exactly kind to me either. The marchioness has let a few things slip. She is fond of Sir Dashiel. A neighbor of long standing, always a gentleman, that sort of thing. My unmarried state embarrasses her, methinks."

Lucien rose and offered Penelope his hand. "The marchioness wanted you nearby, doubtless thinking that you'd be able to run both Lynnfield and the Roost, which you are more than competent to do. Aunt has a pragmatic streak, though she keeps it well hidden. The rain has stopped."

Penelope rose and caught Lucien in a hug. "It might start up again. I am curiously reluctant to brave the elements just now." Also curiously fortified. Encouraged in the old-fashioned sense of having found some bravery.

Lucien rested his chin on her crown. "We will face the elements together, if that makes a difference."

Missing him had left Penelope with a well of longing that would take years to fill, though she comforted herself with the realization that Lucien had carried a similar burden, and for just as long.

"To brave challenges with you will make all the difference in the world, Lucien." She kissed him once more for good measure, then handed him his coat.

They were soon in their respective saddles, trotting for the manor, because the sky presaged more rain, wind, and mischief. They had made it as far as the gate before a wet figure came into view, tramping along the lane toward Lynnfield.

"He's soaked, whoever he is," Penelope muttered. "Caught in the proverbial downpour."

"I know that walk," Lucien replied. "I know that hat. Uncle! Uncle Malcolm!"

The figure trudged onward. Penelope urged Ursuline into another trot. "Uncle Malcolm, wait." She caught up with him, and still he marched along. "You are soaking wet, you poor thing. Lucien and I built a fire in the lake cottage, and if you—"

Lucien came up on his gelding. "What's amiss?"

Malcolm brushed a glance over Penelope, and she felt a chill that had little to do with the nasty weather. "Malcolm is furious."

Lucien swung down. "Uncle, are you in difficulties?"

Malcolm stared straight ahead, a sopping-wet old fellow who yet exuded both ire and self-possession.

"Pen, if you'll take Lorenzo to the stable, I will accompany Uncle to Lynnfield."

Malcolm offered neither support nor protest at that plan. Penelope took the gelding's reins. "You don't want me to send a cart?"

"I suspect the situation calls for discretion. We'll see you at lunch."

Penelope left even as another spate of drizzle commenced. When she topped the next rise, she looked back, half thinking to blow her darling a kiss, except that Lucien and Malcolm were slogging along, heads bent against the wind, and the moment was too disquieting for silly kisses.

CHAPTER EIGHT

"You're leaving us tomorrow?" Lucien asked, passing St. Didier a glass of brandy. "Has the hospitality been lacking?"

"The hospitality has been excellent," St. Didier said, accepting the nightcap. "The company interesting. To journeys safely concluded."

Lucien sipped, more amused than annoyed at St. Didier's allusions. "I am home to stay. You are right about that." Where was home for St. Didier? The family seat where he'd likely been raised was doubtless now in the hands of the Crown.

"What does her ladyship make of your return?" St. Didier asked, starting on a circuit of the library. "Lady Penelope, that is."

"She and I have sorted the confusion regarding the terms of my departure. We are firmly in charity with each other." What a relief to be able to say that.

St. Didier studied a portrait of Malcolm and Purdy done when they'd first arrived from Wales, before Lucien's day. Malcolm had been a tall, serious youth, a glimmer of wildness in his eyes. Purdy had been petite and much given to the elaborate embroidery and excessive lace of an earlier age. She'd exuded timidity even in girl-hood, while to Lucien's eye, Malcolm had been fierce.

"Why doesn't he speak?" St. Didier asked. "Rude of me to inquire, but your uncle is clearly intelligent and observant."

As St. Didier was intelligent and observant. "We don't know. According to Aunt Purdy, Malcolm spoke Welsh as a boy without any problem. When he was brought here, he tried to learn English, then gave up speaking altogether. He reads in several languages and knows every weed and wildflower on the estate, but he keeps his words to himself."

"He wasn't at supper."

"Or lunch. He was caught out in the rain this morning and got quite a soaking." Though Lucien was certain that more than wet weather had put Malcolm in an angry state.

"He sketches," St. Didier said, peering at an exquisite drawing of purple heather finished in watercolors. "Quite competently."

"He was educated as a gentleman until his parents' demise. I gather he did a lot of wandering once he came to Lynnfield, and the old marquess allowed it. Do you plan to lecture me about the betrothal contract that I have yet to rescind?"

St. Didier sipped delicately. "Would lecturing do any good?"

"You will be pleased to know that Lady Penelope and I have embarked upon a quiet courtship."

St. Didier's expression became severe. The change was subtle, a firming of the lips, a slight lift of one dark eyebrow. "Fast work, my lord."

"Having resolved the old misunderstanding, I have leave to discreetly pay Penelope my addresses, nothing more." Though Lucien was troubled by the fate of the note. Who had found it? What had they done with it? He'd written in code, of course, but Theo was a good amateur cryptographer, and Tommie had been underfoot at the time as well.

"I still say, fast work. Why be so precipitous in your wooing?"

That St. Didier took the situation seriously was encouraging. He truly would thrash anybody who offered Penelope insult.

"Sir Dashiel has taken it into his head that he and Penelope would suit. Penelope had begun talking herself into considering the same possibility. She doesn't particularly like Sir Dashiel, but the marchioness favors the match."

"And Lady Penelope has spent her adult years, such as they are, ensuring that the marchioness has no cause for complaint. Old habits die hard." St. Didier moved on to a portrait of Lucien as a youth.

"Is returning to London an old habit?" Lucien asked.

"Oh, perhaps. One has inquiries to make. You were skinny."

"I grew three inches the summer I sat for that one. I could eat banquets without ceasing, and it made no difference." Endless raids on the kitchen with Penelope standing as lookout. Impromptu picnics on every corner of the estate... A lovely summer, full of yearning and sweetness. "The old marquess said my father had been the same way as a boy."

St. Didier treated Lucien to a head-to-toe perusal. "What does Huntleigh make of your decision to leave his employ? He was fond of you, in his way."

"His Grace sacked me for about the seventeenth time. Said I was an idiot not to take my own advice. That I had family, true family, waiting for me at home, and putting off the inevitable never made it any easier. Then he told me I was welcome to remain as a guest in his house as long as I needed to and swept off to Italy with his duchess."

"He's unconventional, but nobody's fool. You'll write to him?"

Huntleigh was another of St. Didier's finds, the heir of last resort to an impoverished dukedom. Also a decent man and a wickedly talented sculptor.

"I will inform His Grace that I am happily established at the family seat and inquire after the duchess, Miss Emily, and her menagerie. Lady Penelope has asked me to remain silent regarding other developments, though she gave me leave to impart the generalities to you."

St. Didier took another measured sip of his drink. "I am honored, also puzzled. Haste on your part, hesitance on hers. She's an earl's daughter and an heiress. You're a marquess without a marchioness. The ladies are supposed to favor vows spoken sooner rather than later. What's holding her back?"

What a sour view St. Didier had of matrimony, but then, his own marital prospects had doubtless plummeted when his family's title had reverted to the crown.

"Penelope seeks to avoid embarrassing Sir Dashiel. He's smitten with her fortune, would be my guess, and prepared to turn up difficult if I come between him and his beloved."

St. Didier left off playing art critic. "I don't care for him, but I don't care for many people."

Did St. Didier envy Sir Dashiel even a lowly baronetcy? "I don't know Sir Dashiel as well as I ought. He's a few years my senior, and he was sent off to public school, while I was educated at Lynnfield. I went to Oxford; he didn't last a full year at Cambridge. He bought his colors. I went on a version of the grand tour."

"And you don't trust him." A statement, not a question.

"I've ridden his home wood, and the windfall and deadfall has all been gathered up. He's either burning that wood to save money, or he's selling it. He is most assuredly not allowing his tenants to have it, and yet, he's a stickler for tradition and custom. His sister should have made her come out last year, but she lingers at home. Why? We're in the time of year when all the byres, barns, and muck pits should be cleaned out and the manure spread on the fields. Sir Dashiel has either sold that resource, too, or he lacks the manpower to see the task done at the appropriate time."

"He's pockets to let and looking to marry money. Is that so puzzling? This is good brandy, by the way. Fournier's stock?"

"Of course. His everyday offerings are better than most vintages I've sampled in France." Which had nothing to do with anything. "Why doesn't Sir Dashiel use his military rank, St. Didier? I'll tell you why. He was nearly drummed out of the regiment for stealing from the quartermaster's stores—not so he could consume the occasional tin of purloined jerky, but so he could incriminate anybody he disliked, from laundresses to lieutenants. The less said about his military exploits, the less likely anybody is to learn of his larceny."

"I thought fighting and philandering were the soldier's favorite pastimes." St. Didier wandered over to the chessboard, where somebody had placed a few pieces as if to set up the king's gambit. "Larceny for the sake of entrapping one's fellow officers is nasty behavior."

"I suspect the laundresses denied Sir Dashiel an opportunity to philander, and he wasn't in uniform long enough to do much actual fighting. He had no need to steal, much less to make others suffer for his convenience. I call that criminal behavior, not mere nastiness."

St. Didier finished his drink and returned the glass to the sideboard. "I want to tell you that you are simply jealous of the man who took understandable advantage of your absence to whisper in Lady Penelope's ear. To some extent, you must be, and yet, I traveled on the Continent as well, trying to locate Huntleigh and bring him to heel."

"I won't like what you're about to tell me, but do go on."

"I frequented the inns favored by English travelers, chatted with any officer on leave I came across, and generally listened at keyholes."

Lucien had suspected that St. Didier's extensive travels hadn't been strictly in pursuit of missing heirs. "One occasionally must listen at keyholes in the course of certain endeavors." One also picked locks, lurked in shadows, and resented the hell out of one's duties.

"Sir Dashiel's superiors were relieved to be shut of him," St. Didier said. "So were the men under his command. When I heard Sir Dashiel's name mentioned in connection with Lady Penelope, and then the lady herself asked me to facilitate her legal freedom from you... One grew concerned."

For Penelope. Truly, she had a champion in St. Didier. "Thank you for that. The puzzle now becomes how to ease Sir Dashiel away from his marital schemes, but Penelope has asked that I leave that challenge to her."

St. Didier glanced at the clock. "You will keep me informed?"

What had it cost him to ask that? "I will do better than mere dispatches. Take a pigeon or two with you back to Town. Make all the inquiries you please regarding Sir Dashiel's situation. If he has markers, buy them up on my behalf. If he owes the shops, get those debts in hand too. If Miss Tabitha Ingraham has settlements—or had settlements—find out the extent of her wealth."

St. Didier looked subtly relieved. "I cannot be in your employ and Lady Penelope's at the same time. Until she releases me from my obligations, I can only make informal inquiries on my own behalf."

Such fine lines he drew. "Then please make those inquiries, and perhaps you can also nose about on behalf of a cordial acquaintance who is head over ears for the lady."

"She has truly given you permission to court her?"

"She absolutely has, to my shameless delight."

"Very well." St. Didier strode for the door. "No need to see me off in the morning. I have some pressing inquiries to make in Town—on behalf of a friend." He disappeared through the door, closing it silently in his wake.

Two seconds later, the door reopened, and St. Didier leaned around it. "Don't muck this up, my lord. Get it right, or go back to your little art business. Are we clear?"

St. Didier was a proper scold when motivated. "We are clear. Good night, St. Didier. Safe journey."

The door closed once again. Lucien finally took a sip of his brandy, enjoying the library's silence and the brandy's smooth burn.

"He meant me," Lucien said to the portrait of Malcolm and Purdy. "He's making inquiries on behalf of a friend, and that friend is... me. Odd fellow, though a good sort."

The chess set beckoned, and Lucien ignored it. He had a report to make to Penelope, and the hour was growing late. He took his brandy with him and made his way to his intended's door.

Penelope was belting her dressing gown when a syncopated four-beat tattoo sounded on her parlor door.

Lucien, using the old signal. She opened the door. "I was just about to head your way, sir." He looked tired by the light of the sconces, also worried. With him, worry was a subtle thing, mostly around the eyes. When fretting over some private anxiety, he became more polite and slightly distant.

"Should I be flattered that you would seek me out?" He stepped into her parlor, closed the door, and offered Penelope the brandy glass he'd been holding. "I enjoyed a nightcap in the library with St. Didier. He is very much your sworn vassal."

"One would rather have him for an ally than an enemy." She nosed the drink, the fragrance hinting at apples, sunshine on weathered oak, and a trace of warm spices. The gentleman had been enjoying the good stuff.

"St. Didier is leaving in the morning," Lucien said, "and he asked that I not see him off. He likes to make his entrances and exits quietly, I gather. How is Malcolm?"

Lucien would ask. That hadn't changed, thank heavens. "Recovering. I don't think a tramp in the rain is bothering him half so much as whatever inspired his temper. I've never seen him so wroth."

Lucien prowled to the hearth and tossed another square of peat on the flames. "Nor have I. Somebody or something mortally offended him. Shall I make inquiries?"

That he would ask her to decide was pure Lucien. No pretenses, no pride when it came to what mattered.

"I think not," Penelope said, setting the drink aside, untasted. "You are the marquess now, no longer young master Lucien. The youth could pry into all manner of odd corners and be regarded with tolerance, if not affection. The peer is a different article." Penelope settled on the sofa and patted the place beside her. "Let's put Theo on to the inquiry. Everybody regards him as harmless, but he can be shrewd."

"When he's sober. Drunk, he's not so impressive." Lucien settled onto the cushions. "I am pathetically tired. No stamina. Being a butler is a soft life in some regards. Long hours, but most of them spent indoors, lifting nothing heavier than a magnum of wine."

"Why did you do it?" She took his hand, though appropriating his lap also crossed her mind.

"At first, because I needed a post other than nosy Englishman who appears to have no purpose in life. Then because I was useful to the war effort even when in Rome, and then because..."

"Yes?"

He kissed her fingers. "I liked the work, and I saw in my employer something of myself. He'd been away from home longer than I had, had traveled more extensively, and actually made something of himself. I decided that I could make a butler of myself, though the title majordomo has more cachet. You don't suppose Malcolm was taunted by schoolboys?"

The worry would not leave him, which Penelope accounted a good thing.

"Uncle shows the children the best berry patches and has rescued more than one of them from the odd scrape. They like him."

"Poachers would leave him alone—he's not capable of giving evidence through oral testimony, and they tend not to be abroad in daylight—but something upset him mortally."

"You are upset too." Penelope could feel the subtle tension humming through Lucien, for all his quiet. "Perhaps I should kiss away your worries."

The words were out, shameless but honest, and then Penelope found herself straddling Lucien's lap, his arms around her waist.

"Your kisses steal every particle of sense from my mind," he said, tracing a finger along the neckline of her dressing gown. "You haunted me when I traveled. You positively possess me here at Lynnfield."

He punctuated that declaration with a kiss to her throat. His silky hair brushed her chin, his breath warmed her neck, and his hands...

"Lucien, we mustn't."

"Why not? We are courting."

Another delicate caress, spiraling heat and languor through Penelope in equal measures. "*Mae angylion yn fy amddiffyn.*"

Lucien went still. "Pen, you don't need the angels to defend you from me. Tell me to stop and I stop. It's as simple as that. Tell me to leave and I leave. Tell me to shed my clothing and I'm naked."

"Don't."

He rubbed his thumb across her nape. "Don't stop? Don't leave?"

"Don't shed your clothes, because then I will be inspired to shed mine, and such behaviors have consequences." She sounded like her old governess, who'd muttered darkly about animal spirits and sneezing men.

"I will be careful, Penelope. We will be careful. No consequences will befall you save those you choose. You are right, though. I did not come up here thinking to anticipate any nuptial vows. Well, not precisely that. I wanted you to know that I asked St. Didier to make some inquiries."

To business, then, and at her insistence. Penelope extricated herself from Lucien's lap, took the place at his hip, enjoyed a hefty sip of brandy, and passed him the glass.

"This meeting will now come to order," she said. "Inquiries in Town?"

"About Sir Dashiel. He was a very naughty fellow when in uniform, but for present purposes, I'm concerned that he's pockets to let."

"Of course he's pockets to let. Half the shire and most of the gentry are pockets to let. We do a little better here in Kent, because we can raise market produce to sell in Town rather than rely exclusively on corn and hay, but very few of the landed class are flourishing." She accepted the glass back and finished the drink. "Lucien, are you pockets to let?"

He tucked an arm around her shoulders and crossed his legs at the knee. His pose was casual, affectionate, and frustrating. Penelope set the glass on the side table as she envisioned hurling it against the hearth.

"I am on solid footing," he said. "The benefit of being the sole offspring of the house is that I have no sisters to dower, and all of the wealth of previous generations has concentrated itself in my hands. But for Tommie, I've not been asked to educate any young men, and the elders incur minimal expenses. Then too, I am flummoxed to report that my art ventures have been lucrative. Did you think I was marrying you for your money, Pen?"

"You would see me a doddering spinster before you'd marry me for money."

Another kiss to her fingers, this one more lingering. "I'm afraid the same cannot be said for Sir Dashiel."

Penelope shifted, draping a leg over Lucien's lap. "I don't judge a man for wanting to marry well. That's what the whole Season seems to be about."

Lucien ran a caressing hand over her calf and ankle. "Sir Dashiel's military misbehaviors mean he cannot go wife-shopping in Town. Too many former officers and even enlisted men might know of his scandalous activities. The only person to suffer if the gossip starts up would be Sir Dashiel."

"I did wonder. I don't think Dash has even gone hat-shopping in Town. This will also make matters very awkward for Tabby."

Lucien was drawing something on the top of Penelope's foot. His touch was maddening, half caress, half tickle, then he grasped her arch in one of those lovely squeezes at which he apparently excelled.

"I will have a word with the marchioness," he said, "about taking Tabby up to Town. Her ladyship will protest that Tabitha has nothing to wear, but we have seamstresses at Lynnfield, and fashionable London has a dress shop on every third street corner."

"You want Tabitha away from her brother. Should I be pleased that you are so considerate of a blameless young lady going to seed in the shires, or worried that you're moving noncombatants away from the battlefield?"

"Mostly pleased. I've asked St. Didier to get us a picture of Sir Dashiel's debts and to listen for any club gossip regarding Sir Dashiel."

To get us *a picture...* Penelope retrieved her leg and peered at Lucien in the firelight. "You think Dash will prove difficult?"

"You believe he'll bow gallantly, cede the field, and find some wealthy widow to court?"

"I want to believe that."

"But you know the man, and you know the extent of your own wealth." Lucien rose and disappeared into the bedroom, then returned with a pair of worn slippers. "Your feet are cold, my lady. While I would delight in warming up each individual toe, mischief lies in that direction, and my reserves of restraint have been tested enough for one day."

Penelope pretended to consider her toes. "You could chase the chill away from one or two, seeing as we're not in a hurry and all."

He knelt and put the slippers on her feet, then laid his forehead against her knee. "You deserve a leisurely courtship, Pen. I know that. Leisurely and thorough, but do show the occasional glimmer of mercy, too, won't you?"

She kissed the top of his head and wrapped an arm around him. "Glimmers, if you insist. I'll be courted only the once, after all. I think you'd best take yourself to bed, my lord, before my merciful inclinations desert me."

Lucien sat back and considered her. "I am endlessly pleased to try your self-control. Endlessly." He rose, planted a smacker on her mouth, bowed, and decamped.

"Not a moment too soon either," Penelope said, shaking the dregs of the brandy into her mouth. "Leisurely *and* thorough. The imagination boggles."

～

To Sir Dashiel's practiced eye, Penelope was looking a bit knackered. Lord Lynnfield's return apparently had put demands on her, and she'd been a busy lady before the marquess had deigned to rejoin the household.

The marchioness presided over Sunday supper as nominal hostess, and Lord Lynnfield occupied the head of the table like some brooding university boy who'd rather be anywhere else.

Would that he were anywhere else.

"Was Italy exciting, my lord?" Tabby asked while her lemon ice melted in the dish before her. "Was it beautiful and fascinating?"

"Italy was lovely," the marquess replied. "More mountainous than we usually think of it, and much of the region is capable of a heartier winter than you'd expect, but the coastal areas are generally mild and the art impressive."

Drivel, and yet, Tabitha looked enthralled.

"I like an Italian wine now and then," Dashiel observed. "As a complement to humbler fare. Lady Penelope, what of you? What aspect of Italian culture interests you the most?" She'd been all but silent during the meal, and a quiet woman was invariably a harbinger of trouble.

Penelope considered a spoonful of ice. "I value Italy's legacy of statesmanship and philosophy. You cannot beat Machiavelli for insights into political workings, and the Stoics were clear-sighted about much of life."

The elders up and down the table all subtly became more alert, even that inveterate sot Theo. The halfwit Malcolm was apparently not displayed at company suppers, though Tommie the Twit had done his best to offer bon mots while inhaling his beef roast.

The marquess poured more wine for Tabitha. "The Stoics were not entirely off the mark, though my lady knows of my quarrels with them."

The elders exchanged glances, some of which might have qualified as smirks.

"You quarrel with philosophers, my lord?" Tabitha asked.

Must she be such a bumpkin? "The marquess speaks metaphorically," Dashiel said. "Perhaps his lordship falls more into the camp of the hedonists?"

"I fancy myself a realist," Lynnfield replied, "and a pragmatist. What of you, Sir Dashiel? Which philosopher provides your ethical lodestar?"

Dashiel took a thoughtful sip of his wine, a pallid sauternes. "One finds some value in almost every school of classical thought." *Carpe diem, carpe pecuniam, carpe mulier.* And if unable to seize the day, the money, or the woman, find a good case of brandy and seize that.

"A generalist, then," the marchioness observed from the foot of the table. "They always have the best small talk. I vow I could not eat another bite."

"My compliments to the kitchen," Dashiel said, "if I might presume to such a degree. A very satisfying meal." Also tedious beyond belief, even given the delicious roast, though useful too. Lord Lynnfield still lacked social polish, the aging oddities were still very much in evidence despite the marquess's return, and Tabitha had managed reasonably well in his lordship's august presence.

She would dine out on that feat for weeks, and Dashiel was pleased to have arranged a small social victory for her.

When even the little auntie who stole sachets and hatpins had finished her ice, the farewell rituals began. The marquess offered Tabitha his escort to the stable, and Dashiel seized the initiative to offer his arm to Penny.

"Walk me to my horse, my lady." He murmured the suggestion while patting the hand she'd placed on his arm.

"You can no longer find the stable on your own, Dash?" Her smile said she was teasing him, or trying to, though her humor missed the mark.

"The assembly approaches, my dear. Will you save your waltz for me?"

They processed out the main door on Lynnfield's east façade, into bright afternoon sunshine. The day was lovely as only spring could be, but the brilliant beams confirmed that Lady Penelope had left the schoolroom behind years ago. She was no longer *dewy*.

"I wasn't aware we were to have any waltzes on the program, Dash. I'll certainly dance the Roger de Coverley with you."

Always the first dance, lively to the point of ridiculousness. "I might not arrive in time for the opening festivities. Tabitha can take ever so long over her toilette."

They descended the terrace steps. Ahead of them, Tabitha laughed at something the marquess said. Smart girl, to flatter the neighborhood's highest title, even if he aspired to Byron-come-lately brooding airs.

"About Tabitha," Penelope said. "I've been meaning to raise a few topics with you, Dash, discussions best conducted without an audience. Who does most of your sewing at the Roost?"

"I have no idea. The maids, I assume, under the direction of the housekeeper. My valet sees to my wardrobe. Tabitha knows how to ply a needle." Either that, or she spent hours pretending to embroider slippers and linen and whatnot. "Why?"

"I cannot go up to Town with the marchioness this year, and I'm sure she will want for female companionship. Her ladyship usually spends a month or two in London when the social whirl begins. I was hoping Tabitha could go with her."

Dashiel took his time considering a reply. Tabitha was certainly old enough for a Season, and the marchioness would be an appropriate chaperone. But the expense of such an excursion could be staggering.

Then too, Penelope mustn't get in the habit of assuming her every wish and whim would be granted for the asking.

"From what little I fathom of these matters," Dashiel said, "a proper Season takes considerable preparation. A girl ought to have her trousseau all but packed, along with enough fripperies and finery to impress any hostess in Mayfair. Tabitha hasn't bestirred herself to make such an effort."

She had lodged a few timid requests for fabrics, and she'd known to ask for muslins rather than velvets or silks.

"We have capable hands at Lynnfield," Penelope said. "The aunties and cousins are all competent seamstresses, and his lordship has noted their idleness. Making up a few dresses for Tabitha is well within their abilities, and the marchioness is *au courant* when it comes to fashion."

As the stable came into view, it occurred to Dashiel that Penelope was engaged in a bumbling game of chess. She wanted Tabitha, who already took a domestic hand in managing the Roost, out of play. With the marchioness—who was also Penelope's chaperone—off in Town, opportunities to advance a courtship dangled close at hand.

What a charming little schemer, though Penelope had a great deal to learn about strategy—a very great deal.

"My dear, I realize you mean well, but I refuse to send my sister off to be paraded before polite society as an unpaid companion to a difficult dowager. Tabitha is the daughter and sister of a baronet. Her gentility is beyond question. You are not to soothe your conscience by subjecting poor Tabby to drudgery you yourself hope to avoid."

Dashiel kept his tone mild, almost amused, but Penelope would grasp his point: She was asking for a very great favor if she sought to have Tabby trotting around Mayfair after the marchioness.

They walked along in silence for a dozen yards, while Tabitha's mirth graced the sunny air again.

"To bear a loved one company is not drudgery," Penelope said. "My apologies if I ever gave you the impression that the marchioness is difficult. I did not seek to subject Tabitha to an unpleasant situation. Just the opposite."

The note of apology was grudging, but adequate. "What else did you seek to discuss with me, my dear?"

"I'm not done discussing Tabitha, as it happens. I had in mind for the marchioness to see to your sister's court presentation while in London. If you'd rather find another sponsor next year, you have only to indicate. I can vouch for the marchioness's willingness and ability to see to formalities now, but going forward, I can make no guarantees. Her ladyship is not young, and with the marquess on hand, other expectations might be placed upon her."

A bit sniffy, but Penelope was making the desired concession. Not a stupid woman, when she stopped being so stubborn. "Expectations relating to Lynnfield's prospective marchioness?"

"His lordship has been home barely a week, Dash. Not even her ladyship is trying to marry him off just yet."

And what a thankless task that would be. "If you can assure me Tabitha will be presented at court and that Lynnfield resources will be put at her disposal to prepare for this excursion, I suppose I can spare her for a few weeks."

"You don't want her to have a come-out ball with all the trimmings too?"

"I would have to attend such an event,"—and pay for it—"and not even for my darling sister can I tear myself away when planting must be seen to. When does the marchioness go up to Town?"

"The Monday following the assembly. If you send Tabitha to us tomorrow, we'll have two weeks to put together a wardrobe for her. That should be enough."

"Send Tabitha to you?" Tabby kept the grumbling from the staff to a bearable roar and maintained the household ledgers, among other duties.

Grooms led out Thor and Tabitha's old mare, and the marquess checked the mare's girth.

"Dresses require multiple fittings, Dash. Tabitha will need everything—a presentation gown, though we might be able to make over the one I wore—day dresses, afternoon dresses, carriage dresses, at least one fancy riding habit, a ball gown, if not several ball gowns. She will need slippers, gloves, and bonnets to match, and underlinen, reticules, parasols... We can outfit her largely from Lynnfield stores, but she must be on hand for the exercise."

Dashiel wouldn't exactly miss Tabitha, but if this London presentation went well, and she managed to bag an offer of marriage, the timing of the settlement negotiations could become delicate.

"Very well. I will send her to you tomorrow morning, but don't blame me if you come to regret this whole scheme, Lady Many Pennies. Was there another matter you sought to discuss with me?"

Penelope glanced around the stable yard. The marquess had assisted Tabitha to mount, and the grooms were loitering about, doubtless hoping to collect gossip.

"About the assembly, Dash." Penelope looked very earnest and determined, and she kept her voice down.

Oh, right. The assembly. "If there is a waltz, will my lady save hers for me?" He owed her that much. All heads would turn, they would make a lovely couple, and then...

The next thought inspired Dashiel to positively beam at his plain, aging, stubborn intended. *Engagements* were announced at the quarterly assemblies. A venerable tradition and an occasion for much goodwill.

Well, of course.

Penelope looked to be filling her sails for a fine diatribe, probably a discourse on the passage of time and gathering rosebuds and life being uncertain for a lady without family. Broad hints that amounted to begging for a proposal now that Lord Lynnfield was so inconveniently underfoot and the marchioness making tracks for Town.

Sometimes, patience truly was its own reward, though before Penny could embark on her speech, the family dimwit Malcolm emerged from the barn. He caught her eye, scowled, and withdrew without even glancing at Dashiel. Either Uncle Muttonhead had a scintilla of sense, or he'd been attempting some sort of cut sublime.

How quaint. "You were saying?" Dashiel prompted.

Penelope's expression lost its seriousness. "Nothing that won't keep. We will look for Tabitha tomorrow morning." She bobbed a curtsey and offered him a smile.

Dashiel bowed, swung into the saddle, and touched a finger to his hat brim. The outing had been worthwhile after all, if Tabitha was to be socially launched without emptying Dashiel's coffers, and Dashiel owed that lovely development indirectly to Penelope.

Not a bad day's work, and the roast had been done to a turn. "Lynnfield, my thanks for a fine repast. Come along, Tabitha. Lady Penelope has proposed a scheme of which you should be made aware."

Tabitha's mare plodded away from the mounting block, and Dashiel considered how best to explain to his sister that thanks to his clever finagling and skillful bargaining, she would have a proper come out, complete with a marchioness for a sponsor and a fashionable wardrobe in the first stare of fashion.

He glanced over his shoulder and saw Lady Penelope standing beside the ladies' mounting block, the marquess in conversation with her. His lordship was utterly focused on whatever Penny was saying, and the blighter stood too close to her too.

Lynnfield would soon learn to keep a proper distance from what didn't belong to him. Dashiel would administer the lesson personally and as often as necessary.

CHAPTER NINE

"All I'm saying, dear boy, is that I had planned to take Penny with me when I went up to Town." The marchioness was whiling away her Sunday evening with a deck of cards, though while Lucien had been observing her, she hadn't found many matches. "Penny hasn't been to London for several years, and she could do with some new bonnets."

"Try the card in the upper right-hand corner if you're looking for knaves," he said, cracking a window to air the otherwise stuffy family parlor. "Penelope has no desire to go to London with you."

The marchioness turned over the card in the upper *left* corner and revealed a two of spades. "Penny told you she'd rather bide at Lynnfield?"

"Yes. Doesn't care for Town in the least. Has no patience with the social whirl, hasn't made friends among the polite set, for all she's an earl's daughter and an heiress." The lack of lady friends might not be so odd—Penelope did not suffer fools—but she hadn't made any conquests either. Why not? For settlements such as Pen had to offer, the swains should have piled up six deep at her feet.

"I won't take Penelope for the duration, Lucien. She can come up to Town for a fortnight or so. Long enough to schedule some fittings, establish order among the domestics, and see the house put to rights. She excels at such tasks."

While Aunt excelled at annoying Lucien. He did not recall her as particularly vexatious, but she'd either acquired the knack, or his memory had failed him for the first time in all his born years.

"You work Penelope as if she were a rented mule. You'd take her to Town for your convenience rather than her pleasure."

The marchioness put down her two of spades. "No need to be rude, sir. I actually have Penny's best interests in mind. When she sees all the interest young Tabitha stirs, she'll realize she's already flirting with spinsterhood. Sir Dashiel won't wait forever, no matter the size of Penny's fortune."

An unpleasant, logical suspicion formed in the back of Lucien's mind. "Penelope nearly gave Sir Dashiel his congé earlier today, but lacked sufficient privacy for a discussion of that nature."

Her ladyship gathered up her cards, though the game was far from concluded. "How on earth could you know such a thing?"

Penelope had told him as much before Sir Dashiel's gelding had disappeared down the lane. They'd sat on the mounting block and discussed timing and strategy, until Malcolm had emerged from the stable and offered Penelope his escort back to the house.

"I am in Penelope's confidence, and she is in mine," Lucien said. "That hasn't changed." What had changed was harder to describe. They'd grown up, and they'd grown apart, but the old closeness had taken on a new sparkle too.

The marchioness shuffled the deck. "I'd ask you to play with me, but you always win."

The elders would soon begin to assemble, and Lucien wanted the conversation with the marchioness over and done with. "I pay attention. I can't help having a good memory."

She began laying out the cards in a grid on the green baize table-top. "Many people have good memories, my boy. They are also savvy enough to know that constant winning annoys others, so they curb their excellent memories for the sake of conviviality."

She described a form of dishonesty that was somehow not cheating. "I understand manners, Auntie, and I understand that Penelope will not be accompanying you to Town. You are to launch Tabitha such as you can on short notice, and I'm sure you will find a way to enjoy that undertaking."

"In truth, Lucien, you seem to have become more dunderheaded than you were as a lad, and that development hardly seems possible. Tabitha is sweet, pretty, good at running her brother's household, and as accomplished in the ladylike arts as she should be."

"But?"

"But her settlements wouldn't catch the eye of a widowed knight with six children in his nursery. Your scheme to see her launched is cruel, creating expectations the girl will never see fulfilled."

The marchioness was very sure of her facts. "Sir Dashiel has confided the girl's situation to you?"

"Tabitha's oldest sister and I correspond. Besides, Tabby turned eighteen last autumn. She should have gone up to Town last year, this year at the latest, and there she sits, embroidering the family crest on pillowcases and making sheep's eyes at you."

The sheep's eyes had been cast in Tommie's direction. "You will please do your best by her in London, nonetheless."

Her ladyship turned over two cards, a three and a nine. "Or what?"

The question crossed a line, from diffidence to defiance. Lucien returned fire. "Or Sir Dashiel will be disappointed in you, which you seem to regard as a consummation devoutly to be avoided."

His arrow hit its mark. The marchioness stared at her mismatched cards. "Truly, you left your manners in Rome, or wherever we are supposed to believe you bided. Sir Dashiel is a neighbor, a gentleman, and the local magistrate. He cares for his sister, and he will expect me to perform a miracle. I have connections and rank, and I can dress the girl in fashion that flatters her, but I cannot change the rules of the game."

The game that played out each spring in Mayfair, or the one

apparently unfolding at Lynnfield? "Intimate to your cronies that I am impressed with Tabitha," Lucien said, "and she'll get a second look from a few of the more ambitious matchmakers."

This suggestion earned him a curious glance. "That might work. Are you interested in her?"

"Not in any marital sense, and if I were, I'd give the whole notion a serious reconsideration because Dashiel is her brother. Your regard for him should be tempered with a little caution, Aunt."

A lot of caution.

"You were always jealous of him. He went to public school, he's charming, he joined the local militia, he's well liked and considered handsome."

Why would the marchioness resort to outright nastiness that could profit her nothing? "What does Sir Dashiel have on you, madam? You sing his praises to Penelope at every turn, probably gave him leave to court her ladyship without even telling her, and now you fear to disappoint him with Tabitha's lack of marital prospects."

Lucien anticipated protests, scolds, even a tantrum, but Aunt merely continued turning over cards in random pairs.

"Hopeless boy. We were managing well enough without you, you know."

Penelope had been managing the household well enough, that much was true. "I wasn't managing."

The marchioness considered the field of facedown cards. "Your delicate nerves troubled you?"

Ask Wellington about my delicate nerves. "I was homesick." Though for what? Not for this difficult old woman, not for a neighbor trying to sneak off with Penelope's future, not for a household full of idle elders.

Homesick for Penelope, of a certainty.

"Right, homesick," the marchioness said, turning over two cards at the same time. "So now you must play lord of the manor. Have you considered how Penelope will feel when you take a bride, my boy? She's in your confidence, and once upon a time she likely would not have objected to being in your bed, but Sir Dashiel offers her a respectful—"

Lucien plucked the cards from her hand. "Rudeness toward Lady Penelope will not be tolerated, even from you, madam. My intentions toward Penelope are entirely respectable."

A bit unclear as to timing and a few details, but deeply, deeply respectful.

By the flickering light of the sconces, the marchioness appeared worn and tired. "You always had a knack for creating problems, especially when you professed to be solving them. Sir Dashiel offers Penelope a storybook future, ruralizing among those who love her. You appear out of nowhere, your past a mystery, your future equally vague. Will you drag Penny up to Town so you can vote your seat? Expect her to hare all over the Continent with you in search of curios and musty royal portraits? What exactly do you offer her that gives you the right to disdain Sir Dashiel's suit?"

Lucien studied his aunt, whom he would have said was a decent enough soul, if a bit spoiled.

"I have no place disdaining or approving Sir Dashiel's wooing. The only opinion that matters on that topic is Penelope's, and she isn't favorably impressed. She will convey her position to Sir Dashiel at the time and place of her choosing, and if you attempt to meddle— to meddle further—I will remove you to the dower house and deny you the use of the traveling coach, the town house, the family property at Bath, and the funds I supply to keep the lot of it in good trim."

Aunt gave up any pretense of attending her card game. "You were a sweet boy, beneath the quirks and queer starts. Now you're overly full of your own consequence. Mind your step, Lucien. I detest bullies. Excuse me." She rose with vast dignity and made a stately march toward the door.

"You *are* being bullied," Lucien said quietly, "but not by me. Whatever Sir Dashiel has threatened or promised, I will do all I can to help if you will put me in possession of the particulars."

She stopped before him. "Be careful, Lucien. Despite what you might think, I do care for Penelope and for you. I've done what I believe is best, and I will exert myself to the utmost for Tabitha, but you underestimate Dashiel Ingraham at your peril."

Lucien allowed Aunt to make a dignified retreat—the least he could do—and gathered up the deck she'd abandoned. Blunt interrogation tactics hadn't worked, logic had failed utterly, threats had been pointless, though really, Aunt lived in a style anybody else would consider lavish, thanks solely to Lucien's generosity.

She'd defended Sir Dashiel's interests to the last, which suggested she found her paragon of a neighbor not merely intimidating, but rather, terrifying. Lucien sat at the table and laid out the cards one by one as he mentally composed a missive to Leopold St. Didier.

Penelope opened the sewing room door to find Lucien, resplendent in his riding attire, standing in the corridor.

"You've been for a gallop." No sedate hack put a man's hair into such disarray or turned his cheeks ruddy.

He sidled past her, and Penelope closed the door.

"I tapped on your bedroom door at first light, and when you did not admit me, I assumed you needed your rest. I needed the fresh morning air rather desperately. Have you been in here all night?"

The sewing room was not exactly topsy-turvy, but fabrics were stacked on one of the worktables, matching thread and bindings arranged atop each choice. Workbaskets had been rifled and stood open around the room, a swatch of silk or satin draped over most of them.

"I told Dashiel that Tabby would have a new wardrobe, and I fear my generosity ran away with my common sense. Making good on my promise will take a deal of hard work."

Lucien kissed her, a disarmingly soft press of lips to her cheek, near but not quite touching the corner of her lips. "Good morning, my darling. I see no *we* working hard. I see only you. What can I do to help?"

The part of Penelope's mind not consumed with velvet, muslin, and embroidered borders was grateful. Lucien had always had a practical streak that nobody gave him credit for. On the Continent, that pragmatism might well have kept him alive.

She used her fingers to winnow his hair into a semblance of order, then passed him a mound of white fabric along with a small tool sporting a curved blade. "Let out the hem, please."

He gave the blade a curious look, sent the same sort of glance to Penelope, then gathered up the froth, lace, and pearls that had been her presentation gown and dumped it on the worktable. He then pushed the worktable next to the nearest window and pulled off his boots. While Penelope watched, he climbed upon the table, sat tailor-fashion, and gathered the gown into his lap.

"I should have thought of that," she said, taking up her embroidery hoop and settling into a rocking chair by the cold hearth. Only then did it occur to her that Lucien had sought her out twice since dawn. "What troubles you, my lord?"

"I wish I had seen you in this dress," he replied. "You doubtless glowed like some celestial being come to earth."

"The pearls glowed, but I was so worried about catching them on a door latch or tripping over my own feet that I would have been a very anxious sort of celestial being. Then too, white does not flatter redheads. That was my presentation gown."

Lucien held up the bodice, the white work and seed pearls catching the morning light magnificently. "You are sacrificing your presentation gown for the sake of Tabitha's prospects?"

He clearly disapproved, but would follow orders nonetheless. Perhaps he'd learned to do that while spying as well, though Penelope had no idea why she was so preoccupied with his Continental exploits.

His *dangerous, solitary* Continental exploits. "I will never wear that gown again. To make it over is no sacrifice. Waste not, want not.

Besides, when I look at that garment, I am reminded that I spent an eternity in the fitting rooms for clothing that was hot and uncomfortable. I could hardly breathe in that thing."

Lucien regarded her long enough that Penelope grasped he was choosing to avoid some sort of argument with her. After an eternity of unspoken reproaches, regrets, or something, he began cutting the stitches that bound the dress's hem.

"Did the Regent speak to you?"

"He certainly did. He always notices the heiresses. He said the circumstances of Henry's death were to be lamented above all things, and I must console myself with fond memories. I'd been out of mourning for only a few months at that point, but Prinny had already filed the appropriate petitions to have the earldom's properties revert to the crown. His condolences nonetheless had a ring of sincerity."

"One underestimates the Regent at one's peril," Lucien said, making steady progress with his little blade. "George is neither stupid nor ill informed, but he likes to pretend he's both. He knows what it is to lose siblings. He would have noted Henry's death the instant the news reached England and been well aware of your situation."

"Relieved he need not have made me a ward of the crown, you mean. What's bothering you, Lucien?" Penelope knew exactly what she was bothered by—the need to spin a heap of fabric into a fashionable wardrobe in a fortnight. If Tabitha was to have only one Season in Town, then turning her out in the first stare had become imperative.

Lucien glowered at yards of pretty fabric and then at Penelope. "When you give Sir Dashiel his marching orders, make your speech somewhere that other people can see you in conversation with him, but not hear you."

Botheration, Lucien had been brooding again. "Why? Such a discussion merits privacy for the sake of Dashiel's dignity, if nothing else. Besides, he and I are not engaged. I can't exactly hand him the you-do-me-great-honor bit." Penelope had almost managed to start the requisite conversation yesterday in the stable yard, but the moment had passed.

I'm saving my waltz for his lordship, Dash. Wish me luck.

Too flippant.

Lucien's return has made me rethink my situation at Lynnfield.

Too meek, and blaming Lucien would never serve.

Dashiel, you bore me.

Too honest, though he did bore her, when he wasn't annoying her. Why must some men have such frail sensibilities? If one offended them, they threatened tantrums and worse, but if one left them to their fancies, their expectations soon departed from any semblance of reality.

Lucien plucked at snippets of white thread. "Plain sight is safer for difficult exchanges, and Dashiel will moderate his responses if he has an audience. When did Dashiel become a justice of the peace?"

What had that to do with anything? "As soon as he mustered out and came home. Former officers often join the commission of the peace, and Dashiel was no exception. He's probably holding his parlor sessions as we speak."

"And he's accorded respect for meting out justice?"

Lucien hadn't been merely brooding, he'd been pondering, as only Lucien could ponder. "No, actually. Within a month of joining the bench, Dashiel sent Mr. Trotter's oldest boy off to the assizes for helping himself to a jar of Mrs. Plimset's plum jam on market day. The lad was nearly transported, but Uncle Theo, Uncle Malcolm, and Cousin Tommie spoke on his behalf. The aunties attended the trial as well. Theo let it be known that you and the marchioness would take a dim view of such harsh measures, so a fine sufficed."

"Who paid the fine?"

Nobody else had asked. Penelope bestirred herself to start on a row of French knots on a golden silk dancing slipper.

"I paid the fine and the lawyer, but you must never tell Dashiel. His theory was that one or two examples of swift justice, and the whole shire would be crime-free in perpetuity."

Lucien's blade paused. "But?"

"But now, we simply don't peach on each other over petty offenses, and if anything, those petty offenses have multiplied because nobody wants to see a neighbor end up before Sir Dashiel. Every mischievous boy and habitual inebriate knows it." Somewhere, beneath inventorying the larders, settling spats among the elders, and keeping the marchioness in fashion magazines, Dashiel's theory had also annoyed Penelope.

"With nobody involving the king's man," Lucien said, "Sir Dashiel has less work to do. His reports make it look as if the shire has turned up Puritan under his watch, when, in fact, discipline in the ranks has deteriorated. Many a regiment operated on a similar scheme. Lawlessness abounded among the enlisted men and even among some of the officers, but the appearances were quite in order for parade inspections."

The fundamental dishonesty of such an arrangement would have offended Lucien. "Did your clandestine activities acquaint you with army discipline? Is that where you learned to have your most dangerous discussions while strolling the village green?"

Lucien collected all the little loose threads into a pile on the table. "You must not bring up that aspect of my past, Pen. What I did was dishonorable and delicate. Henry died a hero's death, while I compromised my integrity for the sake of my pride. Nobody respects a spy."

But he'd been a good spy, because he'd wanted to feel needed. Penelope knew all about the unfortunate results of seeking to feel needed. She brushed aside the guilty possibility that promising a whole wardrobe on short notice had been an exercise in making herself needed.

Another exercise in making herself feel needed.

"Did Henry die a hero's death, Lucien? Nobody seems to know the particulars. Felled by a French bullet is about all I've been told. His commanding officer wrote me a sweet, comforting letter about Henry being a paragon—he wasn't—and a fine officer—he was an inexperienced officer—and Henry being remembered for his valor.

Henry ought to also be remembered for his vanity. He did so love parading about in his regimentals."

Lucien had finished ripping out the hem. From his higher perch on the table, he regarded Penelope over the billows of her presentation gown, a sagacious, sartorial owl in stockinged feet.

The sight of him, limned by morning light, disheveled, occupied with women's work and yet entirely himself, made her heart turn over. All the ways she had missed him—as a friend, a confidant, an intellectual sparring partner, a source of affection, and so much more —settled over her in a silent cascade.

Never leave me again.

"Henry was too young to die," Lucien said, batting down the folds of white around him. "We can agree on that, and when you can bear to recall a person's faults as well as their endearing attributes, your grief is abating. Give me another task."

The moment passed, and like a game horse finding her footing on a sloppy course, Penelope made a leap borne of impatience with herself and with her life.

"Would you undertake some inquiries for me, Lucien? Get me a few particulars regarding Henry's death? He wasn't on any battlefield, and the French were supposedly nowhere in the vicinity, and yet, he was ambushed."

Lucien shook out the gown and began folding it. "I would not know where to begin such an investigation, Pen. I do know that Sir Dashiel will take umbrage when you show him the figurative door. That worries me."

When Penelope allowed it to, the looming discussion with Sir Dashiel troubled her too. "We're launching his sister at no effort or expense to him. Let him be consoled by that dazzling display of neighborliness." Would Sir Dashiel have exerted himself even to the extent of ripping out one seam for Tabitha's sake?

In the privacy of her thoughts, Penelope admitted that where Sir Dashiel was concerned, she'd had a narrow escape. She could have made marriage to him bearable, but why had she even entertained that fate in a theoretical sort of way?

"Aunt claims Tabby's settlements are paltry," Lucien said, tossing the orts and leavings of silk threads into the dustbin. "She had it from one of the older sisters, though as to that, why aren't the older sisters launching Tabby?"

"They did not marry well enough. Good matches, not spectacular matches." Lucien's question touched on a curious point. Sir Dashiel's three married sisters did not visit the Roost, though they all dwelled within a few hours of their brother.

Too busy with their nurseries, perhaps. "I will ask Dash to walk me home after Sunday services and explain to him that I've enjoyed our occasional hacks and picnics and calls, but I will be quite busy for the foreseeable future..."

Lucien's gaze was unreadable. "Once you get Cinderella off to the ball, you will be no busier than usual, Pen. Be honest with the man. Tell him he's too good a friend to be allowed to harbor any mistaken aspirations. You apologize for speaking so plainly to him, and you hope you are mistaken, but the marchioness has been murmuring wrongheaded intimations. You fear she has got above herself and murmured the same innuendos in Dashiel's hearing too. In an abundance of caution, you thus seek reassurances that Dashiel also views the marchioness's clumsy matchmaking as quite off the mark, meaning no insult and so forth. Blushing would make the whole recitation more credible."

"How long did it take you to puzzle that out?" The strategy was brilliant and simple, also close to the truth.

"Half the night. Blaming a somewhat guilty third party saves everybody's pride. If you frame the issue as the marchioness creating mischief, then Dashiel solves the whole problem by admitting that he had the same concern, and nobody should take her ladyship's little schemes seriously. You have relieved his mind, in fact, by confiding your worries to him, or so he can claim."

"Does spying involve diplomacy? I would not have thought to

cast Dashiel in the role of forbearing gentleman, but he'll like that."
Not *like* precisely, but he'd be flattered by it.

"Spying is a form of diplomacy, to hear some people tell it, but
that topic holds no interest. Give me another task, Pen. I can do those
French knots."

She passed him the slipper, thread, needle, and all. "Can you
start those inquiries about Henry, Lucien? If you were so accomplished at your nosing about on the Continent, you must have some
idea where to ask a few questions."

Lucien wound thread around his needle and poked it through the
top of the slipper. "You won't leave this alone, will you?"

"My only brother, my last surviving family member, is dead, his
title obliterated, and I'm supposed to sit in the corner and choose
recipes for syllabub. I stay busy in part because I sometimes fear the
alternative is to go mad."

Now where had that admission come from?

Lucien put the slipper aside, climbed off the table, and knelt
before her. "Don't go mad, but never read another recipe for syllabub
if you don't care to. Exhaustion can serve for a time to dull the
emotions and keep the memories at bay, but it can also become a
habit, like marching or drinking. When I arrived in Rome, I lay about
for weeks. I had to learn again how to sleep for more than an hour at a
time, to waste a morning with the newspapers, to dress slowly, to eat
when I was hungry and not simply because rations were available
and I had miles to cover before sunset..."

He rested his head in Penelope's lap, and she stroked his hair.
"None of us thought our marquess had gone to war, but you had."

"I went completely to hell for a time. Crossing paths with
Huntleigh was the single greatest stroke of luck I've had other than
ending up on the same estate with you. In his way, Huntleigh was as
lost as I was becoming. Organizing his household gave me a place to
start making peace with myself."

That was as close to a speech as Lucien, Marquess of Lynnfield,
was likely to make short of doing his bit in the House of Lords.

And yet, Lucien did not feel at peace to Penelope. More settled than he'd been as a youth, wiser, and calmer, but not at peace.

"If nobody else has said this, Lucien, I'm saying it: Thank you for what you did when you went traveling. You risked your life every bit as much as Henry did, and if the French had caught you, your fate would have been the torments of the damned. I respect you for the courage you showed and the risks you took for king and country."

He lifted his head, scowled at her, then sat back. "This is why the whole estate colludes in running you off your feet. Given time to think, you are far too insightful. Thank you for your kind words."

He made a production out of returning the worktable to its assigned position and tugging on his boots, then he passed Penelope the slipper. "One aspect of Henry's death has troubled me."

"Oh?" The French knots Lucien had done perfectly matched Penelope's efforts.

"You are right that the French had no business patrolling that far behind Wellington's lines. They supported themselves by hunting and foraging, which we English call pillaging. The season was high spring, and we were in relatively lush terrain. Game and grazing were abundant."

Penelope parsed what Lucien wasn't saying. "That patrol was not in search of rabbits or boar or an undefended root cellar."

Lucien stood. "I'm sure there's an explanation—a shipment of cattle promised to Boney's men, some general taking a notion to circle behind the English, a scout getting lost, or a Bonapartist sympathizer with news to pass along. I don't have the explanation, though."

"Can you find it?"

"I don't want to. Wellington made very certain we did not fraternize openly with the enemy, but both armies observed a certain unspoken protocol. If the French and English camps were in proximity, the night pickets took care of exchanges of letters and news, or bread for brandy, that sort of thing. Deserters knew to walk into the opposing camp at the breakfast hour, hands in the air. Amid intermittent barbarism, we found patches of sanity."

"And for Henry to be shot in broad daylight offended those patches?"

"Yes, and for the French to wander so far from their own territory with no apparent objective... I did ask a few questions when I eventually learned of the situation, but by then, nobody admitted to knowing anything."

Penelope rose as well. Lucien had just explained to her a small part of how the passing years—and the war—had changed him. "You didn't want to tell me this."

"No. What purpose could such a disclosure serve?"

"What harm could it do?"

Lucien took her into his arms. "You will be more haunted now. You will beg heaven more fervently for answers that heaven cannot give because they might lie solely within hell's keeping. Your disquiet will increase for knowing I have questions too."

Penelope considered that reasoning and found it sound, also vintage Lucien. "But you contemplated lying to me. As a boy, you would not have lied to me or to much of anybody."

"Not lying outright, but yes, I entertained the possibility of keeping my thoughts to myself."

That skill, he possessed in abundance. "Don't," she said, hugging him tightly. "Don't keep any part of yourself from me, Lucien, save to preserve your own dignity. Don't spare me, don't protect me like that, don't hide behind some misguided notion of manly honor. We will have the truth between us or nothing at all."

Penelope's own daring impressed her, but she would not tolerate being managed by a man who professed to care for her.

"The truth," he said, easing his hold, "is that you need reinforcements, and I intend to see that you get them. Who are the best seamstresses among the aunties and cousins?"

Subject changed, which was honestly a relief. Penelope resumed her seat. "They are all skilled, and even Tommie can sew a straight seam. The same fellow valets for him, Theo, and Malcolm, and needs must occasionally."

"You can't have Tommie. I am meeting with him this morning, but you can have the entire complement of ladies, so decide now how you want to deploy your troops."

"And the marchioness?" The question was automatic. Get her ladyship settled, or not much else could be accomplished.

"She can unearth any relevant patterns from the attics, but you are in charge of actual needles plied and fabric cut. Take the ladies in hand, Pen, and I will try to do likewise with the gents."

The sense of having conferred with a fellow general was novel and a bit heady. "What about Henry's demise? Will you make inquiries?"

"I've already started."

He kissed her again—on the mouth this time—then slipped out the door. Penelope threw the slipper at the solid oak and heard Lucien laugh before his steps retreated.

He had tried to keep his concerns to himself and failed. Penelope decided to be encouraged by that, but that he'd contemplate keeping her in ignorance... not good. Not good for Lucien and not good for her either.

CHAPTER TEN

"Art?" Tommie made the word sound like some arcane turn of law Latin. "Portraits, landscapes, miniatures. That sort of thing?"

"Those all qualify," Lucien said, schooling himself to patience. He'd asked to meet Tommie in the man's own sitting room, a small space, but tidy, comfortable, and, above all, *private*. "I tended to buy what caught my eye, so if an epergne struck me as particularly graceful or a collection of fans impressed me, I picked those up too."

"Fine art and decorative art, both?" Tommie poured himself a second cup of tea, the tray apparently sparing him the need to appear at breakfast.

Lucien wandered the room, looking for clues to the occupant's personality out of habit. "Yes, both. A few snuffboxes and the occasional ornate watch made it into the trunks. Some ivory carvings, candlesticks, standishes, a fair amount of jewelry, though I avoided the finest gemstones."

Tommie sipped placidly. "You indulged your aesthetic whims."

Offered as a theory, rather than an accusation. "I did. Beauty was a comfort at the time."

"Beauty is always a comfort. I'm not in love with Penelope, by the by, lovely though she may be."

Lucien left off studying the titles on Tommie's bookshelf. "I beg your pardon?"

"She's not in love with me either, though she does enjoy ordering me about. I indulge her because heaven knows the woman gets ordered about enough herself. Then too, Penelope's orders are never foolish."

For an impecunious fribble, Tommie had an impressive collection of poetry. "What are you going on about, Thomas?"

"Penelope is fond of me, and I am very fond of her, but only as cousins, or what passes for cousins at Lynnfield. I'm not... You don't have to send me to Town to clear the field of competition."

Lucien chose a volume at random and opened it to the middle. Years of practice kept his tone merely curious when he was in truth utterly flummoxed. "Clear the field?"

"Do have a seat, my lord, and you might ask permission before you handle a fellow's personal effects." Tommie plucked the volume from Lucien's grasp without rising. "An example of my earliest efforts. One appreciates the hard work it embodies, though the results want polish."

Lucien sank into the second wing chair. "You are a published poet?"

Tommie tucked the volume aside, beyond Lucien's reach. "The satirical verse pays more. The crown is cracking down on the best of the political cartoonists, locking them up to hold without charges, that sort of thing. Any illiterate drudge can grasp the humor in an image. Satirical poetry is the safer expression of the same notions. Not as likely to inflame the masses."

Lucien would not have been surprised to see purple parakeets flying out of the wardrobe. "You write political satire?"

Tommie's ears turned a hot pink. "In verse, which makes it poetry. I have written other metrical compositions, all bucolic and symbolic. I'm not from the Lake District, but I can appreciate the countryside as well as the next ruralizing gent."

Lucien took down another volume from the shelf behind him. "Thomas Lynn?" Not exactly subtle, but still a pseudonym.

"Malcolm is my editor. I grew up speaking both English and Welsh, but Malcolm came to his English *cicio and melltithio*. His eye for the details of English, spelling, and punctuation is faultless."

Kicking and cursing. "Have you ever heard Malcolm speak?"

Tommie's blush was fading, leaving a pleasant if unremarkable countenance in its wake. "Our Malcolm talks in his sleep. English, French, Welsh. Sings in his sleep, too—the old psalms. The first time I heard him, I thought Lynnfield was haunted. Theo swore me to secrecy, but I think it's one of those secrets everybody knows."

Everybody except me. The sensation was old and familiar. "His secret is safe with me. Malcolm himself might be unaware of it." And Lucien didn't like holding even so harmless a confidence. "If you are a poet, perhaps you might enjoy taking on my art gallery."

"You have—own—a gallery?"

"I think the polite term is 'sponsor,' and yes. I have also commissioned His Grace of Huntleigh to send me inventory from Italy—I own a number of his smaller pieces—and I have contacts in the German states and France who also provide me stock."

Tommie took an inordinate time to select a cherry tart from the offerings on the tray. "A marquess in trade isn't quite the done thing, Lucien. I hope you know that?" A gentle, even kind question. "Granted, you are the mysterious marquess now, gone for years, popping up unexpectedly, and all the hostesses are saying they knew the instant you returned to London. How droll that you passed incognito as your ducal friend's butler, but still. One can overdo the aristocratic eccentricity."

Lucien was dimly aware that Tommie was being protective of him. Avuncular, though Tommie was barely a few years his senior.

"I am wealthy enough that I will be permitted a few crotchets, I hope, and I truly do enjoy trading in art. I cannot be in London to see to the commercial minutiae, and I'd expect you to hire a gallery manager or two for the actual day-to-day business, but somebody must be my eyes and ears about the place. Somebody must ensure that clients are treated as honored guests rather than *customers*."

This time, Tommie chose an apple tart, though his ears were pink again, and the cherry tart sat uneaten on his plate. "I do miss Town, but one cannot maintain a proper address on a poet's earnings."

"Of course not. The post is salaried, Thomas. As long as you've pretended to kick your heels at Lynnfield while humoring the elders, doing the pretty with the neighbors, and guarding Penelope's flank, I don't expect you to also manage a gallery gratis."

Tommie looked up, the apple tart in his hand. "I'd do it again, Lucien. I'm bored, true enough, but these people have been family to me when I had no other family to claim. Lynnfield has been home. That matters, and I had my poetry. My correspondence is vast and lively, and many of my connections bide in London this time of year."

Tommie wanted to take the job, in other words, which meant...

Lucien named a figure. "Plus, let's say, a ten percent commission on goods sold and the understanding that whatever you personally add to the gallery's collection is your business, save for a ten percent contribution into the operating funds."

Tommie stared at him. "Lucien, that's very generous. One hesitates to offer insult to oneself or present company, but perhaps it's too generous?"

Lucien rose. "I would rather you feel you have to live up to expectations, than think yourself justified in living down to miserly remuneration. If you head to London soon, the marchioness can put the word out that after years of collecting and advising me on my own purchases, you are making a few select pieces available to discerning parties for sums appropriate to their quality."

Tommie stood as well. "Right, quality on both sides of the bargain. But if I'm to go up to London, I might also serve as escort to her ladyship and Miss Tabitha in a fortnight or so, mightn't I?"

The question was posed with exquisite diffidence.

Well, well, well. "I shall rely on you to see the ladies to the town house itself, and you can serve as their escort of choice until other parties come forward to claim the honor."

Tommie grabbed Lucien's hand and wrung it. "And so I shall. Miss Tabitha will be new to Town, and squiring her about will be my dearest delight. She's really quite clever, you know. She's had to be, putting up with that brother of hers."

Lucien retrieved his hand. "Sir Dashiel?"

"Sir Dunderhead. Tabby keeps all the household books, and she intimates that our brave baronet is quite pockets to let. He puts on airs, and he certainly can't afford those hunters, but then, he thinks himself all but assured of Penelope's hand. I have no doubt he's been trading on those expectations with the village shops, if not the London merchants. Puts poor Tabby in quite a bind."

To say nothing of the creditors and staff. Then too, a magistrate deeply in debt could become a nasty situation all too easily.

"Does Penelope know this?"

Tommie made a face. "I expect not. She's our grand lady, more or less, after the marchioness. She doesn't hear nearly as much of the gossip as Theo and I do. Cousin Lark gets all the best village news, provided she leaves Purdy at home when she goes calling. Nobody is exactly thrilled to welcome poor Purdy into their formal parlor."

"Calpurnia steals from *neighbors?*"

"We refer to it as borrowing—when we refer to Aunt's little habit at all. Pen goes through Purdy's reticule of a night and has the purloined articles delivered to the owner by messenger with apologies. Purdy is much better than she used to be. Watches seem to be her only remaining weakness, and everybody knows not to wear a watch to the assemblies. We keep a very close eye on her in situations like that."

We meaning the whole household, from Malcolm to Cousin Lark and likely all of the servants too. *We* had not included Lucien for a long, long time.

"If you go to London..." he said slowly, "when you go to London, we will miss you. You must not be a stranger, and if you bide at the town house while you settle into London life, you must anticipate a lot of Lynnfield company."

That hail-and-farewell was not the best Lucian could do. He considered what he would say if Penelope were standing there, giving him the sort of encouraging look that was half dare, half warning.

"What I mean to convey, Thomas, is my sincere thanks. Thank you for taking the art business off my hands and for keeping such a careful eye on the elders and Penelope. Your patience and loyalty are appreciated."

Lucien departed on that meager effort rather than watch Tommie endure another blush, but Tommie called after him.

"Something else you should know, Lucien," Tommie said, coming down the corridor to close the distance between them. "Old MacGuinness looks after my wardrobe, and he does for Malcolm and Theo too."

Lucien vaguely recalled a venerable figure with snow-white hair and ferocious eyebrows. "Wears a kilt on St. Andrew's Day?"

"The very one. He claims somebody beat the stuffing out of Malcolm. Striped him all over his shoulders, neck, and back. Malcolm offers no explanation, and when MacGuinness advised salve, Malcolm ordered him from the room."

"One suspected something untoward," Lucien muttered. "But not this. I thought Uncle was well liked."

Tommie glanced up and down the corridor. "Malcolm is not merely well liked, Lucien, he is damn near *treasured* in these surrounds. Part precious fool, part Merlin, and entirely our own. He hears secrets the widows and orphans can't tell Vicar. He looks after the small children who oughtn't to be wandering alone, and he can fashion a splint for a lame puppy that will soon have it bounding about again. He rescues kittens from trees and dries as many juvenile tears as any granny ever has. He is well loved, and somebody beat him soundly."

Lucien said the only thing he could. "Thank you for telling me. The malefactor will be punished."

"Good." Tommie clapped him on the shoulder, the first person to ever do so, and jaunted back to his rooms.

Lucien had no more appointments until after luncheon, and thus a quarter hour later, he was in the orchard, watching blossoms drift down to carpet the grass in pink and white.

"I thought they all depended on me," he said to nobody in particular. "They have learned to depend on one another." That should have been a relief—it was certainly a revelation—but to realize that one's standing and resources had been of secondary import was also a trifle lowering.

A trifle bewildering.

Even more bewildering was the notion that Malcolm had made an enemy, one who had waited to attack until Lucien had returned to Lynnfield.

"Avoid the military types lurking among Mayfair's potted palms," Dashiel said, eyeing Tabitha's mare. When had the horse grown so long in the tooth? "They pretend to means they will never enjoy. Half pay is less than half enough to live on."

"No half-pay officers, even for an allemande. I understand, Dash." Tabitha was the meekest of creatures, and yet, Dashiel heard a note of condescension in her reply.

"An alle-what?"

"A boring dance of German origin. It's said to be the grandmother to the waltz, so fashionable hostesses sometimes include it for the sake of the old people."

Where had she come across that bit of arcana? The lending library no doubt. Too many periodicals graced its humble shelves, to say nothing of all the lurid novels Mrs. Dinkle insisted on stocking.

"And do you consider me among the relics and antiques, young lady?"

Tabitha turned a glorious smile on him, and Dashiel was momentarily dumbstruck. That smile was going to London, to *Mayfair*, where it would be noticed. While part of him understood that an advantageous match could well be the outcome of this journey—the marchioness was no fool, and Dashiel was to be congratulated for arranging such a feat, and the war was quite in the past and thoroughly won—another part of him fretted that a smiling, darling Tabitha would stir up talk.

"I think," she said, "that you are the best of brothers and that I will miss you terribly and will write you long, boring letters every day, gushing with wonderment over all the delights of Town. You are a very dear fellow to make this possible for me, Dash."

"Indeed, I am, and very generous, but you may limit your dispatches to weekly summaries. I want the names of all the bachelors, Tabby, and whether their families have means, land, and decent lineages. You are not to fall in love with any Scotsmen or with any impoverished poets."

Her smile dimmed. "Poets are witty. Byron is a poet and a lord, and everybody dotes on him."

"Until he offends them or breaks their hearts. Have a care for your good name, miss, or you will soon see the last of London."

The groom checked the mare's girth and led her to the ladies' mounting block, where both man and beast waited with comparably blank expressions.

"You will come over to Lynnfield to see me off?" Tabitha asked, gathering up the skirt of her riding habit. "Promise you will, Dash."

"I promise, and you shall see me at the assembly as well." The same assembly where his engagement to Lady Penelope Richard would doubtless be announced. That connection—to an earl's daughter and her fortune—all but assured Tabitha of a successful Season.

Very well and cleverly done of him indeed.

"Another quarterly assembly," Tabitha said. "I am so glad to be going to Town at last, Dash. I very much feared... Well, no matter. Will you miss me?"

A second horse, also venerable, stood at a hitching post, hip cocked, head down. The animal swished its tail at an imaginary fly.

"I will muddle on without you somehow, my dear, though you are merely going up to Town for a few weeks."

"I left a month's worth of menus with Mrs. Brook, and we should have some peas and cucumbers soon to liven things up at supper."

Dashiel, feeling old and unaccountably sentimental, escorted his baby sister up the mounting block's steps. "You will come back from Town, spouting off about this peer or that grand ball, and garden vegetables will have flown completely from your mind." As well they should at her age.

Tabitha pulled on her gloves and gave him a serious look. "We rely on that garden for survival, Dash. No grand ball matters more than a good crop of peas."

He grabbed her by the nape, kissed her forehead, and stepped back. "You have always been my most sensible sibling. Away with you, and keep your eyes and ears open at Lynnfield. Penelope is an estimable woman, but the rest of the household leaves much to be desired."

A younger Tabitha might have protested for form's sake. This one settled on her sway-backed mare with considerable dignity and nodded graciously to her brother.

"Good day, Dash. Mind you behave in my absence." She punctuated that startling admonition by grinning again and trotting off in great good spirits.

Ah, youth.

The groom swung up onto the cob and, without so much as looking at Dashiel, plodded after the mare.

"No half-pay officers!" Dash called. "And none of the full-pay variety either. They're even worse."

Tabitha waved without turning back, and Dashiel watched her go until the horses had disappeared around a bend in the bridle path. Tabby would manage. She had the basic pragmatism common to all the Ingrahams, and what a relief to see the fourth and final sister off Dashiel's hands and on her way to holy matrimony.

"They beggar a man," he muttered, taking the path back to the manor house. "Sisters. Most diabolically expensive arrangement ever conceived of." The late baronet had consoled his only son with assurances that land and honors would befall him, but dowering the girls had nearly bankrupted poor Papa. Enough had remained to buy Dashiel a captain's commission, and from there, Dash had had to rely on his own native wit and initiative.

"Unlike certain marquesses, off buying art for years at a time."

Lord Lynnfield had been involved in more than a wartime grand tour, though Dashiel was vague on the details. Lynnfield himself likely was too. The whole lot of them were barmy, in Dashiel's estimation. The marchioness, not a Pritchard by birth, could at least be sensible on occasion, though the poor dear was prone to tippling.

"You have a caller, sir," Jenkins, the butler said, taking Dash's hat from him upon his return to the manor house. "Mrs. Domenica de Plessis. I put her in the formal parlor."

A buxom widow and tiresomely friendly, poor dear. As if Dash would settle for one farm, however prosperous, and a broodmare going matronly about the middle. Still, she had influence in the village, and she could prove useful.

"I suppose we'd better offer the woman tea, though thank goodness it's too early for a luncheon invitation. Have you inventoried the cellars yet this month, Jenkins?"

"I have, sir. You shall have my report within the hour."

"Very good." Dashiel moved off before Jenkins could cough discreetly and murmur something about wages not yet paid. As the head of the domestic staff, Jenkins took his role seriously, but he was also getting on. Thanks to dear Papa, a modest pension was available to get rid of the man at the moment of Dash's choosing.

Today was not that day. Dash ducked into the music room to

check his appearance in a full-length mirror going speckled in the corners, found himself as attractive as ever, and sailed across the corridor into the formal parlor. He adopted the air of a fellow with much on his mind and little time for socializing, but the look in Dommie de Plessis's eyes suggested she hadn't much interest in socializing either.

"Sir Dashiel." She rose and curtseyed, giving him an eyeful of an impressive decolletage, despite the early hour. The good widow de Plessis had been born Domenica Bottledorf. Her family was solid gentry with a baron a few branches up the family tree.

She was also well formed, if a bit generously proportioned. She styled her brown hair in a coronet of braids that tended toward fashionable rather than staid and regarded the world out of tolerant brown eyes. Not a diamond, but easy to look on. Tended to freckles across her lower back, of all the peculiarities.

"Mrs. de Plessis, a pleasure. Jenkins will bring along a tray shortly. You find me without custom for my parlor sessions this week by happy coincidence, and might I say, you are looking well."

It never hurt to compliment a widow, though Dash was careful to keep to the polite side of flattery. Dommie and he had had their fun years ago, and he had no interest in renewing relations, as it were.

Well, little interest. Dommie was still attractive, in a mature way.

"You appear in quite good looks yourself," she said, "but I have sought you out in your capacity as magistrate, rather than that of congenial neighbor. I'd like to lay information against Calpurnia Richard and bring a charge of theft. My late husband's watch has gone missing, and we have searched the entire house for it. He loved that watch, and it's worth a pretty penny. The sentimental value to me is incalculable."

Jenkins arrived with the tray, and Dommie busied herself pouring out while Dashiel considered the advantages and disadvantages of various tactics. He could put Dommie off—the easiest course—or he could charge Aunt Purdy on the strength of facts alleged.

"You do know Lord Lynnfield is back in residence?" Dashiel said as he accepted a cup of acceptably strong gunpowder.

"Of course I know it. You have always been slow to see brains in others, Dash. Now that Lynnfield is back, we can do something about that thieving old woman. She's awful, a local joke. Nobody wears a watch to church because of her."

One wasn't supposed to consult a timepiece at divine services in the general case, which was beside the point.

"Have you seen her with the watch?"

"No, but she and Miss Lark called upon me on Tuesday, which is when I'm at home, and I noticed the watch missing on Wednesday. Purdy Richard took it. I know she did. I leave that watch out on the escritoire in my parlor. It stopped at 3:17 precisely, and Harold was born on March seventeenth. Said his Irish mother planned it that way. I want that watch back, Dash, and I want Purdy held accountable."

Aunt Purdy—Aunt Purloiner—had been a fixture in the village for decades, and her thievery had been viewed with amused exasperation. She was good at slipping a bauble into her reticule even when closely watched.

"Theft is a serious matter," Sir Dashiel said. "A very serious matter. Do you want to see Calpurnia, a neighbor of long standing, hanged for taking that watch? I would have to bind her over to the assizes if I arrested her."

Dommie sat up very tall, which had the effect of thrusting her bosom forward. "No, you wouldn't. A magistrate has latitude. I want my husband's watch back, and I want Calpurnia to stop her nonsense. Everybody says she's not as bad as she used to be, but watches are valuable, and she cannot be trusted around them."

The sooner Penelope was free of the Lynnfield lunatics, the better—after Tabitha had been properly launched, of course.

"I will take the matter under advisement, Dommie, and make some inquiries, but I am loath to send an old woman to her death over a missing watch. The situation wants witnesses, and ideally, I would find the watch in Calpurnia's possession."

"I want my watch back, Dash. Do what you must to sort the matter out. Now, tell me about Tabitha. Is it true Lady Lynnfield is taking her up to Town? However did you manage that?"

The call descended into small talk and flirtation, and when Dashiel had established that Tabitha was already a visitor at Lynnfield and the Roost all but deserted, he admitted to himself that having his sister gone might offer a handsome bachelor a few advantages.

"I've been thinking of having Tabitha's rooms made over in her absence," Dashiel said. "Perhaps you'd be willing to give me a woman's opinion on the matter? Tabby's apartment is toward the back of the house, with a nice view of the pastures and kitchen garden."

A nice rural view.

Dommie gave him a look that suggested she was just at that moment making up her mind to tryst with him, and the decision took some thought. The ladies did cling to their little games.

"If I decline to assist you, you will hang the walls in yellow silk because it can be had for less," she said, rising. "Yellow flatters practically nobody. Let's have a look, though I can't stay long."

"Of course not," Dashiel said, offering his arm. "What colors do you recommend?" Not that he'd be buying any silk this side of his own nuptials.

Thirty minutes later, the color most in evidence was that of pink and white flesh. Dommie was snoring gently beside Dash in the best guest room, and Dash was considering the dark ceiling beams above the bed.

To leave a watch in plain sight all but guaranteed that Calpurnia would steal it, suggesting Dommie had merely sought a socially credible excuse to pay her call. The watch itself—if, in fact, it was missing —had apparently been an acceptable token to exchange for a morning's pleasure.

Dashiel idly stroked the lady's muscular thigh and considered possibilities. A competent officer always had contingency plans ready in the event the accursed French—or his own accursed superiors—disobliged his initial strategy. The London connections were slow to pay of late, the creditors howling, and Tabitha's prospects uncertain.

Then too, Lord Lynnfield was home, and he'd apparently supported the entire collection of misfits through all his years of travel.

Dashiel would take the matter of the missing watch under very discreet advisement, because fate was for once apparently taking his side, and at a very opportune time too.

CHAPTER ELEVEN

"I am kidnapping you," Penelope said, speaking quietly, though Lucien was alone in his study. "I thought you'd never let Uncle Theo go."

Lucien rose and came around the desk. Since Tabitha's arrival two days ago, Penelope hadn't seen much of him, and their most private interactions had been limited to a few good-night kisses. He attended supper with the family, sat sphinxlike at the head of the table, and contributed to the conversation to the extent necessary to entertain Tabitha, but no more.

"I thought he'd never let me go," Lucien said, taking Penelope in his arms. "When sober, that man has a lot to say."

This embrace had a wonderfully mundane quality. In the past days, they'd stolen a few quiet moments, a hug here, a brief clasp of hands beneath the table, a half hour sitting side by side in the family parlor while Penelope embroidered and Lucien read some agricultural pamphlet. Nothing ardent or obvious, but precious to Penelope all the same.

Lucien's presence sank into her body and mind with each encounter. He truly was home.

"Touching you brings me inordinate joy," she said, her cheek against Lucien's chest. "For so long, you were not here to be touched."

Lucien kissed her temple. "Touching you brings me joy as well, my lady. Joy and temptation."

Penelope retaliated by kissing him on the mouth, and what followed was part skirmish, part celebration, until she was perched on the corner of Lucien's desk, her beloved wedged between her legs and her wits flown straight out the window.

"We can't do this here," she said, letting her legs fall from around Lucien's hips. "At any moment, Cousin Lark will tap on that door with plans for the garden, Tommie will seek your counsel on carpets for the gallery, and the marchioness will demand my assistance with her London packing." That her ladyship had not begun to pack for a journey less than two weeks off was vaguely puzzling.

Lucien smoothed a hand over Penelope's hair. "What is it, precisely, we cannot *do* here, Pen?"

Penelope was abruptly as mortified as she was determined. She rested her forehead on Lucien's chest, the better to hide a blush.

"We mustn't tryst."

Lucien bent his head. "Tryst, as in kissing and caressing and embracing?"

They'd become adept at that part, or at least comfortable with it. "I meant the rest of it."

"The intimate rest of it—the part that can lead to procreation?"

Even the timbre of his voice pleased her. "Must you sound so self-possessed?"

"Tell me about the kidnapping part, Pen. Leave nothing out."

"The coach will be out front by now, the hampers packed. I thought we'd inspect Finbury today." Penelope's admission left out a good deal, but Lucien was a smart fellow, good at reasoning from facts to conclusions.

His embrace shifted so his chin rested on her crown. "You seek to have your way with me?" He wasn't laughing, which was fortunate for the marquessate's succession.

"I hope we have our way with each other." Put like that, the plan seemed laughable. "Must we *discuss* this? Can't we simply fall into a convenient bed behind a stout and equally convenient locked door? I go mad at night, touching myself..."

Lucien hugged her as if he'd shelter her from her own awkwardness. "You do me great honor, Pendragon. The greatest honor. If I refuse this generous overture, you'll be hurt, won't you?"

"I will be frustrated and bewildered. We are courting, and courting couples enjoy certain freedoms. I have it in my head that if I can take you to bed, you won't disappear again."

She'd said it. Voiced the fear she hadn't quite admitted even to herself. Penelope yearned to put her imprimatur on Lucien's mind and body, even as she knew that limiting his freedom in any way was beyond her. Her path was illuminated by instinct rather than common sense, and yet, that path blazed brightly.

Lucien gently rubbed her earlobe between his thumb and forefinger. "You have abandoned logic, unless you believe that honor will bind me where devotion and my own self-interest could not."

"Honor is a powerful bond, Lucien. I'm not clear in my own mind why I believe as I do. I just know I've reached for my dressing gown with intent to seek your bed more times than I can count."

He stepped back and kept hold of her hand. "While I have lectured myself about the folly of haste and the need for abundant self-restraint, as if actually embarking on a happy future terrifies me."

"Does it?" How courageous of him to disclose such thoughts, even in the conditional.

He stroked her fingers. "I am afraid I will wake up in Rome, having twitched away another quarter hour in fitful nightmares, the pantry mouser regarding me from the foot of the bed with a feline disdain that approaches pity."

She hated to think of him in those tangled sheets, alone in the dark, only an aloof cat to witness his struggles. Lucien doubtless wished even the cat hadn't seen him in such a state.

"Let's go to Finbury," she said. "The tenants are off at the seaside, I've sent notice that I'm making a visit, and this is an outing you suggested yourself. You can tell me what schemes you and Theo are hatching up."

Lucien scowled over her shoulder at his desk blotter, which was littered with ledgers, sketches, foolscap covered in jottings, and brass paperweights in the shape of dragons.

"I ought to propose," he said. "If we are to make this journey to a destination which you have assured I will never get out of my mind, I should propose. I was working on a speech, complete with topics in order of their importance—your comfort, the good of the household, the stability of the realm, my sanity—and supporting arguments for each one. I owe you that, and a ring, and my personal pledge, but how does one word a pledge of heart and hand without sounding medieval? I sound medieval maundering on about it."

Lucien flustered and casting about for order was a rare and adorable sight. "We are betrothed, sir. A proposal would be redundant."

His brows twitched, and he peered down at her. "So we are. Betrothed. Engaged to be married and entitled to all the blessings attendant thereto."

His smile eased a knot in Penelope's chest. Watching Tabitha count the hours until she departed for London, seeing a new sparkle in the girl's eyes, Penelope had felt bewildered.

Why didn't I ever feel like that? Except she did feel like that when Lucien tugged her into the warming pantry and stole a hug and a kiss, or when he squeezed her hand beneath the dinner table. She felt giddy and special and happy when he smiled at her across the family parlor, and she felt positively delighted when he turned a page of his book and managed to brush her arm in the process.

The emotions—excitement, glee, satisfaction, and, that most daunting of all, hope—had filled her imagination both waking and sleeping. Going to Finbury had become a replacement, cure, and reward for all the times she had instead gone up to London.

Reluctantly, dutifully alone despite the marchioness's chattering company.

"We are engaged," Penelope said, "and I will expect you out front in ten minutes. I've told Tommie my plans, and he will make our excuses if we're not back by supper."

"By supper? Are we to tryst or indulge in a two-person orgy?"

"Why not both?"

She left Lucien looking intrigued and distracted in his study, though, in fact, he was out on the front steps, dignity at the ready, in less than five minutes.

Lucien grappled with the revelation that Penelope expected lovemaking of him, and not merely the pretty kind, with words and caresses and tender embraces. He was learning her preferences in that regard. She didn't like to be rushed, and she needed intermissions to plot her counterstrategies, which was fortunate. Lucien needed intermissions to recover his wits.

But now Penelope expected the carnal kind of lovemaking, too, with trust, pleasure, and intimacy and—she deserved nothing less—exhausted satisfaction.

Lucien watched Lynnfield's stately park from the carriage window and asked himself impossible questions: Where to start? What to say? Chess was no help. Espionage was no guide. The clamorings of lust felt ridiculous in the stately traveling coach.

Ridiculous, not impossible.

"Have I spoiled everything?" Penelope asked, taking off her bonnet and putting it on the opposite seat. "Are you trying to work out some sort of retraction, Lucien?"

"I'm trying to work out a seduction. One hasn't much practice, and five minutes is apparently insufficient notice to prepare me for the challenge." He looped an arm around Pen's shoulders, for his own comfort and to prevent her from leaping out of the coach on a sudden change of mind. "I sound like a curate trying to explain why his sermon on forgiveness lacked inspiration."

"You sound like you want to get this right, and so do I, but, Lucien, might we consider this outing in the nature of a rehearsal? A practice debate?"

She tossed her gloves into the crown of her bonnet. Lucien's top hat sat beside her bonnet, his gloves drooping over the brim. The image of the two hats, side by side, struck him as inordinately touching.

Prosaic and profound.

"You suggest we needn't write poetry for the ages, but merely some entertaining verse?" A tempting approach, though not good enough for his Pen.

"Something like that. What did Theo wring your ear about at such length?" Penelope took possession of Lucien's hand. The result was a sort of circular embrace, his arm around her shoulders, his free hand in hers.

Comfy, particularly when Penelope slouched against him and rested her head on his shoulder.

"I have been racking my brain regarding a constructive application of Uncle Theo's gifts. He's charming, practical, well liked, well educated when sober, and doesn't judge his fellow creatures harshly."

"He's patience itself with the ladies, Tommie, and Uncle Malcolm. Theo would have made a good vicar."

Penelope this close bore the fragrance of roses. Whenever Lucien encountered the aroma lately, he was thrown off stride. For years, that scent had presaged terrible homesickness, regret, confusion, and even anger. Now, the aroma was soothing and reassuring.

I am not halfway across the Continent, possibly never to see her again. I am home. In the next instant, the thought reached its logical progression: *Penelope is my home.*

Her elbow delivered a glancing blow to his ribs as she rearranged herself at his side, and even that soft blow, reminiscent of its sharper, youthful predecessors, pleased Lucien.

"I hope Theo will make a decent steward," he said. "He knows the properties and tenants. As a youth, he thought he'd inherit land in Wales, and thus his interest in farming is of long standing."

"When he falls asleep in the family parlor, he's usually reading some pamphlet or other. The benefits of rutabagas for people seeking healthier bowels, or the ideal arrangement of the goodwife's spice garden. I confess those topics would put me to sleep."

Theo appeared to suffer the excesses of alcohol each evening, but it was possible, perhaps, that he was merely falling asleep at least some of the time.

"Those pamphlets fascinate him, and I'm considering making him an offer: If he can learn the stewardship of Lynnfield and its tenancies in the next year, I will deed him ten acres of forest or arable land per year. If he can competently execute his duties for five consecutive years, he can have his pick of the tenant properties, in addition to his fifty acres."

"That is diabolical, Lucien. You took the whole business of inebriation out of the picture."

"Many a London merchant overimbibes, but he's minding his shop the next morning lest his customers go elsewhere. Theo will sort out the drinking if he has meaningful challenges to deal with instead." A hope, not a certainty. Theo was owed the chance to pursue that hope, though, and the present steward had been grumbling about longing for his pension cottage for years.

"I like this idea," Penelope said as the coach swayed around a turn and the horses picked up speed. "A land steward is a gentleman's occupation. Theo is good at flattery. He never tells anybody what to do, he asks questions. 'Are we trying to find a place for that portrait?' 'What do you ladies think of a picnic luncheon on such a fine day?' Stewards need to be diplomats. I've been trying to diplomatically suggest that the marchioness hire a companion or an amanuensis when she's in London."

A fine idea, though Lucien rather hoped the marchioness would remove to London altogether. She had acquired a subdued air that made him uneasy.

He discussed with Penelope the ideal lady's maid, as well as how to tactfully suggest to Tabitha that her ancient mare ought to be spared the trip to London. By inches and degrees, Lucien's anxiety about how to go forth into new territory with Penelope abated.

She was his home, and his task was simple: He was to become her home in return. Her fortress and refuge, her pleasure barge and summer cottage. The place she went for solace, joy, shelter, companionship, and safety. The words *I love you* came to mind, though he left them unspoken.

He would love her in fact and in bed, rather than natter on about his sentiments. He did love her. Passionately. Always had, always would.

"Are we there?" Penelope rose from dozing on Lucien's shoulder an hour later and rubbed at her eyes. "I vow sewing has exhausted me. You've never seen so many dresses taking shape so quickly. It's as if the aunties and Cousin Lark were waiting for the starting bell or something. Pretty dresses too. I do love this place."

She had raised the shade, and Finbury in all its modest glory sat on a slight rise at the end of a gently curving carriageway. No grand fountain, no strutting peacocks, but instead a lovely planting of Holland bulbs in bright reds and yellows against a backdrop of whitewashed stone. More tulips bloomed in pots on the terrace and its steps, giving the whole place an air of cheerful, tidy welcome. Three stories, fifteen windows across, the front door painted bright red, the shutters white, and the window boxes boasting more tulips.

"Conscientious gardeners," Lucien said as the coach came to a halt before the manor.

"Bulbs are easy." Penelope handed him his gloves, put his hat on his head, and adjusted the angle. "Smart gardeners, I should say, and somebody willing to invest in some beauty. What are you...? Oh."

Lucien had appropriated her bonnet and positioned it on her

head. As he tied the ribbons in a loose bow, she beamed at him, and he knew exactly what she was thinking: *So domestic and so dear, these little mutual courtesies.*

He kissed her on the lips without allowing their millinery to bump, the better to inspire still more shared thoughts, and then passed her her gloves.

"The household is expecting us?" Lucien asked.

"I chose today because it's half day, but yes. We are expected. I explained that we would bring our own victuals and need no escort. I have popped in here from time to time over the years, when I wanted an excuse to get away from Lynnfield."

Lucien opened the coach door and flipped down the step. "Good. If nothing else, you reminded everybody at Lynnfield that you bide with them by your own choice." He climbed out and handed Pen down, his words a reminder to himself: Penelope had options. At any moment, she could swan up to London to buy out the shops or establish her own household in Mayfair.

A sobering thought.

"I want to kiss you," Penelope said, slipping her arm through his. "Instead, I will show you around the place, and when we've enjoyed a picnic in the deer park, I'll acquaint you with the hermit's grotto."

"Out of sight of the house, I trust?" What a talent for planning she had.

"Out of sight of everything and quite commodious. Come along, Lucien, and stop trying to concoct learned speeches in your head. You will be too busy kissing me back to utter a single word other than 'please' or 'more.'"

Lucien stopped thinking of anything other than how much he loved his betrothed and how much he'd enjoy kissing her back until she couldn't utter *even* a single, delighted word.

~

Part of Penelope tried to uphold the tradition that said Lady Penelope Richard was a bustler, a woman who accomplished much in the course of a day. She toured the public rooms with the housekeeper, Lucien trailing behind them, and made pleasant noises about the lack of dust. She stood in the doorways of the guest rooms and complimented the housekeeper on the sparkling windows.

She flattered the butler regarding the thoroughness of his inventories and praised the first footman for the spotless hearths and gleaming andirons.

The whole time, she was also cursing the perception she herself had established. Why couldn't Lady Penelope have been an inveterate daydreamer? A hoyden? She wasted time admiring wainscoting that she could have spent being private with Lucien.

In bed.

Naked.

All the pleasures proving, to paraphrase old Mr. Marlowe, or at least beginning to explore.

"I do believe you've seen the lot of it, my lady," the housekeeper said when their little parade had returned to the foot of the main staircase. "I trust you're finding everything in order?" Mrs. Beadle was a grand specimen made more impressive by a starched and pristine mobcap atop her gray hair and a tinkling chain of keys dangling from her waist.

Old-school and proud of it.

"I'm impressed," Penelope said. "I don't believe we maintain Lynnfield to the standards you uphold here at Finbury."

"Grand manors are such a lot of work," the housekeeper replied, "begging his lordship's pardon, but they are. Finbury's the perfect size to make a gracious impression without beggaring the exchequer. Just the right age, too—a century and a half—to be done with the settling and shifting about without being cramped or dank. You will not find a more commodious nor better-kept dwelling in all of England, my lady."

A short speech, by Mrs. Beadle's standards. She was as loquacious as she was conscientious. A talented bustler. In her care, Finbury would be just as spotless and orderly ten years hence, whether or not Penelope ever saw the place again.

"Perhaps," Lucien said, "I might plead an empty belly, your ladyship, and request that picnic you promised me?"

Oh, thank heavens. "I am a bit peckish myself," Penelope said. "Mrs. Beadle, you have convinced me that the property continues to prosper, and we will leave you to enjoy your half day."

Lucien bowed, Mrs. Beadle curtseyed like a seventy-four gunner dipping in heavy seas, and Penelope all but dragged Lucien out onto the back terrace.

"The deer park is to the west of the parterres. Come along, Lucien. Finbury seems as if it has grown a dozen bedrooms, sixteen pantries, two cellars, and eight attics that I'd never seen before."

"Mrs. Beadle knows when she's in the presence of an expert. You are not merely the owner, you are Lady Penelope and essentially the house steward at Lynnfield."

Penelope stopped halfway down the terrace steps. "That's how you see me? As your house steward?"

"In the normal course, a house steward is remunerated for his services. I thus position you more as Lynnfield's guardian angel-at-large."

They passed through the garden at a sedate pace, Mrs. Beadle and her minions doubtless watching their progress and to blazes with half day.

"I prefer the title house steward," Penelope said. "That has dignity and respect. Guardian angels are ephemeral creatures too much given to virtue."

Lucien opened the door in the garden wall and held it for Penelope. When he closed it, and they stood outside the garden, they had privacy from the house, given the height of the wall and the roll of the land.

"Having second thoughts, Pen?"

"Not second thoughts, but thoughts." She gazed up at him and saw patience in his eyes and bottomless affection. "You would enjoy this picnic and happily escort me back to Lynnfield if I told you I'd changed my mind, wouldn't you?"

His smile was crooked. "I will *politely* escort you home if that's what you prefer, but I will ask for a moment on my own to admire the stables first."

"A moment on your... oh." She ought to be blushing, but the idea that Lucien's animal spirits clamored as loudly as her own pleased her.

"Let's find that picnic basket, my lady, and take it to the grotto, shall we?"

Splendid notion. "The picnic basket is under that leaning oak," Penelope said, dodging around Lucien to lead the charge. "It's the closest to the grotto, which lies below that swell."

Five minutes later, Lucien was peering around the "grotto," which Penelope had always thought of as more of a gatehouse built partially into the side of a small hill. The view from the flagstone terrace was lovely—the homewood in all its verdant spring glory across a sparkling stream, sunlight dappling the water, and wild irises adding dashes of yellow along the banks.

"Oh, to be a hermit," Lucien muttered. "I suppose it gets chilly in winter?"

"I had a parlor stove installed, and what passes for the kitchen has another hearth. Let's have a look."

She took his hand and led him into the shadowed interior. No candles had been lit, but indirect light revealed a miniature parlor that looked out over the terrace. A kitchenish sort of room with table and chairs for dining sat behind the parlor and shared a flue with it. A narrow, tightly curved wooden staircase led from the parlor to a surprisingly airy bedroom above that also enjoyed a view across the river.

"This was built about three owners ago," Penelope said. "Follies and ruins and grottoes were all the rage back then. A great-uncle with bookish inclination used to retreat here, or so the family story went. My mother suspected less scholarly uses for the place."

"How fortunate." Lucien pushed open a bedroom window that had been merely cracked. "I'm not feeling very scholarly. You gave orders for the place to be aired?"

"Of course. Mildew is no sort of aphrodisiac." An unseductive observation. One could not housekeep and bustle one's way into a seduction, and Penelope very much wanted to seduce Lucien. Now that the moment was upon them—the four-poster took up a quarter of the room—awkwardness seized her by the heart.

Lucien strolled across the bedroom, all lazy grace and nonchalance, blast him. "You have made a study of aphrodisiacs?" He kept coming, until his arms were around her.

Penelope relaxed against him, glad for an excuse to hide her face against his chest. "I have, as it happens. The herbal is the province of the lady of the house. One wants to be informed."

"One absolutely does. Might one also want to be kissed?" He spoke near Penelope's ear, the scent of his lavender shaving soap tickling her nose.

"One abruptly wants the earth to swallow one whole. Lucien, I know I planned this outing and made my intentions very clear, but I'm not... That is, I don't know..."

He looped his arms loosely around her shoulders. "I don't know either, Pen. I'm not completely ignorant, but I don't know *you* in this new and wonderful way. I am nonetheless overjoyed to embark on this adventure with you."

Not quite a declaration of love, but reassuring. "Where do we start?"

He kissed her, and she understood that words were no longer the only useful means of communication. When Lucien moved closer, his body told her that desire had already taken hold of him, and the knowledge was a match to the dry tinder of Penelope's own longings.

For years, she'd known that despite time, distance, absence, and even anger, Lucien was the only possible lover for her. Then she'd grown weary and wavering, vaguely considering even the likes of Sir Dashiel Ingraham for a husband. All over again, the sense of having had a narrow escape clutched at Penelope's nerves.

Lucien is home to stay. She pressed against him, wanting greater closeness and wanting their dratted clothing *off*. When he began to deftly undo the buttons down the back of her dress—kissing her all the while—she freed her hands to go after his cravat.

Garments were loosened, then went sailing onto the chair by the hearth until the spring breeze tickled Penelope's shoulder blades, and Lucien stood before her in his shirt and breeches.

"In the race to shed clothing," he said, stepping back and undoing his last two shirt buttons, "you are lagging far behind, my lady. Allow me to assist you." He pulled his shirt off over his head and tossed it onto the pile on the reading chair.

Penelope held up a hand. "Wait."

Lucien went still, his gaze growing guarded. "I'm waiting."

He was also breathing hard, shirtless, and no longer a youth. Lean muscles rippled across his chest and belly and roped his arms. He wasn't hirsute, but the hair on his chest was dark and—Penelope assayed a caress—crinkly.

"My lord will turn around, please."

He complied, making a slow circle, and Penelope was treated to more abundant muscle and male perfection. "What's this?" She traced a finger over a white, puckered line running from his left shoulder down over the left shoulder blade.

"Saber blow. Not deep. Itched like hell when it was healing. Fortunately, a competent medical man saw to it—a Frenchman flying British colors of all things."

Penelope hated that scar and hated even more the casual recounting Lucien offered. She spun him around, and though her dress gapped and Lucien was half naked, she yet mustered a lecture.

"No more of that, Lucien. No more sabers, no more riding off to war and calling it a grand tour. No more trading in art and espionage. You are mine now. I love you, and you will bide *with me*."

He removed a nacre pin dangling behind her ear—a half dozen were doubtless scattered on the carpet. "I will bide with you. Right now, I'd like to bide naked with you in that bed, Penelope. Might I be your lady's maid?"

He hadn't returned her declaration outright, but he'd managed the part that mattered. His place was with her, and on that point he'd given her no argument.

"You shall be my lady's maid, and then you shall be my lover."

He moved around behind her, finished unbuttoning her dress, and made short work of her stays and stockings. When Penelope stood barefoot in her shift, she realized a great deal of her hesitance had fallen away.

They were betrothed. Lucien had *never* made any effort to rescind those promises, and he'd never admitted to so much as speculating about a future with another lady. What he hadn't said told her as much as what he had.

He was hers, and the look in his eyes said he intended in the next hour to prove that conclusion past any and all doubts.

CHAPTER TWELVE

Penelope in pursuit of pleasure was a revelation.

Lucien had seen her spend a whole morning trying to outsmart a grandpapa trout, only to throw her catch back when she'd gained her victory. She'd memorized the first canto of *The Lay of the Last Minstrel* in a week flat. She had decided to take on the violin as a challenge and within one long summer had played well enough to perform at the marchioness's musicales.

Pen was capable of intense, unrelenting focus, but she had never turned that focus on him—not like this.

She stood in her shift and bare feet, her hair a thick braid over her left shoulder, one fist planted on her hip, pirate-captain-on-the-quarterdeck fashion. "Who is overly dressed for the occasion now, my lord?"

"We both are."

Her brows shot up, then she drew the curtains over the window and marched back to the braided rug beside the bed.

"Race you," she said, whipping her shift over her head and tossing the wad of fine linen behind her. The bravado would have been convincing, but for the slight upward tilt of her chin and the way she stared at the bedpost six inches to Lucien's left.

Such courage, such determination. Such *fire*.

Lucien set his pocket handkerchief on the bedside table, then undid his falls slowly, not because he sought to draw out the moment, but because manual dexterity nearly eluded him. Pen was... perfection. Rosy and rounded, sturdy, and spectacularly, robustly feminine.

She watched his hands, then bit her upper lip when he shoved his breeches off and stepped out of them. Before he could pick them up to add to the stack on the chair, Penelope laid a hand on his bare chest.

"The textures of you fascinate me," she said, brushing her palm lightly over his chest hair. "Bristly here, crinkly there, smooth and rough, warm and..." She stepped closer and swiped her tongue over the bump of his collarbone. "A bit salty and redolent of lavender."

"While you," Lucien said, gripping her hand, "provoke me nigh to madness." He kissed her rather than attempt more words, and heaven help him, *she kissed him back*. Passionately, insistently, perhaps even a little vengefully, and Lucien's self-restraint began to unravel.

In his head, he tried distracting himself with this chess gambit and that sequence of moves while Penelope's hands mapped his wildest longings and fondest dreams. Mentally reciting Caesar's Gallic letters proved useless when she decided that the contours of his derriere fascinated her.

When she pushed him back onto the mattress, Lucien fell in a dazed heap.

"Stop thinking," she said, moving around the bed and climbing in on the other side. "Stop trying to cogitate your way through lovemaking. I have given up domestic bustling for the nonce, I'll have you know. You must give up mentally bustling for the next hour too." Penelope straddled him as he lay against the pillows. "*Aros gyda mi.*"

Stay with me. A Walter Scott verse tripped through Lucien's

head, one he'd shied away from for years. Too painful, too apt. *This is my own, my native land...* "I'm here, Pen. I'm here, and I'm with you."

She crouched over him, a lioness preparing to enjoy the fruits of a long and difficult hunt. "And I am with you."

She'd spoken Welsh, and that helped quiet the tumult in Lucien's mind. This was his Pen, and she'd asked only that they make a first attempt at mutual seduction. Typical of her to keep her expectations modest.

Typical and so very *wrong.*

Lucien set aside poetry and strategy and gave himself up to pleasuring Penelope. He learned her every curve and hollow with his hands. He gathered up her sighs with kisses. He teased and tested and tasted, until she was restless and panting beneath him, her braid gone frizzy and her eyes dreamy.

"You could do this all day, couldn't you?" She brushed his hair back from his forehead and tugged on his ear. "Play at being the lover while you drive me mad."

"I have never been more completely in earnest, Pen." Nor had he ever been happier or more thoroughly in the grip of desire.

She cupped the back of his head and drew him down to her. "Stop playing, Lucien, or I will go up in flames of frustration."

The *up in flames* part... "You're sure?"

"Are you?"

How like her, and the question was apt. A pause to unmuddle, to refocus. "Yes. Absolutely certain." Lucien was equally sure he'd dispatch St. Didier to buy a special license before noon tomorrow.

"Fortunate for you, sir," Penelope said, "because I have made up my mind as well." She took him in hand and seated him against her heat.

Lucien resisted the commands of his bellowing animal spirits and resisted even Penelope's demented wiggling. "Hold still."

She complied, and he was torn between closing his eyes, the better to be enveloped in pure sensation, and keeping his eyes open, the better to drink in the sight of Penelope becoming his lover in fact.

He decided to keep his eyes open for as long as he could.

"I like that," Penelope whispered, turning her head on the pillow. "I like..."

Lucien set up a slow, shallow rhythm. He liked using pleasure to steal her words. He liked seeing her gaze go all soft and sweet. He very much liked the hitch in her breathing that told him desire was coursing through her as it ignited every corner of his being.

Penelope muttered something in Welsh, her words too soft for Lucien to make out. He was hanging on by a slender thread of determination when Penelope bowed up and moved against him with the inexorable power of a woman in the throes of intense satisfaction.

When she subsided onto the pillows some moments later, she was flushed and beaming. "*Saint ac angylion bendigedig.*"

Desire beat at Lucien, as did joy. Blessed saints and angels, indeed. "Catch your breath," he said. "That was the appetizer." For her, he'd somehow find the will, the superhuman capability, the... love.

"What of you?" she asked, lacing her fingers with his against the pillow. "You refrained, didn't you?"

"Betrothed is not the same as married."

She moved her hips experimentally, the fiend. "Not a great difference, some would say."

"You tempt me, Pen. Allow me this one scintilla of caution."

Her undulations ceased one instant before Lucien would have had to withdraw. "You were too long wandering in strange lands, Lucien, too far from home. If Wellington should ever cross my path, His Grace and I will have words." She was not in the least teasing or joking.

"Try to have them privately. The duke isn't accustomed to being taken to task."

"And therein lies a problem. Is it safe to move?"

Lucien kissed her nose. "Go gently."

A fine plan, and because Penelope apparently grasped that a slow build of passion could yield an entire blazing sunset of pleasure instead of a mere bonfire, she went gently until she went not gently at all. When she'd ceased thrashing, Lucien held her and waited and waited some more—holding a replete Penelope was a grand delight in itself—then withdrew and spent on her belly.

She watched him—add that to the list of aphrodisiacs quite near the top—and handed him the handkerchief when the last tremor had passed through him.

"I would rather you not leave me," she said when he'd tossed the handkerchief away and cuddled down atop her. "I'm lonely without you."

Lucien buried his nose against her hair. "I am lost without you." Had been lost, for years. Lovemaking with Penelope gave him the courage to admit that to her.

"I'm falling asleep. Will you be here when I waken, Lucien?"

"I will be no farther away than the next pillow, if I make it even that heroic distance."

When Penelope succumbed to slumber, he eased himself off of her and curled up at her side. Something more profound than anticipating vows had happened in this venerable four-poster, not that anticipated vows were a paltry occasion.

Lucien arranged himself around his intended and let his mind drift as it hadn't in ages. Impressions, thoughts, and emotions swirled together in a slow eddy of awareness.

He loved Penelope. That wasn't news. He ought to tell her, though. The verse from *The Lay of the Last Minstrel* meandered back to him, the words clear in his mind:

Breathes there the man, with soul so dead,
    Who never to himself hath said,
    This is my own, my native land!
    Whose heart hath ne'er within him burn'd,
    As home his footsteps he hath turn'd,
    From wandering on a foreign strand!

If such there breathe, go, mark him well...

The wretch, concentred all in self,
    Living, shall forfeit fair renown,
    And, doubly dying, shall go down
    To the vile dust, from whence he sprung,
Unwept, unhonour'd, and unsung.

"You are my own," Lucien said softly. "And I am home."

He dozed off, arms around his betrothed, his spirit as close to peaceful as it ever had been.

"Sir Dashiel, come to call," the butler said, and because Rhian, Marchioness of Lynnfield, knew her butler quite well, she heard the note of disapproval he conveyed in five simple words.

"Show the baronet in." Her ladyship was always home to Sir Dashiel, as the butler well knew. "I will receive him here in my personal parlor." Where nobody eavesdropped, though the chief eavesdroppers were fortunately busy in the sewing room. Theo was off with the steward, assessing the hay crop, and Tommie was absorbed of late with his correspondence.

"Shall I inform Miss Tabitha that her brother is gracing us with a visit?" the butler asked.

Penelope managed the staff, and she did so with a light hand. Sometimes too light. "You shall not. Sir Dashiel might well be making a flying pass on his way into the village, and Tabitha is lately prone to gushing at length." Bless the girl.

"Very good, your ladyship." Kerry bowed low enough that the shining top of his pink head was visible—*when had he grown so old?*—and withdrew.

The marchioness's formal parlor was becoming outdated, but she preferred the exuberant elegance of bygone eras to current fashion's austerity. Everything in the well-appointed London town house was now symmetric, refined, and restrained.

Boring, in other words. Sir Dashiel had grown boring too. Witness, his visit had been all but predictable.

He presented himself with his usual pretense of hurry, taking her hand and bowing smartly over it. "My lady, a pleasure on this lovely afternoon."

"If you say my beauty rivals the sun, I shall smite you." And not with her fan. "Have a seat. The tray will be along in a moment."

In his staid riding attire—sable jacket, buff breeches, plain linen, shiny tall boots—Sir Dashiel was a jarring note amid the cream, azure, and pink hues of the parlor. He'd been a jarring note in her ladyship's life, too, though she'd been lamentably slow to notice his rough edges. Perhaps Penelope could smooth them out before Sir Dashiel charged headlong into real trouble.

"You are gracious, as always. How fares my dear Tabby?"

He played the part of the doting brother convincingly, and perhaps he was a doting brother—the sort who stole his sisters' settlements to feed the hunters he doted upon.

"Tabitha is in alt, of course. A London Season is every girl's dream, and I intend to see that she leaves Town with all the right memories and as many of the right connections as possible."

Conversation paused while the tea tray was wheeled in. Penelope had left standing orders with the kitchen to feed Sir Dashiel, the vicar, and the vicar's wife at every opportunity, and thus the tea cart held sandwiches, tarts, and glazed petits fours.

"A feast!" Sir Dashiel said, just as he said every time the cart appeared. "A veritable feast. No need to hover, my good man. I'm sure her ladyship and I will manage."

The footman, one of several Joneses on staff, stepped back, folded his gloved hands before him, and looked straight ahead.

"That will be all, Jones," the marchioness said. "Thank you."

He bowed to her, nodded to Sir Dashiel, and withdrew, though he wouldn't go far. The marchioness had given a few standing orders of her own where Sir Dashiel was concerned. The baronet closed the door in the footman's wake. Alas for her guest, on such a fine afternoon, her ladyship had opened her parlor windows.

The whole business—Dashiel's mischief and his attempts to be discreet about it, the countermeasures she took to foil him, and the other measures she took to appease him—had grown wearying beyond belief. She was half tempted to dump the problem in Lucien's lap, but then, duels were scandalous, Lucien had no heir, and Penelope would be appalled.

The marchioness was too tired of the entire farce to be appalled. The last indignity would be having to confess her foolishness to Lucien. That humiliation would be worse than appalling.

"So when is the great day?" Sir Dashiel asked, pouring out for himself while leaving his hostess's cup empty. "Monday after next, I believe? I will have the Season's inventory ready to go, though this being the last shipment, I will raise my prices. Those who grumble will find themselves out of luck."

"I cannot dicker like a fishmonger, sir. If you want to raise the price of your brandy, you will inform your usual cohort, and I will see that the proper quantities find their way into the proper hands."

The job of hauling Sir Dashiel's brandy up to Town had started off as a favor. Four years ago, Sir Dashiel had asked her to deliver a few cases of spirits to several trusted friends from his army days. The potation must have been very high quality, because they'd been received with barely contained enthusiasm on every hand.

And yet, that enthusiasm *had* been contained, had been nearly discreet, if not furtive.

Weeks later, her ladyship had caught a snippet of gossip about a Spanish monastery having been raided during the war and nobody knowing what had become of the treasured vintage in its cellars—not that Wellington tolerated pillaging, of course. Soldiers had been hanged for violating that dictate.

The occasional case or bottle showed up at a gentlemen's club or in a peer's personal stores, but nobody knew where or how the brandy had made its way from France.

Her ladyship knew, though she'd never admitted to Dashiel that the rest of the story had fallen into her hands.

"I cannot trust the mails," Sir Dashiel said, biting into a sandwich of beef and brie. "If I need you to convey a change of terms, you will do so in person."

He was growing obnoxiously sure of himself, and that was the marchioness's own fault. "I cannot possibly bargain on your behalf. London is like the world's largest village. Somebody is always watching. I can hardly go around to the back door at White's and have a word with the sommelier, can I? My coach wouldn't fit down the alley, and the sommelier wouldn't be caught dead parleying with a woman on club business."

Sir Dashiel was good-looking, convivial, and possessed of a certain cunning, but he was also hopelessly *rustic*. Penelope might like that about him, but the marchioness found his narrowness of experience tedious.

He paused between sandwiches. "Can you arrange for a few express communications to go up to Town?"

"Why not have Lord Lynnfield frank your letters?" her ladyship asked. "Nobody will tamper with correspondence bearing his hand or seal." She was being naughty, rubbing Sir Dashiel's face in his relatively lowly station, but truly, he was overdue for a set-down.

"As if I want his lordship poking his nose into my affairs. I will send a half-dozen express letters, let's say Friday. With everybody at market, a few riders heading west won't be noticed. I will send my missives here, to your attention, and you can forward them to London for me."

In the normal course, mail was paid for by the recipient. Sir Dashiel would expect the marchioness to pay for these epistles, just as he likely expected Tabitha to come home engaged to a prince.

I have been such a fool. When Penelope married Sir Dashiel, the foolishness would stop. Dashiel's hoard of contraband was apparently exhausted, and Penelope's settlements would keep him in hunters for a good many years.

Unless one of those hunters—please, heaven—took a wrong step and sent Dashiel headlong into a convenient ditch. The marchioness bit into a petit four rather than castigate herself for that unworthy thought.

"Is my darling Penelope spending endless hours sewing in her tower?" Sir Dashiel asked around an apple tart. "The woman really does work too hard, considering the lord of the manor has returned. Let him see to his own pantries and peasants."

"Those peasants are all that stand between you and starvation, sir."

Dashiel smiled over his half-eaten tart. "You sound curiously like Tabby, going on about peas and cucumbers, or was it beans? One forgets. I should pay my addresses to Penelope before I take my leave. She has all but begged me to announce an engagement at the next assembly. I suppose I ought to oblige her."

Penelope was constitutionally incapable of begging, a fine quality in any woman. "She has to marry somebody, you are the only remotely eligible parti, and I sing your praises at every turn, but have a care, Dashiel. Penelope has a contrary streak and independent means. Don't rush your fences."

Then too, Lucien had returned. Sir Dashiel didn't seem to realize that a marquess, one of whom Penelope had always been fond, could be a rival for her affections.

"Rush my fences? I have been dancing attendance on that woman since she set aside her schoolbooks. Rush my fences? Dear Penelope has one foot in spinsterhood as it is, and well she knows it. Besides, she is the only remotely eligible parti in terms of my own marital prospects, and I am too handsome a bachelor to be allowed to maintain my freedom indefinitely."

He was teasing, for the most part. "I still advise caution. Lord Lynnfield is apparently home to stay. That alone means you will have to bargain fairly over Penelope's settlements. His presence also means I'm done delivering your contraband."

The word wiped the smile from Dashiel's blue eyes. "Those who *haul contraband* are more guilty in the eyes of the law than those who purchase it. Your ladyship would do well to recall such details."

And what about those who stole from monasteries? Who brought the contraband into England? How Dashiel had accomplished such feats, she did not know, but he had.

"I do a generous favor for an impecunious ruralizing neighbor. I have no idea of the provenance of the items I'm taking up to Town for him."

"A fine tale, but alas I cannot recall entrusting anything to you, my lady. All those friends of yours on the Continent, the ones you still correspond with, the nephew who roamed France at will during an entire war, might have some idea where you came by such valuable goods."

Hence, Sir Dashiel's great good cheer. He'd convinced himself that if his smuggling came to light, he'd simply blame Lucien. The letters confirming sales would be dispatched from Lynnfield, the wagons bearing the goods would depart from the general vicinity of Lynnfield, and the marchioness would oversee the actual London delivery of the stolen brandy.

"Lucien kept his solicitors apprised of his movements. You will have a hard time proving wrongdoing on the marquess's part, unless a weakness for fine art is now a felony offense."

Sir Dashiel popped the last of the tart into his mouth. "I needn't prove anything. Innuendo, gossip, rumor, a few hints in the right ears. Lynnfield himself is mad, you know. Tainted blood on the dam side. Penelope doubtless feels sorry for him. She's tenderhearted, for all her practicality. I am very fond of her."

Do you always steal from the women you're fond of? "And she is fond of you, I'm sure."

"I certainly hope so. Easier for her that way." He started on a second sandwich, or possibly a third.

"What is that supposed to mean?"

Dashiel looked up, his expression ominously pleased. "Should my intended prove reluctant to speak her vows, I will give her cause to rethink her decision. This house is full of misfits and maiden aunties, all of whom Penelope dotes on. She might come reluctantly to the altar, but for the sake of the Lynnfield lunatics, come she will."

This was a new and different sort of boast from Dashiel. "What are you talking about?"

He tore off a bite of sandwich and considered it. "Justice, my lady. I am discussing justice. If Penelope conducts herself like a biddable and grateful wife, all will be well. If she proves contrary—your word—then I will take appropriate measures to deal with her stubbornness. Fear not, all will be as it should be, and you will be free to find Tabitha a suitably well-heeled, enthralled swain. A longish engagement would suit—I must sort out Penelope's finances before I embark on settlements for Tabby—but a younger son might do nicely if he's truly infatuated."

"Have you even proposed to Penelope?"

"I won't have to. She has all but proposed to me. Where is she, by the by? Wouldn't want my darling to think I'm neglecting her."

"She's off at Finbury for the day. The marquess escorted her." Her ladyship added that last bit out of futile spite. Penelope and Lucien had always been thick as thieves, and they were cousins at some remove. For them to make a joint inspection of Penelope's property was nothing out of the ordinary, more's the pity.

"Finbury will fetch a lovely sum, I'm sure," Dashiel said, finishing his sandwich and dusting his hands over the tray. "Or maybe I'll dower Tabby with it. That could work nicely. Expect letters from me Friday morning, and I'd like them delivered to London by the end of the day. I'll see myself out."

He tossed her a jaunty bow, snatched three sweets from the tray, and took himself off.

The marchioness set the plate of petits fours on the opposite side of the tray and rose. Dashiel was growing worse, and that comment about Lucien's mother... bad form. Very bad form, and cause for regret. The marchioness had let that bit of family history slip late one night over too many hands of cards and far too many glasses of brandy.

She debated again putting the whole matter into Lucien's hands —he did seem more settled—but Dashiel would soon be done with his smuggled goods, apparently, and Penelope was fond of him. Better to let matters run their course, get Tabitha married off, and hope Dashiel was, as usual, far more talk than action.

CHAPTER THIRTEEN

For Penelope, the coach ride back to Lynnfield happened in a very different world from the outbound journey a few hours earlier. In the morning, she'd been anxious, hopeful, uncertain, determined and aflutter. Now she was *happy*.

Simply, completely happy.

She tucked herself against Lucien's side, content to let the miles roll past while she cuddled with her beloved and contemplated a future full of wonderment and pleasure.

"You're quiet," Lucien said, his fingers tracing her jaw. "One worries when you go quiet."

"And yet, you are capable of a silence lasting days. Perhaps you get that from Malcolm." In the past when Lucien had gone all broody, he'd usually been working out some philosophical problem or geometric proof.

"Malcolm is apparently not silent after all," Lucien said, his caresses wandering to her neck and earlobe. "He talks in his sleep. Thomas says it's an open secret."

Coming from Lucien, that was a question. "I suspected. I think he sings too. Very quietly. He loaned me his Welsh psalter, and the book's pages are far from pristine. I've given it back, and he seemed relieved to again have it in his possession. I would love to hear what he has to say, Lucien."

"As would I. Purdy doubtless misses her brother's voice."

"She's helping Tommie with budgets for the gallery." The wagon rounded a curve, throwing Penelope more snugly against Lucien's solid bulk.

"Or Tommie is helping her stay out of trouble. When was the last time she took something?"

"Not for some time. We keep her under guard, as it were. She never goes calling alone if we can help it, and at divine services, we try not to tarry in the churchyard. Purdy is an accomplished pickpocket."

"I'm not half bad at it myself. Needs must."

Another small admission relating to his past. Penelope treasured Lucien's confidences every bit as much as she treasured his kisses. "You'll show me how it's done?"

"If you wish. The skill takes practice and a willingness to violate another's privacy and trust. I found the whole business distasteful."

Despite that distaste, he'd doubtless refined his abilities to a high art. "I'd still like to know how such intimate thievery is accomplished and how to guard myself against it."

"Ah. Of course."

A change of subject was in order, lest Penelope's beloved dwell on gloomy memories. "How do you regard the notion of children?"

She felt the change in him, an increase in alertness, a pause in his caresses. "Whose children? Other people's children tend to be noisy, fidgety, and prone to mischief. Our children will be fascinating little paragons of good conduct and charming curiosity."

Our children. The affection in his tone nearly brought her to tears. "Curiosity and good conduct tend to work against each other." She could see a schoolroom full of little Luciens, all dark-haired, dark-eyed, and full of solemn mischief. Why were children forbidden to take spirits if spirits reliably revived flagging humors? He'd put that question to each of his tutors, and the ones who'd spluttered never lasted long.

"You aren't worried even a little that we'll bungle as parents?" she asked.

"Firstly, my marchioness will be incapable of bungling. Says so in the letters patent if one reads the law Latin very closely. Secondly, we will bungle with only the best of intentions. I am more concerned that we remain extant long enough to see our children both outgrow our errors and appreciate our best intentions and to become the wonderful people we long for them to be."

And now he confided his worries for the future. Lovemaking done right truly did change everything. "We've both enjoyed great good health so far."

"My mother enjoyed great good health, until she didn't."

Penelope waited, but Lucien said no more. Some memory haunted him still. Some snippet of family history bothered him. When he chose to share it, she would honor that confidence too.

"The village approaches," Lucien said, retrieving his arm from around her shoulders. "Why do I wish the journey from Finbury to Lynnfield was a matter of weeks rather than a short hour or two?"

Real regret laced his tone, and that would not do. "Lynnfield is rife with charms, Lucien. Your bedroom is all of fifty paces from my own, for example."

He jostled her gently. "Minx, though what you say is true. Do I have your permission to send for a special license?"

That he would ask her meant worlds. "In case you are inspired to propose? Of course. We owe the rest of the family a wedding, though, Lucien. Banns cried for three successive weeks, Vicar presiding, enormous wedding breakfast, the whole bit."

Lucien gathered her close. "Penelope, please marry me. I will expire of loneliness if you refuse my suit."

A thread of desperation wound through his words. Not quite the proposal she'd had in mind—more of a verbal ambush—but from the heart.

"I will happily marry you, Lucien. Pending that lovely occasion, I expect to see more of you in the altogether, if you please. A lot more."

He took her hand. "You enjoyed yourself with me today?" He didn't bother attempting diffidence. The question was clearly important to him.

"One suspected such pleasures awaited, such closeness. To affix the label 'enjoyment' to lovemaking is too pallid by half, Lucien. Too tame and simple. I *reveled* in the intimacies we shared. They delighted and inspired me. I will never view Finbury as simply a property to be managed again."

"Good. We need a grotto at Lynnfield, by the end of summer at the latest."

"Several grottoes," Penelope replied in all seriousness. "A folly or two and a belvedere wouldn't go amiss either, and one of those graceful Japanese towers by the lake."

"A pagoda?"

"As long as it has a bed in it and the door locks, call it whatever you please."

Lucien turned her head gently by placing his palm on her cheek. "I adore you. I truly, profoundly adore you."

Some kissing followed, which was both ill-advised—kissing inspired desire, and desire in a coach fast approaching home led to frustration—and miraculous. Couples kissed wantonly, because desire frustrated was merely a down payment on a purchase to be redeemed at a later hour. Couples kissed spontaneously because they owned that freedom by right of mutual permission.

And couples kissed because some of the most meaningful thoughts could not be conveyed with words. Penelope had time to vaguely wonder if Lucien would ever tell her he loved her with words, and then the coach swayed around another turn.

The Lynnfield gateposts, blast the luck. Penelope eased away from the kiss and permitted herself a sigh. "Is my hair in order?"

"Of course. You taught me how to braid it, and the lessons took. My cravat?"

"Of course. I tied it."

They reached for each other's hands at the same moment, and that brought Penelope inordinate comfort.

"Nobody can tell, Pen. They cannot tell by looking at you that we've become lovers. Bustle about as you normally do, ask the elders about their day's activities, change for supper. The day at Finbury is ours to treasure privately."

"You can hear my thoughts now?"

"I can hear my own, which mirror yours on occasion. I like that."

Another kiss, this one rendered in words. Penelope pushed aside the curtain to see afternoon shadows lengthening across the park. Lynnfield was such a pretty property, so tidy and peaceful.

"I see a rider heading for the ridge," she said.

"On a skinny bay," Lucien murmured. "Sir Dashiel. And we missed his call. What a pity."

Penelope let the curtain drop. "Probably checking on Tabitha."

"He doesn't care one bent horseshoe how she's faring. He knows she'll be cosseted like visiting royalty. He came to call on you."

Penelope had the gnawing sense Lucien was right. "He does, from time to time, and on the marchioness, too, of course."

"Pen, promise me that when you disabuse the baronet of his matrimonial fantasies, you'll do so where others can see the conversation but not hear it."

This again. "I promise, and I will blame the whole awkward triviality on the marchioness's misguided matchmaking."

"You needn't alliterate, but yes, and then get free of him. Leave him to seethe, pout, regret, and fume in private."

"I'm not disappearing into France in time of war, Lucien." A bit of asperity crept into Penelope's words, but only a bit. She hadn't truly known his whereabouts, but she'd known enough to worry about him.

"Humor me nonetheless." He pressed a soft kiss to her temple. "Be careful."

"Three follies at least," Penelope said, determined to lighten the mood. "And a belvedere and a pagoda."

"As long as I can have my grotto, I will build you all the follies you please."

Penelope let him have the last word, but the enchantment woven at Finbury had begun to unravel, as it inevitably must. One could not float along on rainbows while organizing linen or planning a menu. But one could count the hours and minutes until midnight.

Penelope kissed Lucien's cheek and schooled herself to patience.

One of Dashiel's hunt-mad fellow captains had claimed to be able to tell when a mare had conceived by the look in her eyes. "As if she has a precious secret that puts all of the rest of creation in order for her. She's both at peace and preoccupied with matters known only to her."

Seeing Penelope chatting in the churchyard, he allowed as how Smithers might not have been spouting complete drivel.

The prospect of marriage apparently agreed with Lady Many Pennies. Having made up her mind to meet Dashiel at the altar, she went about her greetings and gossiping with a new air of quiet joy. She was just as poised, just as dignified, but also more relaxed. Her graciousness was a bit warmer, a bit less the lady of the manor mentally counting off the neighbors whom she must be sure to cordially acknowledge.

The marchioness had not attended services, too busy packing perhaps, while Tabitha, looking fetching in a new pink frock, had turned into a chatterbox.

"The fabric is so fine you could draw it through a wedding ring,

Dashiel. Lynnfield has bolts and bolts of it and in the most exquisite colors. Lady Penelope has chosen the best of the lot for me. I am truly and forever in her debt."

"Neighbors are supposed to be generous with one another, poppet. Please don't hang on my arm, you'll wrinkle the line of my jacket."

Tabitha smoothed his sleeve. "Wool isn't that delicate. Why is Dommie de Plessis trying to catch your eye?"

"Because I am the most handsome specimen in the shire, of course." And because the woman was insatiable, given the least encouragement. "I'll see you to the Lynnfield coach."

"You should hear the aunties and Cousin Lark telling tales on each other, Dashiel. They are hilarious, and then Uncle Theo says something naughty, and I laugh until my sides ache."

"Ladies aren't supposed to laugh, poppet." He turned his back on Dommie and led Tabitha through the lych-gate and along the row of coaches parked around the green. "You offer a sweet smile instead of putting your teeth on display."

"How do you know what's fashionable now, Dash? You haven't been up to Town in ages, and one gathers you timed your visits to avoid the social Season."

"Heaven shudders, Tabitha. You're aspiring to be impertinent to your very own brother. I must marry you off to the first drover on his way back to Scotland. I avoid Town during the whirl, true enough, because a handsome, single baronet awash in charm would be expected to make up numbers, do the pretty, and otherwise bankrupt himself for the convenience of the hostesses. You do, however, have three older sisters, and because of them, I am an expert on acceptable behavior."

The monstrous Lynnfield coach was next in line. The vehicle was large enough to tote the entire lot of misfits in their Sunday finery, though it was far from *au courant* in its appointments. Perhaps the marquess was as indifferent to fashion as he was lacking in social graces. The coach was pulled by four matching bays, the most boring sort of team possible. Stagecoaches were pulled by bays, for pity's sake.

"You'll come over to Lynnfield to see me off?" Tabitha asked as a footman opened the coach door and lowered the steps.

"I will see you at the assembly before you leave, and yes, I will wave my handkerchief at you when you depart. Truly, child, you are only going up to Town. You are not marching away to war."

She hugged him, the wayward brat. "Don't say that, Dash, even in jest. You did go off to the wars, and I nearly expired of worry. I am so glad you decided to come home."

In truth, the decision to sell up had been made for him, but the whole episode had turned out remarkably well. A little ingenuity, a little luck, a little derring-do, and the day had been thoroughly won.

"You were glad to see me out of uniform, the French were very glad, and I was rather pleased myself, though one doesn't say such a thing too loudly. Behave yourself at Lynnfield. Stay away from that imbecile Malcolm fellow, and I'd avoid Tommie, too, while you're about it."

"I like Tommie."

"Dearest," Dashiel said gently, "he has *no prospects*. Like him all you please, but don't allow him to nurture futile longings where you are concerned. I forbid it, and to do so would be unkind."

Tabitha climbed into the coach. "If you say so, Dash. Enjoy your walk with Lady Penelope." She pulled the door closed, and Dashiel entertained the notion that his youngest sibling had just dismissed him. Little Tabby was growing up, and while that notion jarred, it also brought with it an element of relief.

She'd soon no longer be his problem to feed, clothe, humor, and house. Perhaps a few weeks in London would impress upon Tabby just how lacking life as the wife of an idle popinjay would be, but even if she did marry one of the Tommies of the world, she'd cease to be Dashiel's responsibility.

He lingered at the lych-gate rather than venture back into the churchyard. Dommie de Plessis had come by the Roost not two days past, ostensibly to query Dashiel on his progress locating her missing watch. Dashiel had made no progress and hadn't intended to make any, but he had consulted Dommie on the bed hangings to be ordered for refurbishment of the best guest room.

The woman had stamina, give her that, but another such encounter would be unkind, to use his own logic.

"There you are," Penelope said, emerging from the churchyard. "I vow pleasant weather makes us loquacious. We chatter on for an excuse to bide in the sunshine despite lacking any topic of real interest. Let's take a turn on the green, shall we?"

She wanted to show him off. Understandable, but Dashiel had no intention of plighting his troth outside the smithy. The path back to Lynnfield was shady and private for most of the way, and a newly engaged fellow was entitled to a few liberties.

Not that Dashiel would anticipate the vows entirely. Penelope would have to wait until the wedding night to see those mysteries revealed.

"One turn only," Dashiel said. "We'll let the coaches get on their way rather than have half the village watch our departure. How did you find Finbury?"

She pulled on gloves, her movements brisk. "In good order. The tenants are conscientious, the staff exceedingly competent. Planting has progressed right on schedule, and all will soon be in readiness for haying."

"How quaint." He patted the hand she'd rested on his arm. "My lady has gone for a farmer." They crossed the street as the first of the coaches rattled off along the green. "Is Tabitha being unbearable?"

"Far from it. She is sweet, funny, charming, and all that is delightful. The marchioness has high hopes for Tabitha's London outing."

They strolled along, Penelope holding forth about sprigged muslins and embroidered slippers, bless her, while the churchyard emptied and coaches, dog carts, and wagons gradually departed for their various destinations.

All the while, Penny was clearly trying to circle around to the topic of the day, and Dashiel gently thwarted her. The conversational game was diverting, but he wasn't about to go down on bended knee with the whole village watching.

"Let's make our way to Lynnfield, shall we?" he said as they neared the bridle path that led away from the village. "And I would not be averse to Sunday supper with the neighbors again, provided you seat me next to you."

Penelope dropped his arm and hopped over a stile. "We're a bit at sixes and sevens at Lynnfield, what with her ladyship going up to Town, Lucien taking up the reins, and Tabitha's wardrobe requiring an all-hands effort. Part of Finbury's appeal was the sheer peace and quiet to be had there."

"What would you think of dowering Tabitha with Finbury? I realize she'll have to find a fellow worthy of such a gem, but if it's her dower property, then her husband won't really have much to do with it unless one of his daughters ends up there."

Penelope had gone striding along the shaded path two paces ahead of him. The view she presented was enticing, and watching her steps slow as the import of Dashiel's words reached her was a pleasure as well.

"A *dower* property for *Tabitha?*"

"You heard me, darling Penny. You've been beating about the bush for the past quarter hour, and while I understand that proposing isn't usually the lady's office, I thought I'd make the job a bit easier for you. I am more than willing to marry you—we have time for a few sons, at least—and as your husband, the disposition of Finbury will rest with me."

She said something that might have been in Welsh, then closed the distance between them. "No, it won't."

She was flustered, the poor dear. "Beg pardon?"

"Finbury is held in trust. I cannot dispose of it. You cannot dispose of it. I gain ownership in fee simple absolute when certain conditions are met, and marrying you doesn't qualify."

That was a blow, quite honestly, but Penelope's real property wasn't her greatest asset by any means.

"My consent to your proposal stands nonetheless, my dear. Finbury is creating income as a rental property, and the income will certainly come under my purview." He smiled at her because she might not grasp the legalities beyond the held-in-trust part.

"The income goes into the trust, but, Dashiel, this whole discussion is moot. I was concerned that the marchioness might have led you to believe my regard for you was..."

She stared past him at the double rows of oaks forming the bridle path.

"My regard for you, Penny, is that of a prospective groom for his bride. You've asked for this private discussion, and a couple are permitted privacy like this for one purpose and one purpose only. I've said I'll marry you, and there's an end to it." Firm speech was often necessary when establishing expectations with a woman or a subordinate.

"Dash, I will not marry you. I have not asked you to marry me. I sought relative privacy—on a path the whole village uses—precisely because I hoped to clear up any misunderstandings you might be cherishing."

Good heavens, what was she going on about? "Penelope, if this is some sort of game or ploy... oh, very well." Dashiel stopped walking and grasped his lapels with both hands. "Penelope, I am asking you to become my wife, the mother of my children, my helpmeet at the Roost. Please say you'll marry me." He'd doubtless come across more peevish than smitten, but the dratted woman had picked the wrong time to turn up coy.

She marched off up the path. "I'm sorry, Dash. You are making this harder than it has to be. I have never led you to believe that your addresses would be welcome, and you never sought my permission to embark on a courtship. That's how it's done. You ask, I grant permission or deny it."

He stomped after her, resentment growing with each step. "You invited me to kiss you."

"I tolerated your forwardness in the name of neighborly affection. I *never* invited your advances."

He caught up to her and barely resisted hauling her about to face him. "I don't go around kissing any young lady I meet!"

"I should hope not. The young ladies would take exception, just as I take exception to a courtship by implication. I blame the marchioness. She has led you to believe my feelings are more than neighborly, and that is her fault, not yours."

The marchioness, blast her, had been charged with abetting a courtship. "What possible objection could you have to a match between us? Nobody else in these surrounds will have you, despite your wealth. You're too high in the instep, too long in the tooth, and no great beauty."

She stopped again, but did not turn. "You need not accompany me the rest of the way, Dash. You are upset, and we must put this whole exchange from our minds. We will be cordial neighbors, and nothing more need be said on the matter."

"Nice try." He seized her by the wrist. "You seem to think you have a choice in the matter, Penny. Set that notion aside, once and for all. I say this with every respect for your future happiness. I have given you time. I have humored your pride. I have tolerated your continued presence among the Lynnfield eccentrics, but no more. We shall be wed, and you will accommodate yourself to a future as my wife. I will do my utmost to make you happy, provided you do likewise where I am concerned."

More Welsh, while Penny twisted free of his grip somehow. "Dash, you cannot force me to marry you."

"The hell I can't." He grabbed her by the arms, a primitive sort of glee welling along with anger and lust, and—

And then somebody hauled him back by the shoulders. The next thing Dashiel knew, his knees gave way, and he was falling onto the dirt path.

"Not done," Lucien, Marquess of Lynnfield, said, "to manhandle a lady when she's making her grand exit." He extended a hand down to Dashiel, which Dashiel disdained to take.

"What the hell?" Dashiel said, scrambling to his feet. "What the blazing, blighted *hell* are you doing here?"

"I was trying to enjoy a homeward ramble on a pretty spring day, and some fool started blathering about being entitled to Lady Penelope's hand. My grasp of English law is rusty, but I'm certain that isn't how the institution of matrimony works. Perhaps you'd best run along, Sir Dashiel?"

"You are the fool," Dashiel said slowly. "A prattling, interfering idiot. What passes between Lady Penelope and me is none of your concern, and if there's any running along to be done, you shall do it, my lord."

Lynnfield blinked at him slowly. "I believe the lady has the right of it. The marchioness has played a little joke on you. Not well done of her. A fellow has his dignity, after all, and you are a good-looking devil, but the fact remains that Lady Penelope isn't interested, at least not at the moment. I'll have a word with my aunt. Perhaps she'll bide in London for longer than a few weeks. Would that suit?"

Through a haze of rage and incredulity, Dashiel seized on two salient points. First, the marchioness had clearly made a fool of him. Petty revenge for her imagined slights, no doubt. Second, the marquess, like the proverbial blind hog, had grasped that Dashiel's dignity was imperiled.

"I care not where the marchioness bides, but she has been no sort of neighbor to me and a poor excuse for a chaperone to Lady Penelope. Do as you like with your aunt, my lord. Lady Penelope, I tender my most profound apologies for this whole situation and will wish you good day *for the nonce.*"

Penelope offered him the barest nod, but he'd done what the situation required, and she owed him that much. Dashiel bowed to her and took himself back in the direction of the village green. He was a mere ten yards closer to that destination before the next phase of his plan became clear in his mind.

Let Penelope make what she would of the day's events, but they were merely an opening skirmish fought to a draw, and Dashiel still very much intended to win the war. As for that prattling lackwit Lynnfield, by the time Lady Penelope had been made to see reason, the marquess might well find it expedient to spend another ten years racketing about on the Continent.

CHAPTER FOURTEEN

"That did not go as planned," Pen said, rubbing her arms. "Not at all as planned, and you knew Dashiel would turn nasty."

Lucien walked beside her, his imagination still caught up in how much worse the encounter could have gone.

"Dashiel broke rules when he was in uniform, Pen. Sensible rules rather than the other kind, and he begrudges even his horse proper rations in spring, when the grass is lush and abundant. It doesn't take close observation to see that he's long overdue for a sound trashing, but nobody has been on hand to put the manners on him." A vast, wide, and deep understatement.

Pen slowed as they reached the part of the path that overlooked the lake. "He frightened me. I've always known him to be cordial, a tad priggish, not as handsome or clever as he thinks he is, but harmless. He's not harmless."

Neither am I. "To realize you've underestimated an opponent is unnerving, but Dashiel underestimated you, too, and—God willing—me as well. He'll probably exert himself to be charming and redouble his attempts to try to entice you into marriage."

"Not if you and I announce our engagement at the assembly."

Perhaps not, but Lucien hadn't wanted to make that suggestion. An engagement announcement should be an occasion of joy, not a *tactic*. Besides, they'd been engaged for years.

Pen stopped at a bench positioned to take advantage of the view. The water was an expanse of sparkling blue, the trees still held a hint of the gauzy, luminous green of new foliage, and a white swan made a stately progress parallel to the shore.

No place on earth held more beauty than Lynnfield in spring, but Lucien saw only the look on Dashiel's face when he'd laid hands on Penelope. Avaricious and determined.

Very, very determined. "I want to end his puling, arrogant existence," Lucien said. "Not very civilized of me."

Penelope took his hand and led him to the bench. "So do I, and Dash is likely just as angry, but who were you when you intervened? You were playing some part, the bumbler, the jester. I haven't seen you take quite that attitude before."

"I was the harmless, half-witted aristo. When I was bargaining over art treasures, a touch of the simpleton usually resulted in a better price. I was also safer if I could be convincingly stupid."

"Now there's a fine irony. Sit with me. I need to settle my nerves."

Lucien's nerves would be settled when Dashiel Ingraham was gelded. "You would have kicked him in another moment, Pen. I doubt you were in any real danger." Ingraham had been in danger, did he but know it. Still was.

"I'm in long skirts, Lucien. Kicking isn't nearly so effective through two petticoats, a skirt, and an underskirt."

How had she learned that lesson? "I truly want to kill him, Pen. Use your knee if a kick won't serve."

"My knee. Right. Good thought."

She sat next to Lucien, her breathing calm, her gloved hand in his, and gradually, the peace of the day caught up with Lucien's battle rage. Ingraham had behaved predictably, and he'd been thwarted by the simplest of schoolyard measures.

Pen was safe. A scintilla of ire drained away on that realization. "We must have a pointed discussion with the marchioness."

"She truly sings Dashiel's praises without ceasing, Lucien. She has persistently advocated for a match with him, no matter how unenthusiastic I've been in response. She probably did mislead him to some extent."

A question emerged from the muddle of upset and relief swirling in Lucien's mind. "Why?"

Penelope slanted a frown at him. "What do you mean, why?"

"Why would an aging, notably self-centered woman willingly part with the person who most reliably keeps that woman's life pleasant? You supervise the staff, you dote on the elders, you fetch and carry for her ladyship. She might manage well enough without you, but her life is in every way easier with you on hand. Why give you up to a mere baronet?"

Penelope wrinkled her nose. "Perhaps the marchioness sees my spinsterhood as a failure of her matchmaking abilities?"

"If you are a spinster, Pen, I'm the dowager queen. The marchioness sings Sir Dashiel's praises for a reason. I confronted her previously on her partiality to the baronet, and I went as far as to suggest he'd bullied her into taking on his cause. Her ladyship swanned off in high dudgeon on that occasion, but I watched her when Dashiel came for Sunday supper. She truly does not care for him."

"How can you tell?"

Valid question, and Lucien took a moment to come up with an answer. "Do you recall our great cribbage tournament?"

The reference earned him a ghost of a smile. "A whole summer of pitched battle. Thank heavens we decided to switch to memorization."

"I realized about thirty games in that when your cards were poor, you breathed differently. Not a huff, not a sigh, just different. When your cards were excellent, you went still before you rearranged them. The marchioness has a habit of looking down and inhaling when she's marshaling her patience, as if she's fortifying herself to be gracious. Every time she had to concoct a reply to Dashiel, she went through the same little ritual."

"She'd lose a packet to you at whist," Pen said, tucking an errant curl back into her chignon. "Maybe she's lost a packet to Sir Dashiel?"

Interesting theory. "Does she gamble excessively?"

"You watch her breathing but not her pin money?"

"The pin money is hers. I cover her major expenses, and we don't question each other beyond that. What sort of hold could Dashiel have on her?"

The swan reached the shore, where it became a more ungainly creature, flapping and waddling instead of gliding.

"Dashiel has made himself privy to some sort of scandal involving her ladyship, would be my guess," Pen said. "The marchioness treasures her friendships, and when she's in Town, she rubs elbows with duchesses and archdukes. She isn't unduly snobbish. Those are simply the people who knew her in her youth, the ones who recall better days, before the king went mad and France fell to pieces. Anything that lowered her in the estimation of the old guard would cut deeply."

What could that *anything* be? The marchioness, having failed to produce a viable heir, would not have shared her favors outside her marriage. A love child was unlikely. A scandalous liaison at this phase of her life was nearly her right if she chose to indulge.

"We'd best talk to her," Lucien said, rising. "If nothing else, we owe her a warning. When Dashiel does finally grasp that his suit is doomed, he might take his disappointment out on her."

Lucien offered Pen his hand, and she took it, then tucked her fingers around his arm. "The marchioness holds Tabitha's future in her hands. Why would Dashiel jeopardize his sister's happiness and security over a courtship with me that happened mostly in his mind?"

"You put your finger on the crux of the matter. Knowing that Tabitha's marital future is in the marchioness's hands, knowing that I will be compelled by honor to protect the aunt who opened her home to me when I was an orphaned boy, knowing that I will for damned sure brook no nonsense when it comes to your happiness, Dashiel might still try to charm or compel you to the altar. For him to press his suit under those conditions, he must be very certain of his cards."

Penelope laid her head on Lucien's shoulder. "Such a pretty day and such an ugly muddle. The marchioness has been Dashiel's staunch supporter for at least the past three years, though she was equally vociferous on behalf of some of the bachelors I met in Mayfair. Whatever influence Dashiel has over her, he laid his traps carefully and at least several years ago."

Penelope was thinking critically, assessing facts, and applying logic. Lucien forced himself to attend to the same exercise.

"You will solve nothing by marrying him, Pen." Lucien made the point as calmly as he could. "Dashiel would use your wealth and standing to lay other traps. I would not be at all surprised to learn he's taking bribes in his capacity as magistrate."

"Another reason not to report alleged crimes. I am sorry you have come home to such a mess, Lucien."

"I came home to you, Pen, and about that, I am not sorry at all."

She favored him with a smile, and Lucien walked the rest of the way to Lynnfield in a silence both thoughtful and worried. The objective was to keep Penelope and the Lynnfield household safe from Sir Dashiel's presumptions, but the best path to that goal had grown considerably more difficult to discern.

"You turned him down?" The marchioness enthroned herself in her favorite wing chair, her skirts swishing about her slippers. "Sir Dashiel is a baronet, Penny, not some bumbling squire or knight. In case you failed to notice, we haven't many earls or dukes running about Lynnfield."

We have a marquess. Penelope glanced at Lucien, whose expression was nearly bored.

"My lady seems to forget," Penelope said pleasantly, "that I disdained the attentions of a ducal heir and at least two earls when I went up to London. Sir Dashiel had no right to assume that I'd favor his suit, but you led him to believe otherwise. Why?"

They occupied the marchioness's old-fashioned private parlor. Penelope took the second wing chair, not as close to the windows. Fatigue dragged at her—fatigue and worry—though the hour was barely past midday.

Lucien prowled the room, peering at this botanical sketch or that framed arrangement of dried, pressed roses.

No sketches of children here. Her ladyship kept several of those on the mantel in her bedroom, and how painful it must be for her to see them each night and morning.

"Why would you refuse Sir Dashiel?" the marchioness asked. "He is the closest thing to an eligible to be had in this shire, and you are determined to dwell in the country. I had no doubt you intended to bide where you could both set up your own nursery and keep a close eye on the household here at Lynnfield."

This was pure evasion. "I can dwell in the country at Finbury, if rustication is the pinnacle of my ambitions, and the household here will run well enough without me."

"You're too young to dwell alone and too old to be this stubborn, Penelope. You gave Dashiel reason to hope, and that has nothing to do with me." The marchioness was prone to peevishness, but this display approached venomous.

"If he treasured hopes of the matrimonial variety, then he should have asked my leave to embark on a courtship. He never did that."

"Because he asked *my* permission to court you as soon as he returned from Spain."

Lucien propped himself against the mantel, all lazy grace and ennui. "You didn't think to alert Penelope to that development? She was of age by then and in control of much of her wealth."

"Young women take odd notions. If Penelope believed that Dashiel had sought my permission before approaching her, she would have held that against him. Even the highest sticklers admit that a fellow ought to test the waters with the young lady before approaching those in authority over her."

"You are not now, nor were you ever, in authority over me," Penelope said slowly. "You were my chaperone in name only."

"And as such," her ladyship spat, "I was in authority over you as far as Sir Dashiel was concerned. I vow you've become clodpated, Penelope."

"That will suffice." Lucien stalked away from the mantel. "You were well aware that Penelope was betrothed to me and that the documents were binding unless repudiated. You never thought to mention that to Dashiel?"

Penelope hadn't forgotten about the betrothal, exactly, but she hadn't thought to pose that question.

"Neither of you was of age when that arrangement was concocted, and then you were gone for years, Lucien. How was I to know that you hadn't set aside the agreement immediately upon reaching your majority? If you two are done haranguing me, I will avail myself of a nap before supper. Tabitha's chattering is enough to give anybody a megrim, and she will doubtless be in good form after showing off her new frock in the churchyard."

Her ladyship rose and strode off for the door.

"Before you go," Lucien said, "be aware that if Dashiel has threatened you, if he is holding notes of hand over your head, or has otherwise brought untoward influence to bear on you, I am fully prepared to deal with him on your behalf. You are the closest thing I have left to a mother, and I will not see you ill-used for the convenience of a petty rogue."

Whatever broadside he could have fired, the marchioness had clearly not expected that, nor had Penelope seen it coming.

"And that sort of lordly interference is exactly what I must not allow." Tears welled in the marchioness's eyes. "You always were a peculiar boy. Penelope, please make my excuses at supper. I vow I cannot wait to leave this house for London."

She swished through the doorway, a lace-edged handkerchief clutched in her hand. Lucien closed the door in her wake and took the chair she'd vacated.

"If you say that did not go as planned," he muttered, "I will agree with you. She has always been something of an enigma to me and still is."

"She doesn't move one square at a time in predictable directions, does she?" Penelope murmured. "She is by far the ranking lady in the shire, and she is scurrying off to London as if she's..."

"Afraid," Lucien said. "Angry and afraid."

Penelope considered that description. "More afraid than angry, but you are right. She is out of charity with us and possibly with Sir Dashiel. She did not appreciate that reminder of our betrothal." Penelope took a piece of horehound candy from a silver dish on the low table. "I used to view those agreements as the last insult. I thought you were so indifferent to me that you'd not even bestir yourself to acknowledge what our expectations had once been."

Lucien crossed his legs at the knee. "Now?"

"The betrothal protects me," Penelope said. "Dashiel is the rubbishing magistrate. He cannot ignore a legally valid agreement, and isn't he open to some sort of lawsuit if he entices me away from you?"

Lucien's brows rose, and then he beamed at her. "My darling intended, I believe you have hit upon an argument even Sir Dashiel cannot attempt to gainsay. I suspect he knew nothing of that old bargain, and it does indeed protect you, albeit indirectly."

Indirectly was better than not at all. "How?"

"If you marry another while betrothed to me, the tort of breach of promise arises. I can sue you for the loss of your settlements, essentially, and the loss of you as my chattel."

"Delightful. I'm a prize heifer before the edifice of the law. This would cause a great scandal, I take it?"

"Great expense, certainly, and redound to my great discredit, because a gentleman is supposed to be discreet about these things. Leave the lists quietly, wishing the lady well."

Lucien's mood had brightened, probably because he'd seized upon a potential solution to a vexing puzzle. Penelope's mood was not improving.

"What scheme are you hatching, my lord?"

"I used to hate it when you 'my lorded' me. You 'my lorded' me when we enjoyed the grotto at Finbury, though, and thus I now place the honorific in the endearment category when it comes from you."

"Lucien, cease trying to distract me with a mention of grottoes. You are considering some deviousness that directly affects me. Out with it."

He turned the candy dish ninety degrees. "I will pay a call on Sir Dashiel and politely inform him that you and I are betrothed. He might know or suspect, but we cannot confirm that. I am inclined to think he's been kept in ignorance, which is interesting in itself. I will delicately sketch out the fuss to be made if you refuse to honor the agreement."

"Dash did ask me if you and I were betrothed, though he couched the query in roundaboutation. I was too annoyed to give him a direct answer at the time. The betrothal is still valid, isn't it?"

"You can repudiate the whole business now that you are of age. So can I. You haven't, though, and Sir Dashiel has loudly proposed to you before a witness. I can work with that. He has attempted to poach, Pen, and regards me as a titled eccentric unlikely to acquit myself well on the field of honor. For me to bring suit would not be out of character."

"Yes, it would. You are among the most private of men, and a lawsuit brought against a former intended... I do not like this scheme at all, Lucien. Dashiel is a neighbor, and I agree with the marchioness that stirring up trouble with him is ill-advised. Can't we simply let him lick his wounds in peace?"

Lucien sat forward and took her hand in both of his. "Your

instinct is to overlook his disrespect of your person, to be tolerant and forbearing yet again. I treasure your fundamental kindness and decency, Pen, but that man is neither kind nor decent. I saw his face when he seized hold of you. His intentions were vile, and he must be firmly dealt with. I will be discreet, and he will grasp the advantages of keeping his mouth shut."

Such confidence in Sir Dashiel's common sense was surely misplaced. "I don't want to let you out of my sight, Lucien. If Dashiel challenges you, you could find yourself fleeing to the Continent, and I will not tolerate being left behind again. That, I vow."

Lucien patted her knuckles. "I have left you behind for the last time, and let us not forget, as far as I knew, you were all but sending me away." He kissed her cheek, a mere buss. "Trust me, Pen. I will have a private chat with the baronet, and he will rethink his matrimonial ambitions."

Unease that had followed Penelope from the churchyard became outright biliousness. "I trusted you before, Lucien. To turn your horse around and come back for me, to write, to send for me, to show up in every London ballroom where I was forced to dance with some leering viscount or ham-handed heir to an earldom. My trust has been tried, though I realize you were not to blame."

He released her hand and sat back. "Correct. Your trust was tried by circumstances, Pen, not by me. I am planning to jaunt over to the Roost and have a quiet word with Sir Dashiel. I am not taking ship for Calais."

Promise? Penelope refrained from begging for that assurance on the strength of dignity alone. "Did you ever find the letter you left for me?"

"I haven't looked for it. After all these years, why?"

His favorite question. "Whoever took it has much to answer for."

"Somebody might well have considered such an epistle incriminating. The text was clearly in code, and we were at war with France. The coast is less than five-and-twenty miles away, and London closer than that."

A plausible explanation, but hardly satisfying. "There you go, being logical again. Not your best feature when reassuring a lady, my lord."

Lucien fiddled with his cuff. "What is my best feature when attempting to offer a lady reassurances of my devotion?"

Oh, he had many. His honor, his patience, his kindness, his intelligence, his *touch*...

"Come to my room tonight, and I'll be happy to show you." Penelope rose and quit the room and heard soft laughter in her wake, but she was far from happy with the discussion. The purpose of the conversation had been to get answers from the marchioness—no luck there—and now Lucien was intent on intimidating Sir Dashiel into retreating meekly from the marital lists.

Lucien had a sort of innocence, expecting people to deal as comfortably with sweet reason as he did, when, in fact, few mortals were as fond of logic as he was. As for Sir Dashiel, meekness was beyond him. Of that, Penelope was certain.

She was prevented from brooding on the matter further by Aunt Purdy, who accosted her three steps shy of the warming pantry.

"Oh, my dear Penny, you must spare me a moment. I'm afraid I've been a bit foolish." Aunt Purdy, whose yellow bandeau was no sort of complement to gray curls, pulled Penelope across the corridor to the music room. "Just a bit foolish, but foolish nonetheless, and I have been so good lately too. I'm very disappointed in myself."

For the merest instant, Penelope understood why the marchioness, why Lucien, why *anybody* would be relieved to quit Lynnfield.

"What did you take this time?" she said when the music room door was closed. "And from whom did you take it?"

～

Lucien decided to give Dashiel all of Monday to lick his wounds. Then too, Lucien had needed the day to think, to take stock, and to consider.

Penelope's lovemaking following Sunday's developments had been nearly desperate, pushing Lucien to the very edge of his self-control. The passion was amazing, but the worry driving it had created an edge he hadn't cared for. Penelope apparently did not trust him to thwart the presuming baronet, and Penelope's instincts were formidable.

Lucien also spent Monday night with his beloved, who'd expected him to blow retreat because her courses had arrived. Instead, he climbed into bed with her, and they'd cuddled and talked, about the elders—who had delivered such a drubbing to Uncle Malcolm? About Tommie, who appeared head over heels for Tabitha, and about anything and everything except Dashiel Ingraham's violent advances.

Tuesday dawned bright and mild. Lucien slipped from Penelope's bed and silently commanded her to sleep as late as she pleased to. He spent the morning with Uncle Theo, who'd come up with a plan to rearrange the home farm's sluice gates, the better to irrigate the kitchen garden.

The early afternoon was spent with Tommie, who was full of ideas for the gallery and even more enthusiastic about places Miss Tabitha might like to see during her London visit. Lucien sent Tommie on his way and wondered what Sir Dashiel would think of Tabitha marrying a mere mister.

When Lynnfield business had been attended to, Lucien had Lorenzo saddled and took a wandering path to the Roost.

"My lord." The butler, who'd been venerable in Lucien's youth, bowed slowly. "An honor, my lord. A noteworthy honor to see you on our doorstep. If you'd like to wait in the formal parlor, I will inform the baronet that he has a caller."

No seeing if the baronet was in, which would have been the routine fiction expected of a London servant.

"My thanks, Jenkins, but if Sir Dashiel is in the midst of some-thing, I'm not in a hurry."

Mention of the man's name occasioned some blinking. "Very good, my lord. The formal parlor is this way." The butler's progress was stately in the extreme. Lucien took the opportunity to study the Roost's appointments. The place was tidy, but the wallpaper hadn't been changed since Lucien's boyhood and was thus faded from its once lustrous forest green to a sort of new-pea color. The landscapes and still lifes along the corridor hadn't been cleaned in some time, and the runner, while clean, was worn down the middle.

On the one hand, the Roost might simply be showing signs of Sir Dashiel's protracted bachelorhood. On the other, a paucity of coin also explained the details Lucien noted.

"Here we are, my lord." The butler opened the door to a sunny, pleasant parlor done up in much the same style as the marchioness's private retreat. Pastel blue and pink with white trim, dried hydrangeas on the mantel, lace curtains filtering the afternoon sun.

Though here, too, the carpet showed some wear, the dried hydrangeas were a bit bedraggled, and the curtain lace sported a few snags.

"Shall I bring a tray, my lord?" Jenkins asked.

"No need for that. This is a mere neighborly chat. I won't be staying long."

"I see." Jenkins creaked toward the door, then paused. "Might I presume to inquire, my lord, how Miss Tabitha is faring. We do miss her."

"She misses you, too, and daily threatens to trot over here and see that you're all managing. She is a delightful guest, we are spoiling her rotten, and London will soon be reeling with delight at her charm. We'll take very good care of her, Jenkins. I promise."

Now the old fellow was sniffing and blinking. "One is relieved to hear it, my lord. Wonderfully relieved. I shall inform the house-keeper, who has missed the girl terribly." He paused, a veined hand on the door latch. "Might I also presume so far as to offer felicitations on your lordship's safe return to Lynnfield? I am doubtless trespassing beyond all bounds of a butler's station, though my excesses might be excused considering the length and nature of your lordship's absence, when I say we are glad to have you home, sir."

He tottered off before Lucien could frame a reply. Like most butlers, Jenkins apparently knew a great more than he let on, and he clearly cared about Tabitha.

Lucien was admiring the view out the slightly dusty windows—a tidy formal garden complete with sundial, stone benches, and birdbath—when Sir Dashiel sailed through the door.

"My lord, good day. A pleasure and a surprise to see you at the Roost. I've informed the kitchen that the equivalent of two fatted calves are to appear instantly on the tea tray, or at least some sandwiches. I'm famished, so your call is timely. Do have a seat."

They were to take the hale and hearty route. Let bygone be bygones. No need to belabor any minor unpleasant moments. Very well. Lucien chose a corner of the blue tufted sofa.

"A busy time of year," Lucien said as his host took the only wing chair. "If I'd used more common sense, I would have come back to Lynnfield at the conclusion of harvest."

"But what need has a marquess for common sense, eh?" Sir Dashiel replied, smiling. "I'm surprised you aren't accompanying the ladies up to London, my lord. Your escort would lend Tabitha's arrival quite a bit of cachet."

Was that flattery or a hint that Lucien's presence in the neighborhood was *de trop*? "London is always worth a look, but as it happens, Thomas has volunteered to see the ladies to Town. I will be reacquainting myself with Lynnfield's practical workings, and with my betrothed."

Sir Dashiel looked honestly pleased. "And who, precisely, has the honor of your affections, my lord?"

"My affections?" Lucien arranged his features to reflect puzzlement. "I'm fond of the whole lot at Lynnfield. Sweet souls, for the most part, though Cousin Lark tends to sermonize. When I refer to my betrothed, I mean Lady Penelope. She and I were matched years ago by the old marquess. He had our engagement reduced to settlement agreements and contracts and whatnot. Penelope is an heiress," he added, completely unnecessarily. "They aren't often permitted much sentimentality when it comes to marriage. You understand all about that, I'm sure."

Sir Dashiel's posture, chin propped on his hand, elbow braced on the arm of his chair, shifted. He sat up straight and began tapping a middle finger against the armrest.

"You and Penny are still betrothed?"

She's Lady Penelope to you, sir. "Have been for ages, I'm afraid. I thought you should know before there's more awkwardness. She probably forgot—we were quite underage when this arrangement was settled—but I've reminded her." Lucien added a bashful smile for good measure, while Sir Dashiel stared daggers at Lucien's cravat pin.

"Women don't forget things like that. I'd heard a few old rumors, but assumed they amounted to nothing. Penny went up to Town, and why do that if the young lady already has a match with a marquess?"

"To the world, I am Lord Lynnfield, but to Lady Penelope, I'm just Lucien. That fellow who bested her on horseback from time and time and who was always bringing up politics at supper. We'll rub along tolerably well, I'm sure, but I thought somebody should put you on to the facts. Decent thing to do and all."

Sir Dashiel swung his gaze to meet Lucien's apologetic eye. "I appreciate that your lordship is attempting to deal from honesty—so few people do these days—but you really need not have bothered. Penelope will be repudiating the betrothal agreement, as is her right."

"She will? Can she do that? Are you sure, Sir Dashiel?" The baronet apparently was sure, appallingly so, given the difference in their stations and the binding nature of legal agreements.

"Lynnfield, I'm the ruddy magistrate, for my sins. Trust me when I tell you that contracts executed when the parties are underage can be repudiated upon their majorities."

"I see. What if Penelope doesn't want to repudiate—was that the word?—this contract? She wasn't exactly encouraging your advances on Sunday, was she?"

Sir Dashiel offered Lucien a dazzling smile. "I bungled that. I concluded that Penelope wasn't much of one for protocol, that we had an understanding. In the way of such things, the details could be assumed, or so I believed. I'll put it right, and she will see the benefit of a union with me."

Sir Dashiel was much too confident of his appeal, considering he was at best solvent, he'd been turned down by the lady in no uncertain terms, and he was blithely dismissing the appeal of a wealthy, if somewhat dimwitted, marquess.

What in blazes is he up to? "I wonder where your sandwiches are," Lucien mused. "I grow light-headed when I'm peckish. Been known to fall off my horse if I go too long without food."

"Have you really? How unfortunate for you."

"Wasn't any too lucky for my hat either, and it was a new hat."

Sir Dashiel looked as if he was barely containing his laughter, which was precisely the effect Lucien was striving for. "One hears you enjoy the occasional game of chess, my lord."

"I do. I very much do. Do you play?" Lucien allowed the question to brim with eagerness.

"The occasional informal game only. I really do think you'd best accompany the ladies to London, my lord. Lady Penelope might be accepting my suit as soon as the assembly on Saturday, and you'll need to confer with your lawyers when that happens."

Whatever hold Sir Dashiel had over the marchioness, he somehow intended to extend his grasp to include Penelope too.

"Hadn't we best put the boot on the other foot?" Lucien asked. "I'll sort out the legal fellows, and then Penelope will be free to accept your suit or renew her agreement with me?"

"Sort the lawyers out by express. I might even go through the bother of a special license. By the time you return from London, her ladyship and I might well be enjoying wedded bliss."

Lucien rose and pretended to consider the hydrangeas. "She's stubborn, you know. Her ladyship can put artillery mules to shame when it comes to digging in her heels. Been that way all her life."

Sir Dashiel rose as well, as manners required when one held the lesser rank. "I can make her see reason, have no doubt of that. Penelope is fundamentally softhearted, and that collection of oddities you harbor at Lynnfield is very dear to her."

A frisson of dread prickled over Lucien's nape. "They are dear to me as well, and most of them are family or as near as makes no difference."

"Then you will be pleased to know that I have no intention of cutting Penelope's ties with her friends at Lynnfield. Her first duty will be to me and the Roost, of course, but one should remain cordial with one's neighbors."

Sir Dashiel was beaming, and Lucien was longing to throttle the man.

"Let's have a brandy," Sir Dashiel said. "I know the hour is early, but the day has been long, and it's not often that the Lynnfield peer graces the Roost with a call. I well know the disorientation that comes from returning home after a protracted absence. I sailed back from Spain, and you'd think Napoleon's army had crossed my acres. Place was a complete ruin."

He fiddled at the sideboard, eyeing decanters and lifting a glass stopper or two. "The occasion calls for a celebration—you do take spirits, I trust?"

"On occasion. Never too much. Spirits can muddle the old brainbox." Lucien mentally thanked Thomas for that term.

"So they can, but this brandy is not to be missed."

Dashiel's insistence on a brandy in the later afternoon was odd— a stirrup cup before a morning hack or a digestif after supper would have been more the thing—and his graciousness also had the quality of the serpent tempting Eve to sample the apple.

Perhaps the baronet wanted to gloat that Lucien had toasted an engagement between Penelope and Sir Dashiel? An odd boast, but then, Sir Dashiel felt his station in life keenly. He poured out two modest servings of dark amber potation.

"You've never had anything quite this fine," Sir Dashiel said, "and you never will again. Drink up."

More pressure to taste the apple, and perhaps a passing reference to Penelope's impending engagement to Sir Dashiel.

Lucien nosed his drink somewhat affectedly and got an intriguing surprise. The bouquet was exquisite, perfectly blending apples, caramel, vanilla, and a hint of spices. The aroma put him in mind of sentimental poetry read on a winter night beside a roaring fire, which was ridiculous.

Sir Dashiel waited while Lucien tried a sip.

"Tell me, my lord, is that not the most exquisite libation you've ever had the good luck to sample?"

"Quite lovely," Lucien said, admiring the play of sunlight on the glass's contents. "Quite, quite lovely. How on earth did you come by it?" The brandy was far too fine for a baronet who couldn't afford to have his paintings cleaned.

"That is a tale best left for another day, my lord. Suffice it to say, this brandy saved my life, and there isn't much of it left, alas."

The brandy was *French*. Lucien would bet his entire art collection on that. "I'm honored, Sir Dashiel. One envies you your cellar."

"And my future too. Penny will be very happy here at the Roost, and I'm sure you're of the same opinion."

Perhaps the brandy was some sort of truth potion, because Lucien was sorely, sorely tempted to share an honest assessment of just how a future at the Roost would suit Lady Penelope.

"My opinion doesn't matter," Lucien said, sipping primly. "Yours isn't of any moment either. We're the fellows. The choice belongs to the lady, and thus there's no point in either one of us putting on airs. May the best man win and all that."

"Very civil of you, my lord. Very logical."

Lucien lifted his glass in acknowledgment of the compliment, if a compliment it was. Sir Dashiel finished his brandy and returned the glass to the sideboard. More cordial blather followed, with Sir Dashiel alternately thanking Lucien effusively for hosting Tabitha's visit and urging Lucien to see the ladies up to Town himself.

Lucien allowed himself to be escorted to the front door by his fawning host and refrained from pointing out that a fellow had hoped to cadge a sandwich or two before riding back over the ridge.

He mounted up as Sir Dashiel waved him on his way and let Lorenzo saunter down the drive. At the gatehouse, Lucien stopped, turned his horse around, and considered the aging edifice that was the Roost.

Two aspects of the visit stood out to him. First, Sir Dashiel was up to absolutely no good where Pen was concerned. Whether he had a signed confession from the marchioness implicating her in highway robbery, or he'd found a trio of witnesses willing to attest that Cousin Lark was an accomplished forger, Sir Dashiel was certain of victory, despite Penelope's unequivocal refusal.

That was bothersome enough to give any besotted swain nightmares.

The second item on Lucien's list had to do with the brandy. The brandy didn't fit. Not with the fading wallpaper, the tired carpets, or the neglected paintings. Not with Dashiel's fundamentally avaricious character. That brandy was exquisite, well-aged, expensive, and *French*.

Lorenzo swished his tail at an imaginary fly and stomped a back hoof. Lucien could give no logical explanation for his next decision, but he sent Lorenzo ambling back up the drive in the direction of the Roost's somewhat dilapidated and understaffed stable. There, he found a groom and sent a note by way of the kitchen to old Jenkins.

Not five minutes later, Lucien had his reply. He cantered off this time, having no desire to linger in the vicinity.

CHAPTER FIFTEEN

"Lynnfield is coming to resemble a circus," Penelope informed her mare. "The marchioness is packing and repacking her trunks by the day or, more accurately, having her sorely tried lady's maid pack and repack. Tabitha remains in voluble good spirits, abetted by Lark, Phoebe, and Wren. Tommie keeps popping into the sewing room on any pretext, Malcolm glides about like a restless shade, Theo has taken up *whistling*, and Purdy frets."

Ursuline maintained her brisk walk away from the stable yard, but Penelope wasn't done with her lament.

"Dommie de Plessis had gone off to visit a sister in Bath, and thus returning the watch—why am I always charged with restoring the purloined goods to their owner?—is temporarily impossible."

Ursuline gently suggested that the time had come to trot, but Penelope kept her to the walk. "Lucien is preoccupied. He says I need my rest." For two nights, he'd not come to Penelope's bed, the blighter. "I'm not ill. What I need is him, his arms around me." She fell silent as Ursuline gained the wooded lower reaches of the ridge.

A night with Lucien was magic, even without lovemaking. He

had a way of rubbing Penelope's lower back with an exquisitely firm touch that turned her boneless and sighing.

"I will tell him as much tonight, if I have to traipse down the corridor at midnight to do it."

Lucien's visit to the Roost had merely confirmed what they'd already known: Sir Dashiel was intent on mischief, and his objective was Penelope's hand—and fortune—in marriage. Whether Dashiel had known about the betrothal previously was immaterial when he was intent on ignoring it now.

Lucien had been preoccupied when he'd returned an hour ago from calling at the Roost, suggesting he hadn't disclosed the whole of the exchange to Penelope.

"I'd know if Lucien were packing his bags."

Ursuline made another polite suggestion, quickening her walk, unbidden.

"Oh, very well, but you keep to a ladylike canter."

A fine plan, except that before the mare had crested the ridge, Penelope had given her her head, and a sedate canter had escalated to a pounding, earth-shaking gallop. The trees whipped past, the cares of the day fell away, and Penelope emerged at the summit in a less gloomy frame of mind.

"You were right," she said, patting Ursuline's shoulder. "Blow away the cobwebs, and the troubles disappear too." For a time at least.

Ursuline shook her head and pranced a little. *Let's do it again.*

"Catch your breath, my girl, while I enjoy the scenery." And put off returning to Lynnfield for another quarter hour. The view was magnificent, Lynnfield in all its state glory presiding over a patchwork of fields, pastures, woods, and lanes.

Home, and showing to wonderful advantage, more wonderful because somewhere down there, Lucien was patiently listening to Theo's raptures about irrigation or having a word with the butler about the piping in the distillery.

"I do love him," Penelope murmured, patting Ursuline's shoulder again. "Very much." And that complicated life and simplified it too.

The thought of Lucien disappearing again haunted her with irrational intensity, and even worse was the notion that Sir Dashiel might have some scheme in hand that would ensure Lucien's departure.

Penelope was about to turn Ursuline back the direction they'd come when Sir Dashiel emerged from the Roost's side of the hill. He rode the skinny bay, who'd apparently also been galloping, if lathered flanks and heaving sides were any indication.

Speak of the devil... "Sir Dashiel, good day."

"Penny. Might I hope you were wandering about up here on the off chance we'd meet?" He flashed her the smile Penelope was coming to hate. Superior, unctuous, and watchful at the same time.

"You may not. I simply needed some fresh air. Lucien tells me that you expect me to break my engagement to him and accept your proposal in its place."

Dashiel turned his gelding to fall in step with Ursuline. "Plain speaking, my dear, but the marquess does not lie. Somebody should tell him he's fair to a fault. I'm not sure the poor lad is clever enough to lie, to be honest. You and I will announce our engagement at the assembly the day after tomorrow."

Like hell we will. "After having pointedly refused your advances, why on earth would I change my mind?"

"You will waltz with me, and only with me, and then we will announce our betrothal, because if you refuse me, I will arrest Calpurnia for stealing Mrs. de Plessis's heirloom watch. Then I will bind dear Aunt Purdy over to stand trial at the assizes. I will have Malcolm put into an asylum—he's an imbecile, you know. Blood will out. Theo is a habitual drunkard, and if given some time, I'm sure I can come up with criminal wrongdoing on the part of the remaining oddities."

"Those oddities are my family."

"Lord Lynnfield said much the same thing and seemed utterly oblivious to the insult he did himself. The man's not too bright, Penelope. You truly do not want your children calling him father, and thanks to me, they won't be."

The urge to slash at Dashiel with her whip flitted through Penelope's mind, and Ursuline danced a few steps sideways.

Think, Pen. Dashiel believes he has the upper hand. Think. "What of the marquess? Have you some dire mischief planned for him?"

"You're protective of him? Very sweet, but his lordship truly didn't fuss much when I told him you'd be tossing aside that old betrothal agreement. He does pride himself on his logic, for all he hasn't much in the way of cleverness."

"And yet, you are doubtless willing to attack him, too, if it means my fortune falls into your hands."

Dashiel's smile became, if anything, merrier. "Don't sell yourself short, my darling. I want you falling into my bed as well, though your fortune does have its appeal. Has nobody told you that Lynnfield spied for the French? His ability with languages served him well, and all the time he was pretending to buy snuffboxes and miniatures, he was carrying information for Old Boney."

He was not. "How could you know such a thing?"

"We heard everything in the quartermaster's office. Who had ridden a horse to death on dispatch, who was contemplating French leave because the woman he'd left behind had written that she was in an interesting condition. An English marquess scampering about in proximity to enemy forces could mean only one thing. If you'd like to see Lynnfield hanged as a traitor, then by all means, reject my suit."

As the horses walked the spine of the ridge and the shadows grew longer, Penelope comforted herself with the knowledge that Dashiel was bluffing. He could arrest Purdy and menace Malcolm and probably even bring charges against Theo, but threatening Lucien was a pure, reckless bluff.

Overconfident, yet again. "Can you prove Aunt Purdy is a thief?"

"Dommie de Plessis is ready to lay information, but I don't have to prove anything. The law requires only that I find probable cause to believe Calpurnia committed a crime. She will then be bound over to languish until the quarter sessions, and not a single person in this shire will object. The woman's a nuisance. Jails, in case you've never had occasion to frequent one, are lamentably violent, unhealthy places, and quarter sessions just passed, so your dear auntie is looking at weeks of incarceration."

Purdy would not survive the ordeal. Bodily, she might come through in one piece, but mentally...

"She stole nothing."

"She stole an exquisite heirloom pocket watch of great sentimental value. Mrs. de Plessis can name no other suspect, but she knows of several other occasions when items of value have gone missing after Calpurnia Richard paid a call. Very sad, very felonious."

Ursuline, a lady to her bones, snatched at the reins.

"You need to put better manners on that mare, Penny, or I'll take the beast in hand myself."

"She knows we've been too long away from home."

"Accommodate yourself to the fact that the Roost will soon be your home, my dear. I've been thinking of procuring a special license. Five pounds isn't too much to pay for a lifetime of wedded bliss, is it? Then too, the longer you bide at Lynnfield, the worse effect it seems to have on your disposition."

Lucien had spent the past two days pondering what specific threats Dashiel would use to coerce Penelope to the altar, and yet, so far, Dashiel had yet to mention the marchioness.

"Has it occurred to you, Dashiel, that Tabitha will depart for London in a very few days, and her fortunes there rise and sink on the Marchioness of Lynnfield's whim?"

"You believe the marchioness would serve me such a turn? Of all people, she is the last one who will thwart my wishes, Penny. Suffice it to say, her ladyship has more to fear from the local magistrate than anybody, but why are you so loyal to that lot? They practically advertise a legacy of bad blood. You're better off far, far from the whole sorry bunch."

In other words, Dashiel had convinced himself that he was doing Penelope a very great favor by threatening her loved ones, stealing her fortune, and appropriating her future and her bodily freedom.

"The Pritchards are an old and respected family both here and in Wales. You slander them at your peril, Dashiel."

"*Sir* Dashiel, my darling, unless we are very, very private, which we will soon be on countless occasions. I had it from the marchioness herself that the present titleholder's mother took her own life. Laudanum, of all the unimaginative measures. Grieving, supposedly, but doubtless as wanting for sense as her son clearly is. You will send off an epistle to the lawyers posthaste putting to rest any rumors about some musty old betrothal agreement."

Ursuline tugged subtly on the reins. "Lord Lynnfield's mother did not take her own life."

"He was a child at the time, so of course nobody would have told him the worst of it. He's still childlike, which does not speak well of the peerage, does it? Write to your lawyers today, Penny, and wear your prettiest frock for me on Saturday."

He looked as if he was contemplating a horseback kiss, an inanity he'd attempted before, and Penelope wanted to be sick.

"I cannot rescind a betrothal to a peer with a simple letter. The business wants legal draftsmanship and signatures and witnesses."

"Then see to it, because I've been patient long enough. Besides, you could not have been seriously considering marriage to such a dimwit, even if he is a marquess. He'd expect you to play chess on the wedding night, for pity's sake, and he's a traitor to the crown."

Penelope longed to argue, to fight, to whip the smile right off Dashiel's face.

Back away slowly, Pen. Now. The voice in her head was Lucien's at his most serious.

"I'll wish you good day, *Sir* Dashiel, and take this conversation into most careful consideration."

He saluted with his crop. "I knew you'd see reason. Until Saturday, my darling. I'll be counting the hours."

Penelope nodded and turned Ursuline down the track. When

Dashiel's hoofbeats had faded, she cued the mare into the trot. Not the canter—Penelope was too distracted for the faster paces—but a brisk, businesslike trot.

When she returned to the manor, she made straight for Lucien's study, her heart thumping as if she'd just finished another hair-raising gallop. What she had to say left her angry, frightened, and ready to curse fate in several languages.

"You must leave, Lucien." She advanced on his desk, skirts swishing, even as she felt a pang to see him looking so much of a piece with his elegant, masculine study. "You must saddle Lorenzo as soon as darkness falls and get as far from Lynnfield as you possibly can."

Lucien was on his feet before she'd finished speaking, and then his arms were around her. "I'm not going anywhere without you."

"Yes, you are. You must." Penelope began to cry as she hadn't cried since she'd lurked in the orchard all those years ago and watched him canter out of her life.

"Pen, please don't cry. You break my heart. Calm yourself, *fy nghariad.*" Broke his heart and terrified him. Pen wasn't given to lachrymose dramatics, and damn anybody who drove her to them.

She lifted a tear-stained face from his shoulder and glowered at him. "Don't call me your love thinking to distract me, Lucien. I met Sir Dashiel on the ridge, and his schemes exceed all bounds. If I refuse to marry him, he'll have Purdy arrested for theft and bound over for the assizes. She's guilty as charged, drat the luck, and transportation isn't out of the question, if she even survives to stand trial."

Lucien led his beloved to the sofa. "I can have Aunt Purdy in Scotland by Monday." He'd even managed to sound halfway calm.

Penelope sat, accepted Lucien's handkerchief, and dabbed at her eyes. "You'd best escort her, and take Malcolm and Theo too. Malcolm is to be confined as a lunatic, and Theo is a habitual drunk. Cousin Lark is doubtless a scold, Wren a counterfeiter, and Phoebe a housebreaker. Dashiel is the magistrate—though I'm to call him *Sir* Dashiel unless he's rutting on me—and he can wreak all this mischief in the king's very name."

Lucien dropped down beside her, felled by Penelope's furious recitation. "He will never... If that presuming rodent lays a hand on you, I will gut him."

"Not if I beat you to it."

Pen's anger reassured Lucien inordinately. "Dashiel is desperate," he said. "St. Didier writes that the baronet is bobbing about in the River Tick and has been for some time. The report arrived today. Dashiel will prettily beg this merchant for a bit more time and send a few pounds to that one, then open up a new account with an unsuspecting bootmaker who's pleased to have a baronet's custom. He seems to have a bit of coin in the spring, which makes no sense when most gentry see an influx of cash only around harvest."

Penelope rose and paced before the desk. "He's anticipating a huge influx of cash the moment he dragoons me to the altar. I nearly horsewhipped him, Lucien, and you were right that he apparently has some desperate hold over the marchioness. He bragged about it. Said she'd be the last to gainsay him."

The marchioness went to London each spring. Coincidence? Was she paying off his bills? Pawning her jewelry to keep him afloat?

Lucien retrieved St. Didier's report from the desk. "I'd like you to read this when you can give it your full attention. I noticed that if Dashiel paid any bills, he did so between late March and mid-May."

Penelope took the report. "When her ladyship is in Town. This explains why Tabitha has rusticated at such length. Dashiel doesn't dare get in hock to the modistes and milliners on top of everything else." She set the report on the mantel. "None of this truly matters, though."

"Dashiel can be jailed for debt. He isn't a peer. That matters."

Penelope came to a halt and crossed her arms. "Dashiel claims you spied for Bonaparte, said the quartermasters heard everything. A marquess fluent in several languages flitting about France with impunity and pretending to collect art had only one explanation. This is why you need to leave, Lucien. Get to Scotland or France or Portugal. Dashiel truly does have the upper hand."

Penelope believed he did, and that was bad enough. "Purdy's situation notwithstanding, in my case, Dashiel doesn't remotely have the truth."

She studied him, expression solemn, and Lucien realized that Penelope would not care if he had spied for the French. She'd have trusted that he'd had his reasons and let little bygones like treason and abetting the enemy be bygones.

"He has credibility," Penelope said, stalking to the sideboard and sniffing the stoppers of each of the three decanters one by one. "He bragged about that too. He made me cry, the blighter. I could horse-whip him for that too. Theo is a sot, and so are half the gentlemen I danced with in Town. Purdy borrows trinkets without permission, albeit not to keep. The very realm of which we are subjects prospers by plundering its colonies, but let's not mention that, shall we? Dashiel has to remove you from the equation, so of course he'll tell any convenient lie about you that he pleases. That Dashiel would threaten our Malcolm, though... How dare he, when Malcolm's sole offense is that he's quiet?"

She poured two generous measures of a fine old Andalusian brandy and brought Lucien one.

"He dares because he can," Lucien said. "Whatever mischief Dashiel got up to in the quartermaster's ranks, the only consequence was passage home. Nobody in the local surrounds will confront him, and he's too smart to go near London."

Penelope nosed her drink. "Maybe you should go to London. He'll be reluctant to follow you there."

"To your health," Lucien said, gesturing with his glass, "and to Sir Dashiel's comeuppance."

Penelope drank to that and with no missish airs. "He will attack you, Lucien. He knows I'm fond of you. We can send Malcolm,

Theo, and Purdy to Scotland, but getting you out of the picture has to be on Sir Dashiel's agenda too."

"I did not spy for Napoleon, Pen. The deaths that fiend caused, the destruction of his own country, the pillaging and slaughter... While Sir Dashiel sat on his horse, safely counting barrels of rum far from any battlefields. What I saw, by contrast, will haunt me until my dying day."

"And you pretended you were haggling over snuffboxes." She sipped her drink again. "You cannot stay at Lynnfield, Lucien. I hate the notion of parting from you ever again. I dread it. I'm sick at the very thought, but you must listen to me."

The brandy was exquisite, benefiting from a unique blending process that used spirits of varying ages to create a mature, complex, luscious result, and yet, all Lucien sought was the burn.

"Dashiel does want me gone, you are correct," he said, setting his half-empty glass beside St. Didier's report on the mantel. "He urged me at least three times to accompany the marchioness to Town. With me out of the picture, you are without a champion, meaning no disrespect, and it's you Dashiel is determined to marry."

"By special license, the rotter. Five pounds to buy him a lifetime of wedded bliss."

More evidence of desperation. "I can buy up his debts, Pen. In fact, I've already begun that process."

"He can arrest Purdy *tonight*, and she's guilty, Lucien. She told me so herself, and Dommie de Plessis, her supposed victim, has gone to Bath, so I can't return the watch and claim the whole business is yet another misunderstanding."

Weariness came through in that recitation, and weariness could be a harbinger of defeat. "You go to London," Lucien said slowly, the words as unnerving as they were sensible. "Dashiel won't expect that. I'll remain here, tending to business as usual. You take Purdy, Malcolm, Theo, and the others and get up to Town tonight. The marchioness and Tabby can follow on Monday as planned."

"Leave Lynnfield? Leave you here at Lynnfield to deal with that boar hog in breeches?"

Lucien pushed that image aside and mentally examined his own suggestion. "I've dealt with worse. For you to decamp gives us an element of surprise and takes the fight off Dashiel's preferred turf. I have allies in Town more highly placed than Dashiel can dream of."

"I thought His Grace of Huntleigh was on his wedding journey?"

"He is, but His Grace of Wellington bides in England. If he's not in Town, he's no farther away than Stratfield Saye House, a day's journey into Hampshire from London."

Penelope's temper appeared to give way to surprise. "Lucien? Are you telling me you can summon the Duke of Wellington?"

"'Summon' overstates the matter, but I'll have His Grace's support if I need it. I was very good at playing the wealthy, titled English fool, Pen. I don't intend that either of us play the fool for Sir Dashiel. You have been very good at being anything and everything Lynnfield needed. You took every burden onto your own shoulders, from keeping the house to keeping the peace. You were prepared to sew Tabitha's whole wardrobe yourself if you had to go two weeks without sleep to do it. This time, it's you who must blow retreat."

He'd spoken in plain English, but Pen regarded him as if he'd dropped into some arcane dialect of Latin.

"You expect me to *leave* Lynnfield?"

"Leaving Lynnfield is hard," Lucien said. "I know how hard, but retreat is not surrender, and you will find safety in numbers if the household goes to Town with you." Perhaps she'd find comfort in numbers, too, as Lucien had found comfort under Huntleigh's roof.

"I don't want to go," Pen murmured, running her finger around the rim of her glass. "I truly don't want to leave Lynnfield, Lucien. I hate London, and you've fought too many battles in solo combat too. I don't want to leave Lynnfield and I assuredly don't want to leave you. You don't even take snuff."

Which had nothing to do with anything, but was indicative of Pen ruminating on a decision. "I didn't want to go either," Lucien said. "Not truly, but I was young and at my wits' end." And so in love he hadn't known up from otherwise.

Before he could find words to convey that truth, the door opened.

"Oh, don't mind me." Tommie sidled into the room. "Came by to borrow the big abacus. Had an idea. We could loan out art to all the gentry coming into Town for the Season. Charge 'em a bit for some genuine, high-quality pieces, help them do the pretty for their entertaining without breaking the bank, then put the pieces back in inventory or ship them off to a gallery in Scotland or York. Renting art. I don't know as it's done, but warehousing the goods costs money. Renting brings in money. Are we having an aperitif? Pen, you look a bit peaked, also piqued. All that sewing must be driving you daft."

"Renting art is a fine idea," Lucien said. "A lucrative, fine idea, Thomas. I will be pleased to discuss it with you at some other time."

"But that's the thing," Tommie said, propping a hip against the desk. "We haven't another time. You're promised to Theo and the steward tomorrow, Saturday is the assembly, Sunday is final preparations for the jaunt to Town, though we're not supposed to be exerting ourselves on the Sabbath."

"Tommie," Penelope said, "we have greater concerns than how quickly you can afford to propose to Tabitha. Her brother will never give you leave to court her unless I agree to marry him, and I am unwilling to accept his suit."

Tommie looked from Penelope to Lucien and back to Penelope. "Varlet. Don't care for the man myself, though he's Tabitha's brother. She says she hasn't a dowry because Dashiel had to spend it on seed. He purloined the older sisters' settlements as well. He spent it on those wretched hunters, Hoby boots, gold cravat pins, and French sleeve buttons. A gent don't dress in the first stare of even rural fashion for free. The man's a thief. Theo could tell you stories."

Not for the first time, Lucien had the sense of seeing Tommie anew. "What sort of stories?"

"Bribes, of course. Justice of the peach, they call him in the village. He's bribed witnesses to shore up his cases and looked the other way for coin. I know it happens, but it wasn't happening here until he joined the Commission of the Peace. Theo has the details, and Cousin Lark has picked up a few tales too. Heaven alone knows what Malcolm has seen and heard on his rambles, and he might be willing to swear out an affidavit if he can't exactly testify from the witness box."

Lucien felt an odd frisson of joy. Surprise figured into his emotions too. "You've been keeping Sir Dashiel under surveillance?"

"He likes to accost Penelope when she's stealing some solitude on horseback. Malcolm noticed it first. We don't care for that sort of behavior."

Penelope sank into the chair behind Lucien's desk, and he liked the look of her there. She was calmer and more thoughtful than she'd been even a quarter of an hour ago, and yet, Lucien wasn't ready to let her go bustling away on some domestic errand.

"Thomas, would you excuse us for a moment?" Lucien asked. "Take the abacus, and we'll talk about your art rental tomorrow after breakfast."

"I thought perhaps after supper—"

"Tommie, go," Penelope said, shifting back to her perch on the sofa. "Explain your scheme to Tabitha, and she will think you the cleverest fellow in England."

"Might she? Might she, really? Don't see why. Tenants have been renting land for generations, and it's always the squire who profits. Nothing very original about renting. The squire keeps the rent and the land, the tenant does the work. Should be illegal, but there you have it."

"Shoo," Lucien said, opening the door. "We'll see you at supper." He closed the door after Tommie went muttering on his way. "What are you thinking, Pen?"

"I don't want to go to London."

"I don't want to let you out of my sight either." Hated the very notion.

"But here we are." She patted the place beside her. "I keep

thinking about the last time one of us left, Lucien. We didn't fight then. You let the tutors and solicitors and matchmakers drive you from your home, and I let you go."

"I certainly blew retreat." Though Pen's words were more accurate. He'd not retreated that time. He'd quit the field altogether. A defeat of sorts, if not a complete rout.

"Maybe this time, I do have to be the one to leave. I cannot believe I said that, but you are right that Dashiel won't expect such a maneuver. Lady Penny adores rural life. Ask anybody."

Lucien crossed the room to sit beside her. "We didn't fight. We were too young, too inexperienced. I've been to war, though, and you've fought battles without number here at Lynnfield. If you tell me that you are determined to marry Sir Dashiel, that is your decision, but it won't solve anything. Nobody in this shire will be safe once the baronet gets his hands on your fortune. I cannot allow Dashiel to prosper, whatever you decide."

"To marry that man, to be his wife..." She shuddered. "Defeat on that scale is unthinkable. I'll go anywhere you wish to take me, Lucien, if we need to regroup and take stock, but I say we fight."

I love you. He kissed her hand and kept hold of it. "I agree. This time, we fight." *I love you. I will always love you.*

"And we win free," Penelope said, "or we go down swinging, and cursing in Welsh so loudly they'll hear us in Cardiff."

"We'll win," Lucien said, as much a prayer as a prediction. "But Thomas has me thinking."

"You excel at thinking. He's a clever lad, our Tommie."

"He is, and a sweet fellow, and I will dower Tabitha if her idiot brother has truly bankrupted her. Tommie is clever, Malcolm observant, Lark well informed, Theo well liked. St. Dider has given us interesting ammunition too."

"You're saying we shouldn't fight alone. I like that notion, and I suspect the elders will love it." She started to rise, doubtless intent on sallying forth and rallying the troops, but Lucien stopped her with a hand on her wrist.

"Before we make battle plans, would you stay with me here for a bit? Once we decide on next steps, life will become busy and fraught, and if we divide and conquer, we'll be parted for a time. I want... I need to hold the woman I love."

He'd fallen short of the traditional declaration, but Penelope sparkled as if he'd spouted odes and panegyrics.

"How convenient. I need to hold the man I love." She bundled close, and Lucien's joy was almost limitless.

CHAPTER SIXTEEN

The coach was old but clean, and the kitchen had packed a hamper sufficient to feed the entire troop of yeoman warders guarding the Tower of London. Anybody observing the trunks piled on the roof and the boot would assume another toff was sending his luggage on to London.

And yet, Penelope dreaded to begin her journey.

"In you go," Lucien said as a porter handed another hamper up to John Coachman on the box. "You'll be in Town before dawn."

The hour approached midnight, the perfect time to depart for London if one had the luxury of traveling when the roads were least crowded.

Nothing about the situation felt perfect to Penelope. "I will miss you." She stood close enough to Lucien that she could smell his lavender shaving soap, close enough that she could have leaned against him and reprised her tears from earlier in the day. "I'll miss all of you."

Lucien took her gently in his arms. "The elders were magnificent, weren't they? They've had Dashiel in their sights since he came home from Spain, and they've been discreet about it."

"I thought I was looking after them, and the whole time... I've underestimated our family, Lucien."

"As have I, but isn't family supposed to look after one another, Pen? Family isn't like Tommie's squire renting acres to the tenants. We're to muddle on more like a herd of goats. This one excels at opening gates. That one has the keenest hearing."

"Goats, Lucien?"

"They're clever and resourceful."

"If we're reduced to discussing the merits of caprines, it's time I was on my way."

Lucien's embrace became more snug. "Go straight to St. Didier, before anybody knows you're in Town. Once you've delivered your report, then and only then do you roll into the Lynnfield House mews."

"Where Wren and Phoebe will soon join me, and Purdy, too, though she will play least in sight for a time. I know the plan, Lucien." Lark would follow with Tommie, Tabitha, and the marchioness on Monday. The older ladies would travel up on Sunday, violating every dictate of genteel propriety and making swifter progress than they would on any other day of the week.

Lucien spoke near her ear. "And you know I will not fail you."

This time. The words hung silently in the air, and Penelope's heart nearly broke. "I won't fail you either. Lure Sir Dashiel to Town and have him arrested for debt. Strip him of his magistrate's honors and cover him in disgrace. We shall marry, and the elders will be safe."

The plan was sound, though not exactly satisfying. The elders had approved, though, and had been fiercely willing to take on their assigned roles. The marchioness and Tabitha had been kept in the dark by design.

Lucien kissed Penelope on the mouth, then stepped back and produced a bound book from inside the coach.

"Some light reading in the event you can't sleep. It's a first edition, so please look after it for me."

Evelina, Mrs. Burney's most successful novel. "Our old friend?"

"I was so busy using it to decode our missives, I never actually read it. We can remedy the oversight now, in our separate venues."

Penelope took the book from him. "Is this a race?"

"It's a gift." His expression by the flickering torchlight was oddly solemn. "Be safe, Pen, and please be in London when I've finished my assignment here."

Ah. So Penelope wasn't the only one thinking of previous partings. "It's hard, isn't it?" she said, leaning against him, the book in her hand. "To be left behind?"

"*Mae'n uffern.*" It's hell.

Their next kiss was desperate, passionate, and too brief, and then Penelope was sitting in the old coach, clutching her novel, and knowing she must not look back, must not wave, must not call farewell as the horses lifted from the trot to the canter. How in the name of all that was heroic had Lucien had the fortitude to ride away all those years ago? The courage and determination?

His heart must have fractured anew with each passing mile, and all the while, he'd believed Penelope had sent him on his way *alone.*

She set aside the book, intent on finding a handkerchief. A slim sheet of fragile foolscap drifted from between the pages onto the floor of the coach. The paper was slightly yellowed and covered in familiar writing.

By the light of the coach lamp, Penelope peered at the date, then whirled around to open the slot that let her see the stable yard growing smaller in the coach's wake. Lucien stood beneath a torch, still and alone, and then he lifted one hand and blew her a kiss.

Before she could thump on the coach roof to stop the blasted vehicle, Lucien had slipped into the darkness.

"He found the letter," she murmured, closing the slot and turning up the lamp. "That wretched, wonderful man, after all these years..." He'd found it and, in typical Lucien fashion, had made sure she'd have privacy when she decoded his previous farewell to her.

The amenities in the old coach included a traveling desk. Word by word, Penelope translated numbers into words, words into sentences, and sentences into sentiments.

Please come with me... I'm begging you, Pen... I love you and always will...

The letter filled her with joy and regret—how Lucien must have suffered to think she'd been indifferent to his pleas—and with determination. If she had to haul Lucien bodily to the Hebrides, they would have a future together, and Dashiel Ingraham would rue the day he'd attempted to meddle with that dream.

Lucien made his way to the orchard by the light of a waning moon. The notion of going back to a house without Penelope in it... He sat on the low stone wall, feeling empty and exhausted, though Penelope hadn't been gone but five minutes.

Watching the coach sway down the carriageway had been hard. Knowing he'd once again failed to give Penelope the words *I love you* was harder.

"I'll tell her when I get to London." Lucien was rehearsing that moment when he realized he wasn't alone. A hint of lavender wafted on the night air, along with a subtler scent bringing to mind lush meadows and quiet woods.

"Uncle, show yourself."

Malcolm emerged from the shadows, not so much as a cravat pin showing in the darkness. He bowed slightly and gestured to the stone wall.

"Of course you may join me, though I'm poor company at the moment. Pen has decamped for London." Uncle doubtless knew that, just as he knew so much that nobody attributed to him.

Malcolm squeezed his shoulder and perched beside him.

"I found the letter," Lucien went on. "Purdy had it. She's kept it all these years. Thought I might be communicating with smugglers, allowing them to use Lynnfield as a storage depot on the route to London. Your sister is a fanciful creature."

A fanciful creature so homesick for Wales that as a young girl, she'd reasoned she might be sent back there if she only behaved badly enough. Stealing had become a habit, though, and a comfort once Purdy had realized she'd never be sent back to Wales, even if she purloined the crown jewels. The whole tale had come out between sniffles and apologies, and Lucien had found himself patting Purdy's hand and feeling sorry for her.

"I want to go to London right now," Lucien said softly. "Purdy is still homesick for Wales. I am homesick for my Penelope, and she's not been gone a quarter hour."

Malcolm made a motion with both hands like the flapping of bird wings.

"Yes, I sent pigeons with her. St. Didier has some too. If all goes well, I will be in London by sunset on Sunday, Sir Dashiel hot on my heels, and the birds won't be necessary."

Malcolm shook a fist in the direction of the Roost. Ire and loathing gave the gesture more than theatrical power.

"Sir Dashiel beat you, didn't he?" Lucien murmured. "You were on foot, he was on horseback, and he took his riding crop to you."

Malcolm shrugged.

"It happens regularly?"

He held up four fingers.

"Malcolm, why not pull the blighter from the saddle and beat the stuffing out of him? In a fair fight, you're bigger, smarter, and far more fit."

Malcolm took out a penknife and scratched a word into the dirt at their feet. *Drwg.*

"Evil," Lucien said. "Bad, wicked." The import of Malcolm's opinion took a moment to sink in. "If you struck him and there were no witnesses, he could claim he was the victim of an assault and insist he'd been defending himself against a violent madman. He's been plotting to send you off for some time, then."

Malcolm nodded.

"He's told you as much?"

Malcolm stuck his chin in the air and curled his lip.

"Bragged of it to you." Lucien recalled Penelope telling him that Dashiel had insisted that even his prospective wife address him by his honorific *unless he was rutting on her.* "He's even worse than I suspected."

Malcolm nodded, and a moment later, he rose and scuffed out the scratchings in the dirt with his bootheel.

"I'll come with you if you're going back to the manor." Lucien stood as well, still missing Penelope, but comforted too. Even Malcolm in his silences and wanderings had been keeping watch over Lynnfield and over Penelope. "I will not like leaving you here when I go up to Town on Sunday, Malcolm."

Theo would stay behind as well, because somebody had to keep an eye on Dashiel. Phoebe, Wren, and Purdy would leave for Town directly after services, which Purdy would miss due to the same severe megrim that had kept her from attending the assembly.

If Sir Dashiel cherished a prayer of marrying Penelope before summer, he'd need to pursue her to London posthaste. Penelope's conference with St. Didier would ensure that Dashiel's creditors knew of his insolvency, his lack of marital prospects, and his expected arrival in London.

"The wheels of justice cannot grind quickly enough," Lucien said as the manor house loomed against a starry sky. "I vow, Malcolm, I feel as if I'm once again back at war."

Malcolm stopped him with a hand on his arm, pulled him into a hug, thumped him on the back, and then resumed walking.

"You are right. I am not at war. I was alone then and didn't much care if I lived or died. I have family now, and I very much want to live. That makes a difference."

Malcolm cuffed him once on the shoulder and strode ahead, and Lucien let him go. *I love you* once again remained unspoken, but not unacknowledged. That was something.

"I thought London gentlemen slept until noon," Penelope said, taking in the appointments in St. Didier's breakfast parlor. The room looked out over a small back garden beginning to fill with light and already awash in birdsong. A cracked window let in a breeze that fluttered the lace curtains, and the sideboard was brightened by a bouquet of red and yellow tulips.

The overall effect of the room was pleasant, but the lone place setting at the head of the table struck an off note. Such a room was meant for chatter and good cheer rather than a solitary plate of eggs served with a side dish of financial news.

"Some London gents do sleep until noon," St. Didier said. "Tea or coffee, my lady? Or do you prefer chocolate?"

Penelope would have preferred that Lucien was with her, that she hadn't spent the night jostling about alone in an old coach with the sweetest love letter ever penned by the hand of man, and with memories so dear they'd brought her to tears all over again.

"Strong China black if you have it," she said as St. Didier held her chair. "And some buttered toast wouldn't go amiss."

St. Didier filled her a plate at the sideboard, with modest servings of omelet, sliced ham, and buttered toast. He put a trio of cherry tarts on a second plate and brought her both. A tea cup and saucer followed—buttercups adorning both—along with a pristine linen table napkin.

"The China black is in the pot decorated with buttercups. The gunpowder is in the pot covered with violets." He rummaged in the sideboard as he spoke, then passed Penelope a handful of cutlery and took his place at the head of the table. "I was half expecting you this morning. You or Lord Lynnfield."

Penelope poured herself a steaming cup, and the aroma alone helped revive her. "Why now?"

"Because your local assembly looms at hand, and betrothals are usually announced at such gatherings, unless the countryside has changed a great deal in a short time. Jam?" He set something like a miniature epergne by her plate, except that the three small jam pots did not sit on tiered shelves, but rather, occupied a frame that made it possible to move all three jam jars at the same time.

Penelope chose strawberry. "Lucien will attend, as will our elders, and they will make my excuses. Is there anything more restorative in all of creation than jam and buttered toast with a cup of hot tea?"

St. Didier sipped his own tea, also China black. "Good company," he said, saluting with his cup and offering Penelope a surprisingly charming smile. "Good company can be very restorative. You would not have recognized the Lucien Pritchard I met here in London."

"All serious and busy? Thinking too hard and seeing every pothole in every plan?"

"Exactly, and incapable of simply admitting he was worried, if lecturing his pet duke would serve instead. Huntleigh owes his former majordomo a great deal. How is the omelet?"

Penelope hadn't thought she'd had much of an appetite, but one bite of cheesy eggs and she was glad St. Didier had put them on her plate.

"Hot," she said. "Marvelously hot. One grows so accustomed to cold and tepid offerings that one forgets what a pleasure hot food is."

"My lady has the gift of speaking metaphorically as well as literally."

The wretched man added a dab of extra butter to his toast and took a bite, as if he hadn't just offered an insight into Penelope's life since Lucien had left for the Continent.

"You are forward in your observations, sir," Penelope said. "If this weren't the best breakfast I've had in ages, I'd douse you over the head with my tea."

"Having consumed a few tepid meals myself, I know the look of one mending and making do, my lady. That Lord Lynnfield has put the fire back in your eyes, and that you have similarly inspired him to hurling epistolary thunderbolts, warms an old bachelor's heart."

St. Didier looked to be about thirty, and yet, he did have the air of one who had seen and suffered much. As if hot breakfasts and fresh flowers were statements rather than amenities.

"You've read Lucien's letter?"

"While you were freshening up. I'm to alert Sir Dashiel's creditors to the baronet's impending arrival in Town and keep a close eye on your ladyship. If possible, I'm also to arrange invitations for you and keep Sir Dashiel in my sights once he comes to London."

Penelope had finished her eggs and started on her ham. Not too salty, not too smoky. "You are only one man. How can you accomplish all that when we have mere days to put Lucien's scheme into place?" Lucien's scheme, but refined by the counsel he'd sought from Penelope and the elders.

"Lord Lynnfield had me laying groundwork from the moment I returned to London," St. Didier said. "Then too, Sir Dashiel has been trespassing on the patience of his London creditors for years, and very skillfully. My job will be in the nature of removing the last cotter pin holding the floodgate closed. He's put it about that you have accepted his proposal, by the way, and done so without precisely committing himself."

"In case a better heiress comes along?"

"In case he's accused of fraud outright. If he makes no clear promises, then he's simply a debtor obligated to pay. If he trades in falsehoods to secure goods, then the situation becomes more serious."

Some part of Penelope did not want Dashiel in any more serious trouble. She simply wanted him to leave her in peace. Another part of her knew Dashiel had earned all the retribution coming his way.

"The baronet is badly off," she said. "He's all but forcing me to the altar, he's taken his sisters' dowry funds, and he insists his hunters be fashionably skinny. That makes no sense when it's spring, and no true huntsman begrudges his horses spring grass after a winter of galloping over fences. Dashiel simply lacks adequate grazing and must conserve what he does have for the farm stock." Theo, steward-in-training, had put that much together.

"Were you truly considering marrying this pusillanimous poseur?"

Penelope barely knew St. Didier, but she'd trusted him to find Lucien and to deal with him discreetly. Her confidences were safe with St. Didier, and she'd pondered his question at length herself.

"I was entertaining the notion of marriage to Sir Dashiel in the theoretical sense. *If* I married him, would he be sufficiently grateful to have my money that he'd treat me decently? *If* I married him, would I have the independence that I lacked at Lynnfield, or would I be trading one set of obligations for another?"

"Or simply adding obligations? You never considered him as a man?"

The question brought Penelope up short as she reached for a cherry tart. "No. He is polite enough, clean about his person, but I... There was no attraction, if that's what you're too polite to ask. None." Lighting upon that conclusion pleased her inordinately and made her sad.

"One surmised as much, and at the same time, dispatching me to have Lynnfield execute legal documents was all but guaranteed to send his lordship pelting for home."

The tart was luscious. Warm, flaky, sweet, and pungent. "Because?"

"Huntleigh and I have shared a few brandies late at night. The entire time Lucien Pritchard, as he was known at the time, spent in Huntleigh's household—years, my lady—the man never so much as looked at another woman, despite many a lady casting sighs in his direction. His lordship is smitten, and thank heavens he has the brains to finally admit it to the one person to whom the news matters most. More tarts?"

He admitted it to me years ago, in writing. To hear Lucien say the words would have been lovely, though. "These will do. They are quite good."

"My grandmother's recipe. The Scots know their way around a sweet."

"Your grandmother is Scottish? You seem so... so..."

"English? My mother certainly was, vehemently so, for all the good it did her. More tea?"

St. Didier was a gracious host, his hospitality effortless and informal, and yet, Penelope sensed that questions about St. Didier's lost loves and romantic compromises would meet with vague poetical quotes or platitudes about the weather.

She finished the meal in better spirits than she'd started it, despite the fact that breakfasting alone with a bachelor was the stuff of hopeless scandal. That Sir Dashiel was abusing his office as justice of the peace, had stolen from his own sisters, and was scheming against the elders, Penelope herself, and Lucien put a friendly meal of ham and eggs in a more acceptable light.

"Now you will sleep," St. Didier said when Penelope had finished a second cup of tea. "It's a mistake to neglect the victuals after a forced march, though tempting. I sent your coach to Lynnfield House without you and will lend you mine for the last leg of your journey."

"But—"

"My conveyances are all unmarked by crests or flourishes, and I change teams regularly so my horses aren't recognizable either. My coachman will set you down in the mews, and you will wear the hood of your cloak pulled up as you hurry into the house, ready to put right all that baggage her ladyship sent up in the less commodious vehicle."

Lucien had the same ability to think up plausible stories on the spot. Penelope was too tired to join in the game.

"Very well, I will enjoy a brief nap once I reach Lynnfield House." Three hours was brief, in some contexts. "While you do what?"

"I will appoint watchers at the turnpikes leading to Kent and Surrey, and make the rounds of the places gentlemen stay when they don't want in-laws or creditors to know they're in London. You're sure you won't take some of those tarts with you?"

Penelope helped herself to one more and rose without assistance. "You are a bad influence, sir."

"High praise from you, my lady. I will also send a pigeon to his lordship, who is doubtless fretting about highwaymen and bandits and brothel-keeping abbesses. Lynnfield will appreciate knowing you have safely arrived in Town."

"John Coachman keeps a brace of pistols up on the box. I have my peashooter, and the grooms all carry knives."

St. Didier stopped at the parlor door. "Peashooter?"

Penelope swept through the doorway before him. "They are notoriously inaccurate, but they do fire bullets. I am a dead shot, though I've never taken down a living target."

"Remind me to be on my best behavior the next time I go calling at Lynnfield."

"One senses you are on your best behavior at all times, St. Didier. That must be tiring and a bit dull. One knows the look and so forth."

His brows rose, and he looked as if he was about to say something, then changed his mind. How satisfying to have had some version of the last word with a man who could put half of London under surveillance on any random spring morning.

"What's this?" St. Didier asked when he'd escorted Penelope to the foyer and helped her into her cloak. He'd also opened his own front door to her, meaning not a butler, footman, or chambermaid had seen Penelope pay her call.

"An empty brandy bottle," Penelope said, pulling on gloves. "Lucien asked me to give it to you so you could investigate its provenance."

St. Didier held the bottle up to the window and rotated it half a turn as he peered at the label. "Is this from his lordship's cellars?"

"From Sir Dashiel's. Lucien sampled the brandy when he paid a call and found the vintage far above what Dashiel ought to be able to afford. Lucien found that odd."

"This brandy is rare. I know that much," St. Didier said, putting the bottle back on the foyer's sideboard. "Rare even in France, but then, Sir Dashiel served in uniform, and some of those fellows acquired Continental tastes."

Penelope had eschewed a bonnet and instead pulled her cloak up over her head. "Lucien said the brandy was exquisite, some of the best he's ever come across. He suspects Sir Dashiel extorted it from some nabob, or stole it from the quartermaster's stores in Spain."

"I promise you, my lady, this bottle has never graced any quartermaster's stores. Royal cellars, perhaps, and then only for a princely sum. You are leaving out the back, as the saying goes."

The sun was coming up. Wheeled traffic was even at that moment clattering past St. Didier's front door.

"Out the back will do nicely," Penelope said, taking St. Didier's arm.

He led her through a house of a piece with the breakfast parlor—elegant, comfortable, spotless, and somehow lonely. Penelope stopped before a portrait of a red-haired beauty in Highland tartan.

"Who is she?"

"My grandmother. Left a trail of broken hearts wherever she went, if the stories are true."

The young lady was lovely, with blue eyes and a smile at once demure and mischievous. "One sees a resemblance."

"Cease needling me, your ladyship." St. Didier resumed his progress down the corridor. "Or I will not tell Cook to send you over a basket of tarts."

"Disguised as a satchel of documents, no doubt."

"Or a pair of boots returned from the cobbler's. Soon, you will know all my secrets."

Penelope let that bit of nonsense conclude the exchange, but as she waited with St. Didier in the alley for his team to be put to, she wrestled with the urge to hug him. The man was lonely and trying desperately to tell himself he was content.

She knew the look. Lucien would know it too.

"How will you track down a brandy that's reserved for royalty?" she asked as St. Didier's coach clattered up the cobbles. The vehicle was dark, not too large, and pulled by sturdy matched bays of about sixteen hands. Utterly unremarkable.

"I will pay a call on Xavier Fournier, a Frenchman well established here in London who trades in wine and spirits and does so without running afoul of the excisemen. He's something of a fairy godfather and watchdog over the émigré community, and if anybody knows the details of that brandy, he will."

"Lucien said the brandy was out of place—badly, badly out of place—at the Roost, and thus it piqued his curiosity. He had Dashiel's butler bring him the bottle on a whim." Though Lucien didn't have whims. He had inspirations.

"Perhaps Sir Dashiel extorted a case from some Spanish bandit. We might never know." St. Didier opened the coach door and offered Penelope his hand.

She kissed his cheek and nipped into the coach, shutting the door behind her. The shades were pulled down, but she could see through the crack between the leather and the glass that she'd surprised her host.

He stood alone in the morning gloom, smiling at the cobblestones and looking for all the world like his Scottish granny had in her prime. Irresistibly sweet and bent on mischief. Penelope hoped he looked that way more often in future, because when he did, he was gorgeous.

CHAPTER SEVENTEEN

"All this hopping and stomping about," Lucien drawled. "Enough to give one a megrim." He smiled placidly at Sir Dashiel and pretended to sip his punch. The stuff was three parts rum, one part cherry cordial with a dash of lightning, and four parts celestial wrath come Sunday morning.

Delicious and perfectly suited to Lucien's mood.

The assembly had inspired the baronet to trouble over his appearance more than usual. His curls were perfectly arranged over his forehead, his cravat was tied with intricate precision, and his smile put the sun to shame.

"I'm told your Aunt Calpurnia has indeed come down with a megrim," he replied, "even without any hopping or stomping. Such a pity to miss all this gaiety." He lifted his glass in the direction of the dance floor, where Dommie de Plessis—suddenly returned from Bath for no apparent reason—was being flung about by the blacksmith's pride and joy amid a dozen other couples.

"Lynnfield is still well represented," Lucien said. "Your Tabitha is the belle of the ball." She'd worn one of her new frocks, and between Thomas's doting escort and the sighs of the local beauties who would never have a London Season, Tabitha was radiant.

"As well she should be. Youth adds such a glow to any woman's attributes, don't you agree?"

By youth, Dashiel doubtless meant naïveté, the lack of experience that made the young gullible. "I prefer some wisdom in a lady," Lucien replied. "Tabitha is adorable, but conversation focused on the qualities of velvet as opposed to satin soon pales. She will nonetheless make quite an impression in Mayfair. You should be proud of her."

Dashiel shifted so Lucien was between him and the dancers. "Speaking of admirable women, where is my dearest Penelope? I know all about making a well-timed entrance, but the evening advances, and I have so looked forward to waltzing with my intended."

Lucien sidled a step to the left, blocking Dashiel's view of the door. "Her ladyship has flown the coop, as the saying goes. Mind of her own and all that. She took a notion to go up to Town, or so she claims."

The dazzling smile vanished. "*What the devil?* Gone to London? You're sure?"

"Half the dratted household is bound for London. I show up, the prodigal peer, and the lot of them bolt for Town, and yes, I'm sure. One doesn't confuse London with, say, Edinburgh in the ordinary course. I excel at map reading. All that racketing about the Continent where even the signposts were burned for warmth. Bleak business, that."

"When did she go?"

"Recently." Lucien nodded agreeably to the vicar's daughter.

"Recently when, precisely?"

"Thursday night? No, last night. Said there's less traffic in the dark, and it's the full moon, so away she went. Never been any point telling her ladyship what to do." And never would be.

"The marchioness ordered Penny about a good deal, and as my wife, Penny had best learn to heed the occasional order."

The set came to an end, and a general stampede in the direction of the punchbowl ensued. The vicar's wife was opening every available window, and Dommie de Plessis was staring daggers at Sir Dashiel.

"Penelope humored the marchioness," Lucien said. "Easier to manage the household if nobody is engaging in tantrums and sulks. I'm sure you'd agree. Why is Mrs. de Plessis rubbing at her eye with her fan?" Her right eye, which in the language of the fan was a request for an assignation.

"How should I know?"

"She's looking right at you." Glowering, while young Danny Smith passed her a small glass of punch.

"Perhaps her eyesight is going. She's getting long in the tooth. Thirty if she's a day. Did Penelope say why she left for London?"

The widow had switched to opening her fan, fluttering it a few times, and slowly closing it. *I will marry you.* Dashiel took to studying his glass of punch.

"Mrs. de Plessis is *still* looking right at you, old man," Lucien said. "Handsome woman too. Perhaps you'd best put thoughts of her ladyship out of your head. Opportunity in the hand and so forth."

Dashiel looked up sharply. "Are you daft? Penelope and I have a firm understanding. Our betrothal was to be announced at this very gathering, and now you tell me she's off to Town."

"She said something about scouting the terrain for the marchioness and Tabby, but the marchioness knows London blindfolded. I suspect 'scouting' is a lady's code for 'shopping.' Heaven knows Pen could use some new finery."

Dashiel's gaze became considering. "How much luggage did she take?"

"Whole coach's worth. Took the porters hours to secure it all." A vast and strategic exaggeration.

"What of her personal effects? Is that chestnut mare of hers going up to Town?"

The slightest, most welcome breeze stirred through the room.

"Do you suppose me capable of talking to animals? As far as I know, the mare has no engagements in Mayfair. Best go easy on the punch, Sir Dashiel. I've been meaning to ask you, where did you come by that exquisite brandy you served me the other day? I would like to get my hands on at least a case. Excellent potation."

Mrs. de Plessis had taken to slapping her closed fan against her palm. The gesture translated easily enough.

"I came by that brandy at great risk to my person, and you will never find its like again. Please make my excuses to the committee. I fear I'm developing a megrim myself."

"You don't look ill, and you haven't danced a single set."

Dashiel took a gulp from his glass. "You prancing nitwit, Lady Penelope has taken her entire stock of clothing and jewelry, but left that flashy horse behind. What does that tell you?"

"That she'll use a lady's mount from the Lynnfield House stable in Town."

Dashiel set aside the dregs of his drink. "No, my lord. She's not *staying* in Town. She's going up to Town, which also happens to be a busy port and a fine place to confer with one's bankers. She's trying to bolt on me. Bridal nerves are the very devil. Fortunately for me, you've put me wise to her scheme, and I can intervene before Penelope does something she'll regret very, very much."

"Bankers? Her ladyship keeps them on a short leash, always writing back and forth to them. She might be meeting with the lawyers, though."

"Whyever would she do that?"

Lucien glanced around—Mrs. de Plessis had positioned herself near the only exit—and leaned closer. "A gentleman doesn't cry off."

"What are you going on about now?"

"A gentleman," Lucien said, emphasizing each syllable, "does not cry off. The lady does that part. That's how it's done, if an engagement is to be broken. To break ours, her ladyship would have to meet with the lawyers and sign papers before discreet witnesses and whatnot. The lawyers are in London, unless I summon them to Lynnfield.

Then they are underfoot, eyeing the silver and eating like
stevedores."

Don't overplay the role. Penelope's voice echoed sternly in
Lucien's head. *Dashiel is desperate but not a fool.*

"I can believe her ladyship is terminating her dealings with you,"
Dashiel said slowly. "You might have guessed that part correctly."

"I think Mrs. de Plessis wants you to dance with her."

"To blazes with Mrs. de Plessis."

"I thought you were concerned about her missing watch? Ready
to seize Aunt Purdy in the king's name and bind her over like a
common crook, despite a lack of witnesses or a confession? Isn't the
new fashion innocent until proven guilty?"

"I am not a barrister, my lord, but I suspect Mrs. de Plessis seeks
to dance with you."

The sets were forming, slowly and amid much chatter and laughter. The open windows dissipated some of the heat, and Danny
Smith was bowing awkwardly over Tabitha's hand. Lucien was struck
by how easily Penelope would have fit in. She would have seen the
windows opened a half hour earlier, would have danced with Danny
and convinced the lad she'd enjoyed every moment.

"Mrs. de Plessis doesn't look in a dancing mood to me," Lucien
said. The widow swiveled slowly from side to side, visually
canvassing the room and drawing her closed fan through a curled fist.

"When she does that with her fan," Dashiel said, taking another
gulp of punch, "it means 'please ask me to dance.'"

That particular gesture meant *I hate you.* "Does it really? How do
you keep all the social arcana straight? I suppose that's why you're
the magistrate. You have a good head for rules and regulations."

"So I do. Be a good fellow and stand up with dear Dommie, won't
you? And make my excuses to Tabitha, too, please. I won't be on hand
to see her off on Monday morning, but I expect our paths will cross in
Town."

"She needs you to see her off, Sir Dashiel. I well know how difficult leave-taking can be when loved ones aren't on hand to wish us farewell and safe journey."

"I'll see Tabby in London, I promise. Now put Mrs. de Plessis out of her misery. You're the marquess, and you're supposed to be charming."

"Where does it say that?"

"I just said it." He plucked Lucien's drink from his hand and set it on the nearest table. "Be off with you, or the music will start without you."

The line was forming the length of the room, heralding the ritual hilarity of the Roger de Coverley. Enough punch had been drunk that somebody was certain to end up on the floor, and crashing into one's neighbor was all part of the fun.

Only for you, Pen. As Lucien led his abruptly smiling partner to join the line, Sir Dashiel slipped out the door. He'd taken the bait, the elders were safe for now, and Lucien had a long ride to London ahead of him.

"My lord has such a lovely smile," Mrs. de Plessis observed as the fiddles began the introduction. "What can you possibly be thinking about?"

"A betrothal waltz with my intended. The notion has sustained me through many a dull and despairing hour." He bowed, she curtseyed, and the tune began in earnest.

"You could use a restorative," St. Didier said, passing the Marquess of Lynnfield a generous portion of brandy. "You must have quit Lynnfield directly after divine services." And traveled at a gallop on the Sabbath. Not the done thing, but then, Lord Lynnfield was not the typical peer.

"The brandy is appreciated. I could use a soft pillow on the seat of yonder wing chair too. I'm not the traveler I once was." Lynnfield waited for St. Didier to pour himself a drink before gesturing with his glass. "To your health."

St. Didier was not in the habit of taking spirits before supper, but by country hours, supper would already be on the table. He'd once delighted in country life.

"To happy endings," he said, sipping politely. "My cellar cannot possibly measure up to the vintage Sir Dashiel served you at the Roost, but I assure you that chair is much softer than any saddle. Shall we sit?"

The marquess took his seat with the economy of motion that had characterized him when he'd been in service to the Duke of Huntleigh. Quiet moved with him, along with the self-possession of a man who'd learned to be comfortable in his skin and cautious in nearly all settings.

How tiring, to be ever alert and always prepared.

"My thanks for your gracious hospitality to Lady Penelope," the marquess said. "What have you learned about Sir Dashiel's extraordinarily fine and undoubtedly expensive brandy?"

Straight to business—not the typical peer again. St. Didier took the second wing chair and mentally organized his report.

"We'll get to that part. You are more concerned with how her ladyship is settling in."

This earned St. Didier a faint, tired smile. "Lady Penelope has been in London for an entire day. By now, she will have put the fear of dust and idleness in the town house staff, started teaching the boot-boy his letters, revised and much improved Cook's menus, and collected every shred of useful gossip from St. George's churchyard."

"You miss her, and you've been separated for all of one night."

"I excel at missing her ladyship, and the sooner I conclude my business with you, the sooner I can clap eyes on her."

And hands and lips no doubt. Ah, youth. In the marquess's defense, at the sight of him, her ladyship would doubtless do some clapping of her own.

"Very well, my lord. To begin at the beginning. Sir Dashiel has

taken rooms at The Pelican, a modest inn on the fringes of Knightsbridge. Handy to Hyde Park and Mayfair, slightly out of the way.
Affordable rather than fashionable. He has not yet called at Lynnfield
House. I have notified a dozen of his largest creditors that he's
ventured into London. I further intimated that I would inform them
of his whereabouts when I'm certain of his direction."

"Thank you. I have little experience with traps and ambushes,
preferring a direct confrontation in most cases. That Dashiel is
accommodating this plan is both unnerving and reassuring."

St. Didier had little experience with peers expressing gratitude.
"Traps and ambushes are the baronet's preferred strategies. Your only
hope is to beat him at his own game. He doesn't fight fair. Just ask his
creditors and his sisters, all of whom he has apparently robbed. I've
recruited Moreland to assist you in catching your weasel, or I should
say, Moreland and his duchess."

"The Duke of Moreland? I don't know His Grace well, but we're
acquainted."

Did Lynnfield know any of his peers well? He'd perhaps rubbed
shoulders with some younger sons in uniform and was said to be well
thought of by Wellington, but did Lynnfield have friends? Did Lady
Penelope have friends?

St. Didier batted aside those questions as irrelevant to the present
report and irrelevant in the general case as well. Mostly irrelevant
anyhow.

"Moreland knew your father," St. Didier said, "and Her Grace of
Moreland is acquainted with the marchioness. The two ladies are not
of an age, but as the numbers thin, the old guard closes ranks."

"They think they failed Pen when she made her come out. They
didn't fail her, I did. She wasn't about to accept anybody else's offer of
marriage while engaged to me."

"Lady Penelope was *and is* bonnet over boots for your handsome
self, my lord. The whole business makes me feel old and sentimental." Old and weary. Perhaps there was another word for when the
heart felt hollow and creature comforts provided little solace.

"You are lonely," Lynnfield said. "You should find a wife. I was lonely for years because I'd parted from my best friend, confidante, fellow adventurer, and dearest love."

Good heavens, the man must be beyond exhausted to be spouting that kind of talk. "About Sir Dashiel... I will contrive to get word to him that Lady Penelope and the Lynnfield entourage are invited to Her Grace of Moreland's grand ball and intimate that he could get past the footmen by claiming to be a member of that party. The affair is legendary. Not particularly lavish, though the hospitality is impressive."

"Legendary, how?"

"If given a choice between divine absolution for all sins and an invitation to Her Grace's annual ball most of polite society would grab the invitation and take their chances with Saint Peter's good nature. Spectacular matches are made at that ball, fortunes expanded, futures secured." And more to the point, the evening was usually enjoyable.

"High-stakes gambling?"

"No, and don't get distracted. If Sir Dashiel's creditors have the bailiffs lying in wait on Tuesday night, they can catch him while half of Mayfair looks on." Half of London, really, because crowds always gathered at the Moreland ballroom windows to watch the spectacle within.

"You've been invited?"

"I have." And not because St. Didier had called in any favors. Her Grace invited whom she pleased, and when St. Didier was in Town, that included him.

"Have I been invited?"

"Of course. I am nothing if not thorough."

"Terrifyingly so." Lynnfield sipped his brandy, the clock ticked, and St. Didier waited for the next question.

"How exactly will you contrive to lure Sir Dashiel to the ball?"

"That part is simple. I'll run into Sir Dashiel in Knightsbridge. He's a few streets from Tatts, and he'll want to be seen there for bragging purposes. Please recall he's soon to be married to an earl's very wealthy daughter."

"Right. Of course. Remiss of me to suppose otherwise."

"I will let drop that Lady Penelope is starting off her London tour in style and add that one cannot refuse the Duchess of Moreland's invitations, which is true enough. The rest is so much more playacting. Pretending to spot a blackleg or tipstaff and suggesting they haunt Tatts, which they do. They never arrest anybody on that hallowed ground, but they follow their quarry to quieter surrounds and haul him off to the sponging house all the same."

"You give Sir Dashiel a reason for urgency. He'll have to secure a betrothal posthaste or quit London. Why shouldn't I simply have him hauled away from Tatts?"

St. Didier had to think for a moment. "Timing. The bailiffs and blacklegs are busy fellows, and waiting hours or days for Sir Dashiel to show up asks a lot of them."

"He owes a perishing fortune and a half."

True. St. Didier, privy to many a lord's financial situation, had been staggered to see the extent of the credit that had been extended to a mere baronet in the midst of a disastrous economy. But then, Lady Penelope's wealth was also formidable, and Dashiel had repeatedly intimated that her fortune was soon to become his.

"He owes so much," St. Didier said, "that even if he sells the Roost outright, he will likely die in debtors' prison. That will have consequences for his sister."

"Assuredly. Consequences I will mitigate, assuming all goes to plan, and as to that, Sir Dashiel might have the sense to avoid Tatts. What then?"

No wonder the marquess prevailed against most opponents on the chessboard. "Then, I will casually encounter him at The Pelican. They haven't the staff to bring meals up to the guest rooms, and even if they do, they know not to bring meals up to him."

Another smile, this one a bit more vigorous. "Well done, St. Didier. Remind me never to cross you."

"Stay in Lady Penelope's good books, and I will have no quarrel with you."

"I'm supposed to stand now, aren't I?" Lynnfield said, finishing his brandy. "One is daunted by the prospect. Hard riding is no longer in my gift as it once was." He rose nonetheless, and if his hips, ankles, and knees screamed in protest, his expression remained mild.

No wonder Wellington had appreciated the marquess's talents.

"Get some sleep," St. Didier said, rising and accompanying his guest to the parlor door. "Don't go off on any goose chases, and by Wednesday morning, life will look much rosier."

"Waiting does not agree with me. Drives my Pendragon half daft too. We're not a patient pair."

He called his intended Pen and Pendragon. "One does what one must, unless one is a scoundrel like Sir Dashiel."

They ambled down the corridor at a tired pace.

"About the brandy, St. Didier? What have you learned?"

This was another reason the Marquess of Lynnfield had been such a valuable resource to British intelligence. Even exhausted, preoccupied, and in love, he kept hold of the details.

"Interesting tale there. The vintage in that bottle, Château de la Forêt, is no longer made. Napoleon tried to protect France's wine-growing resources, but with limited success. Between the revolution, the reprisals, the aristocracy being hounded from their ancestral possessions and loyal retainers going with them, the French country-side took a beating even before the Grand Armée opened for business."

"All of Europe has been taking beatings for centuries. Please get to the point before I fall asleep on my feet."

So polite. "The main points are as follows: The winds of war were blowing, and the family who owned the la Forêt vineyard, having seen the same weather in many a previous generation, arranged to send their entire inventory into the safekeeping of a Spanish monastery dedicated to St. Agnes of the Goats, or some-thing. By dark of night and disguised as window glass and tent stakes, the brandy made the journey. The château itself eventually went up in flames, et cetera and so forth, and the decision was made to sell off the greater portion of this liquid treasure and bring the remainder home."

Lynnfield put on his top hat. "Allow me to conjecture. Bandits intervened, or Spanish monarchists, or a besieging English army, and the remaining brandy was thought lost, when, in fact, it was sold by the bandits who gave up their thieving ways and became monks in the order of St. Agnes. Though Agnes means lamb, not goat."

"Not quite." St. Didier passed over a pair of dusty spurs. "English forces gained control of the land on which the monastery sat. The monks, being thoroughly disenchanted with storing contraband spirits, arranged to smuggle the brandy out the cellar door and into French hands, where it rightfully belonged. Or perhaps somebody alerted the French to what treasure lay in the monastery cellars, and Boney's boys retrieved it. In any case, the brandy was spirited away. Shortly thereafter, reports sprang up of French soldiers using that brandy to barter with their English foes for bread."

Lynnfield wiped his spurs on his sleeve. "Ah."

He bent to put on a spur, paused, and steadied himself against the sideboard. In another five minutes, the marquess would be snoring genteelly on St. Didier's parquet floor.

"What does my lord mean with that 'ah'?"

"Sir Dashiel committed treason. As a member of the quartermaster's staff, he would have been among those sent to reconnoiter the monastery's stores, and he's enough of a snob to have known what the brandy was worth. He allowed the French to have most of it—doubtless in exchange for a fortune—knowing full well they'd use valuable spirits to supplement their meager rations. That's the treason part. He kept enough for himself to sell a bit off every spring when fashionable Society gathers in London. My dear auntie has probably been inveigled into smuggling his contraband up to Town for him."

"You can't prove any of that."

The marquess stashed his spurs into his jacket pocket. "I don't have to prove anything. Sir Dashiel was all but hurled from camp on short notice, though he was neither stripped of rank nor court-martialed. That tells me his senior officers had already discovered the brandy-for-bread scheme Dashiel put in motion. They knew and kept it quiet, lest morale or parliamentary support falter. Proof exists somewhere, and that's all that's necessary for my purposes."

"Why don't you look like a man whose suspicions have just been vindicated?"

"Because I am exhausted, and because I have the sense that I'm still not seeing the whole picture. I'm too busy examining snuffboxes."

Incoherence was a harbinger of collapse in the overly tired, though in Lynnfield's case, the same symptom apparently went hand in hand with brilliance.

"Take my coach, my lord. You're dead on your feet, and one doesn't like to think of a marquess fainting on the streets of London."

"Thank you, but the walk will revive me."

St. Didier respected Lynnfield's dignity almost as much as he respected Lady Penelope's temper.

"Must I knock you flat? If any harm befalls your lordship between my doorstep and Lynnfield House, Lady Penelope will take her wrath out on me, and understandably so. I will not survive the encounter with my self-respect intact. Ergo, you will take my coach."

His lordship blinked, he frowned, he scowled, and then he nodded. "Valid point. The oversight is mine. Your coach will be much appreciated."

Five minutes later, St. Didier bundled his guest into the cozy confines of the town coach. His lordship slumped against the squabs, and St. Didier would have bet his favorite spyglass that the marquess was asleep before the horses picked up the trot.

CHAPTER EIGHTEEN

Penelope was aware of the bed dipping as the scent of lavender wafted about her. *Lucien.*

"You're here," she said, opening her eyes to behold her beloved braced above her. His features were drawn, his hair damp and combed back, and he wore not a stitch. "Welcome home, Lucien. You caught me napping."

They weren't *home* home, of course—Lynnfield was home—but he'd come home *to her.*

"Lucky me." Lucien offered Penelope a soft, peppermint-flavored kiss on the lips. "St. Didier sends greetings. The rest of the family will be along in a few hours. I wanted you to myself for a time. I nearly took a nap in the bath."

The kissing recommenced, becoming exquisitely languorous. Then Lucien cuddled close, a warm and welcome blanket of much-missed lover. Penelope stroked his damp hair and gave silent thanks that he'd made the journey from Lynnfield safely.

She was trying to get a peek at the clock on the bedroom mantel—how long had she been asleep?—when it occurred to her that Lucien's breathing had become deep and even and his weight inert. As she rolled him to his back, he barely stirred.

"You poor, dear man." And despite his exhaustion, he'd bathed before coming to her. Penelope drew the covers up over him, tucked herself along his back, and schooled herself to patience.

The shadows in the room had lengthened considerably when Lucien stirred. He muttered something—agate, *agata*, perhaps a Spanish word?—and then he laced his fingers with Penelope's and kissed her knuckles.

"Guarding me while I dream of you, Pen?"

"Enjoying a snooze with you, my lord. You were up most of the night, I take it?"

"I had a long discussion with Uncle Malcolm, who condescended to scribble in a copybook lest I spend the evening playing charades with him. Very interesting discussion, too, given what Malcolm has observed on his rambles. I also had to finish Mrs. Burney's novel, lest you beat me to the end. Then too, I wrote out directions for Theo and the stewards, brought the ledgers up to date, and generally prepared for travel. I missed you."

He'd put his affairs in order, an exercise he was too familiar with for Penelope's comfort.

"And after an hour's nap, you're fighting fit again?" He'd had the same ability as a youth. Nod off for forty winks, then be immediately alert and ready for the next debate.

"Fighting fit, also loving fit, if my lady is so inclined."

Penelope eased her fingers free of his grip and went exploring. "You *were* dreaming of me."

He rolled to his back. "The reality is so much lovelier, but if you keep that up, the reality will be short-lived."

Short did not apply in any regard. *Lovely* surely did. "You are in my bed in broad daylight, Lucien. We are taking a risk."

"Shall I leave and come back at midnight?"

He'd do it, too, the wretch. "You shall not leave now, and you shall come back at midnight." Rather than allow him an opportunity for argument, Penelope straddled him and silenced him with kisses. He answered her in the language of caresses, sighs, and smiles, until Penelope was half mad with yearning.

"I missed you for so long, but, Lucien, had I known I was also missing this... The whole Continent would not have been large enough to hide you from my wrath."

He ceased his attentions to her breasts to brush a lock of hair back from her brow. "I've thought about that, about what if I hadn't gone, what if you had come with me, and it would have been wonderful, of course, but I would not have known the joy of our reunion, Pen. I would not have known that I could be useful to my country, in all my peculiarities and privileges. I would not have seen just how formidable you are when given room to manage life on your own terms. You found a good measure of happiness and purpose for yourself without any help from me, and for me to see that has been important."

Penelope's body hummed with longing, but her heart appreciated the words. "I needed you, Lucien. I need you, but you're also right. We grew, we changed, we are different and *more* for having weathered those years, but I never want to lose you again."

"Nor I you."

His determination was evident in his lovemaking, which progressed from leisurely and sweet to passionate and relentless, until Penelope gave up the debate and surrendered to pleasure. When he would have withdrawn, she wrapped her legs about his waist and stopped him.

"This time, you stay with me. Together, Lucien. Please."

He drew a fingertip along her lips. "You're sure? I have the special license, Pen."

"I'm sure, and I would be even without the special license."

Lucien was apparently sure, too, because he began all over again, building desire and delight to impossible heights, until Penelope could not resist the pleasure. To her amazement, pleasure shared with Lucien was truly pleasure multiplied. She floated in the warmth of his embrace, awash in contentment and wonder.

He remained above her, his weight on his forearms. "I should move. I've already fallen asleep on you once, and I have no excuse now save for complete, ecstatic satisfaction. Push me off of you for the sake of my pride."

Penelope hugged him. "Next time, I'll fall asleep on you."

He lifted his head. "Next time, Pen?"

"Oh, very well. We can take turns. The elders aren't due for hours, and I told the kitchen a cold collation would do for supper."

The moment called for lightness, for laughter and joy, but Lucien's expression sobered. "I have something to say to you."

Whatever he meant to say, he'd chosen a moment when Penelope could not busy herself inspecting a spotless mantel or adjusting the nearest curtain.

"Say it."

"I love you, Pen. Always have, always will."

Oh, Lucien. "I love you too. I tried to set my feelings aside, tried to distance myself, but it was no good. I prayed for your safety. I talked to you when you weren't there. I argued with you in absentia and seldom won. The love would not let me go."

"I hope it never does. I understand that now. The words are a gift, meant to be treasured. They can't promise anything, they don't come with conditions, but we get to keep them forever."

This had to do with his mama, assuring him of her love, then departing the earthly realm. "We have the words, and we have the love, and nothing can take that away."

They held each other for the space of three heartbeats, and then Penelope felt Lucien's mind catching at a thought.

"Do we even need the special license, Pen?"

"No, but the world needs us to use it at some point. Sooner would be better than later. I have plans for Tuesday evening, but other than that, my schedule is flexible."

He rolled, taking her with him. "As it happens, I have plans for

Tuesday evening too. Would it be too gauche of me to acquaint you with my latest discussion with St. Didier? I am not properly dressed, in case you hadn't noticed."

"You will not be properly dressed until I assist you into your clothing, and I have no plan to undertake that task in the immediate future. What did St. Didier have to say?"

"He's in love with you too, poor sod. Or at least fiercely loyal. I like that, for the most part. In any case, Sir Dashiel is in Town, we know his whereabouts, the creditors have been notified, and, Pen, there's more."

As they cuddled this way and that, he told her about what Uncle Malcolm had seen and noted in his journal, about the brandy, about colluding with the French and inveigling the marchioness into delivering stolen goods.

"Her ladyship probably did it as a favor the first time," Penelope said, "then learned she'd been duped into trafficking in dangerously rare contraband. Sir Dashiel doubtless threatened to pin the whole thing on her and perhaps even arrest her for it."

"In addition to arresting Purdy, charging Theo with habitual drunkenness, having Malcom declared insane... You'd think a man with that much imagination could make a going concern of his inherited acres."

"You'd think a man with that great a capacity for underhanded schemes would have had his lights put out," Penelope replied, stroking Lucien's back. They'd returned to the Lucien-superior position, and sunlight was fading to shadows. "I'm growing peckish. We'd best get dressed."

"Must we? Such interesting things happen when I'm naked with you, Pendragon."

Penelope smacked his muscular bum, then petted him. "Interesting, scrumptious things. Seeing Sir Dashiel hauled away to the sponging house will be interesting, too, also a bit sad for Tabby."

Lucien hoisted himself to the side, then climbed from the bed. "We will make sure Tabitha isn't a witness to that part. Perhaps I should throw my clothing out the window. You could hold me hostage then and make me pay a ransom in kisses."

Penelope bounced to the edge of the mattress and sat up, feeling slightly dizzy. "Love makes you whimsical."

He drew her to her feet and hauled her into his arms. "Love makes me happy, Pen. Scarify-ingly happy."

"And honest," she muttered, nose pressed to his chest. "I'm a tad unnerved too, Lucien. Perhaps that special license is for us too."

He rested his chin on her crown. "Agreed. I love you."

Penelope kissed his cheek. "I will somehow resign myself to hearing those words from you as often as you care to give them to me. I love you too."

Her tummy growled, which made them laugh, and soon Lucien was lowering her afternoon dress over her corset and shift, and Penelope was fastening his sleeve buttons into his cuffs.

"I cannot have my marchioness padding about barefoot when I have to clomp around in my riding boots," Lucien said, peering around the room. "Where are your slippers, Pen?"

"Under the bed. They're lined in lamb's wool, and I vow I dread the thought of ever wearing boots again. I forgot I'd left them here the last time I was in Town."

Lucien produced the requisite footwear and ran his thumb around the soft wool tufted inside. "*Lamb's* wool."

Penelope took the slippers from him. "A baby sheep is called a lamb in English. We use the term *oen* in Welsh. What are you staring at?"

"I thought of something as I was falling asleep the first time. *Lamb.* St. Didier mentioned a monastery, St. Agnes of the Goats, but he was off. The brandy was stored at a convent, not a monastery. St. Agata's. Humble establishment, been there for centuries. Rambling old place that doubtless has vast and venerable cellars."

Penelope set the slippers on the cedar chest at the foot of the bed. "Why does this matter, Lucien?" Because it did, his abruptly serious eyes told her that.

"We'll need to revise our plans for Tuesday night. Let's find some food, and I will explain."

Food appealed, but even as Penelope passed Lucien his boots and accompanied him down the footmen's stairs to the deserted kitchen, she knew that food had also been offered up as a distraction. Lucien was organizing his thoughts, deciding the best way to present to her what had to be bad, if not awful, news.

Lucien had seen ballrooms from Saint Petersburg to Salzburg to Salamanca, and each one was unique. The fashions varied, as did the music, the topics under discussion, and even the dances preferred, but they'd all been lacking in one vital regard: Lady Penelope Richard hadn't seen those ballrooms with him.

She ascended the curving steps of the Moreland mansion on Tuesday evening, looking quietly resplendent in a gown of imperial purple velvet, a discreet dusting of amethyst pins in her hair. She'd chosen a half-up, half-down coiffure, both demure and feminine. A single amethyst on a purple velvet choker adorned her throat, and white gloves covered her arms past the elbows.

A corsage at her wrist combined a single violet orchid, thistles, and gentian in a cluster of pinks, blues, and lavenders. Let Sir Dashiel make what he would of the corresponding sentiments—love, determination, and victory.

They passed through the reception line without incident, Moreland greeting them as the old lion he was—tall, white-haired, with snapping blue eyes. His duchess, a statuesque blonde of mature years, conveyed genuine warmth toward Penelope.

"Your ladyship must keep a close eye on Lord Lynnfield," the duchess said. "He is not well acquainted with Mayfair's formal entertainments. Perhaps we'll remedy that oversight with your ladyship's assistance."

A scold, but also a welcome. Lucien replied in the requisite platitudes, and the line moved on.

"We start with punch," Penelope murmured when the herald had
announced them. "I thought that line would never move."

"Sir Dashiel will wait until there's no formal receiving line to get
past," Lucien murmured as Penelope steered him to a side of a ballroom illuminated by blazing chandeliers and graced with the soft
strains of one of Herr Beethoven's piano sonatas.

"Lord Valentine is playing," Penelope said, cocking her head.
"He's wonderfully gifted, but limits his public playing. Sad music for
a ball, though."

Lucien would have called it peaceful music, intended to blend
into spoken conversations rather than do battle with exchanges
shouted amidst a crush.

"The violins will commence soon enough, and I would dearly
love to dance with you."

They were spared having to wait in line at the punchbowl by a
footman who offered them glasses of champagne. That was Moreland's doing, no doubt, or his duchess's. Lucien would avoid any
activity that kept him and Penelope pinned in a single location. They
would not sit at the card tables, would not occupy a bench in the
torchlit garden.

A moving target was harder to strike, and if Sir Dashiel had to
track them down, then he made a target of himself while he was in
pursuit.

St. Didier, by contrast, had been in earnest conversation by the
door to the cardroom with an older lady, whose plumed headdress
nodded slowly in time with Lord Valentine's adagio.

"Would my lady care to dance?" a tall, chestnut-haired
gentleman asked—without benefit of an introduction.

"Westhaven, a pleasure." Penelope curtseyed, her smile radiant.
"Doing the pretty for a change? Lynnfield, may I make known to you,
Gayle, Earl of Westhaven. Westhaven, this handsome devil is my
dearest friend Lucien, Marquess of Lynnfield. Westhaven rescued

me from more than one fortune hunter, and I returned the favor where the diamonds and originals were concerned."

Pen had *conspired* with the earl to foil Society's machinations. As Lucien bowed, resentment flared, followed by grudging gratitude. Westhaven was Moreland's heir and would have been a suitable match for Penelope, and yet, he'd kept his handsome paws off of her and her money.

"Westhaven, my thanks for sparing her ladyship from tedium. Who guards you from the diamonds and originals now?"

"My countess." The earl's smile revealed a resemblance to his ducal father. "She guards me very, very well." For all his dignity, Moreland's heir had clearly made a love match. "I understand we might have an interlude of unscheduled entertainment later in the evening, courtesy of some mischievous baronet. Be assured that Their Graces will have all in hand and are likely looking forward to the excitement. If you will excuse me, somebody needs to tell Lord Valentine to cease his dirges and give us livelier music. A pleasure to see you, my lady, and to make your acquaintance, my lord. Mind the punch. Her Grace's recipe has ambushed bishops, and their heads are notably hard."

He glided off in the direction of the piano, a duke-in-training who was also, despite his reserved demeanor, a happy man.

"I thought he'd never surrender," Penelope said, "and one hears all sorts of stories about how he and his countess met, but no man will put the earl and his lady asunder, of that I'm certain. Try the punch."

Lucien complied. "Go carefully. Slowly and carefully."

They were still going slowly and carefully, fielding a few conversation sallies from the bolder beldames when Lucien spotted Moreland in conference with his duchess by an enormous spray of delphiniums. Her Grace's cordial expression never faltered as she leaned nearer her duke. She nodded, he patted her arm, and they parted like a pair of spies pretending they'd been discussing when to bring the coach around rather than how to move a herd of mules across an armed border.

"The baronet has arrived," Lucien said as a pair of footmen heeded some invisible signal given by the duchess and made straight for Lucien and Penelope. "Blighter broke every rule of polite behavior and crashed a duchess's gate."

"I forget which of the elders told me the high sticklers bear the closest scrutiny because they are usually dealing off the bottom of some deck or—he's at the top of the steps, Lucien, and trying to look nonchalant."

Sir Dashiel was largely succeeding. He'd turned himself out in regulation evening attire, complete with a red carnation boutonniere. He surveyed the ballroom as if looking for familiar faces while giving the entire assemblage a moment to behold him.

"I want to knock him arse over dancing slippers down those stairs, Lucien."

"We agreed to eschew violence, your dragon-ship."

Penelope set her half-empty glass of punch on a passing footman's tray. "You agreed. I made no such promise. Purdy is cowering behind a locked door, scared to death because of that man. The marchioness has been under his thumb for years at least."

The marchioness was doing a magnificent job of shepherding Tabitha about, and at present, Tabby was twirling down the room with a viscount's heir, bedazzling half the lordlings and spares who saw her.

"Let's greet him," Lucien said, "before Tabby sees him, before he can choose how to create a scene."

"I want to create a scene. A nasty scene, but I won't. He's coming down the steps."

"And trying to ignore us. Too bad for the baronet." Lucien offered Penelope his arm, and nearly had to trot to keep up with her progress among the other guests at the side of the ballroom.

They were met at the foot of the grand staircase by Sir Dashiel and no less person than Percival, His Grace of Moreland.

"Lady Penelope." Sir Dashiel bowed. "A pleasure. Lynnfield, a surprise. I have a few things to say to you, my lord, my lady, the first being that I come bearing a warrant for the arrest of one Calpurnia Richard on charges of felony theft."

Moreland, looking quite severe and a bit like his heir, pretended to examine the red gem winking from the folds of Sir Dashiel's cravat.

"See here, sir. You have trespassed on private property to violate the hospitality of this house. I don't care if you have a warrant for the arrest of the sovereign, you are not making a spectacle in front of my duchess's guests. To my study, you lot, now."

Former military. Lucien knew the tone, and so, apparently, did Sir Dashiel.

"My warrant is valid," Sir Dashiel retorted, but he got moving before the two enormous blond footmen could hasten him along.

"Would my lady prefer to remain in the ballroom?" Moreland asked.

"Not on Your Grace's life," Penelope muttered, charging after Sir Dashiel.

Lucien fell in behind Penelope, the duke at his side.

"Puts me in mind of Her Grace," the duke murmured. "Splendid marchioness you have there, Lynnfield."

The old matchmaking rogue. "So I do, and she has me."

One of the footmen opened the door to an opulently comfortable study sort of room. Laughter from the terrace below floated up through an open balcony door, and portraits of handsome young people—lordlings and ladies—adorned the walls. A painting of Her Grace as a younger woman with several children about her held pride of place over the mantel, and a massive carved oak desk sat before an equally splendid hearth.

A bouquet of pink roses on a table by the windows added a graceful touch, though the room was coolish.

Moreland motioned to the second footman, who closed the balcony door, a prudent measure.

"You, sir," Moreland snapped, "spouting off about warrants in the middle of a polite, private entertainment, introduce yourself."

"Sir Dashiel Ingraham, late of the Raven's Roost, and I am on the king's business."

"On the king's business, are you? Well, you will be in my duchess's bad books if you think to cause any mischief this evening. A fate to be avoided, regardless of which king you claim you're serving. I will leave you to state your business to Lynnfield and Lady Penelope, but bear in mind that those two handsome louts in livery, upon whom my duchess dotes shamelessly, will be just outside the door. They have orders to quell any untoward disturbances. Lady Penelope, I bid you good evening."

"Your Grace will not support the king's man in the course of a lawful investigation?" Sir Dashiel asked as the duke turned to leave.

Of course Dashiel would want witnesses to his grand finale, and a duke was more than a witness. A duke was an arbiter of truth. If Moreland examined the warrant and found it valid, all of Society would find it so as well.

"Are you daft?" Moreland replied. "Half the peerage is about to be knocked on its collective fundament by Her Grace's punch. The other half will find itself engaged to be married before the good-night waltz if I tarry here. Besides that, my duchess has promised me a dance, despite all convention to the contrary. I'll send Westhaven to handle bets and referee the match, but my money is on Lady Penelope."

"Perhaps Your Grace might also send us St. Didier?" Penelope asked.

The duke bowed with exaggerated graciousness. "Of course, my lady. Shall I tell the Regent to step 'round as well? He makes a predictable appearance at midnight, in the tradition of all legendary curses, just as the buffet is put out. Perhaps you'd like me to flag down some strolling players while I'm wandering aimlessly about? You'll have Westhaven and St. Didier, but more than that will attract notice, and that we cannot have."

"Your Grace is not interested in seeing justice served?" Sir Dashiel said as the duke made another try for the door.

Moreland turned, and while a hint of humor had laced his earlier asperity, he was every inch the autocrat now.

"Cease your importuning. If it's justice you're after, then I trust Lynnfield to see to the matter. Wellington trusted him too. Still does. You'd do well to recall that. The sort of justice that does not rely on paste rubies for its cravat pin and mendacious warrants that threaten harmless, aging spinsters."

On that telling shot, Moreland took his leave. Westhaven strolled in, took a seat on a pink tufted Queen Anne chair, and consulted his pocket watch. St. Didier followed, and the footmen decamped, closing the door silently in their wake.

"Before these witnesses," Sir Dashiel said, "I inform you, Lady Penelope Richard, and you, Lord Lynnfield, that I have a warrant for the arrest of one Calpurnia Richard, late of Lynnfield Hall. She is suspected of having committed felony theft of a gold pocket watch inscribed to Mr. Roland de Plessis on the occasion of his twenty-first birthday. Anybody harboring said Calpurnia Richard will be considered to have interfered with a lawful investigation and be charged with abetting a known felon."

"You're wrong on the law," Lucien said, strolling across the study to the sideboard. "I could accuse anybody—even you, Sir Dashiel, of stealing a watch, and that does not make me a convicted criminal, much less a known felon." He managed to pass close enough to Sir Dashiel that he could have picked the man's pocket, had he chosen to.

Which, of course, he had not, despite the temptation to lift the warrant from Sir Dashiel's person and destroy it in the nearest fire.

"I am not wrong about Calpurnia's suspected activities," Sir Dashiel retorted. "Your best course, my lord, my lady, is to turn her over to me. I will see her held in reasonable comfort until she can be bound over for the assizes."

"At which time," Lucien said, "you will commend her to the keeping of some corrupt jailer until the quarter sessions. Not very gentlemanly, Sir Dashiel. Would anybody else care for a drink? Lady

Penelope, I know strong spirits are not a lady's typical preference, but we find ourselves in an unusual and vexing situation."

"A medicinal restorative would be appreciated," Pen said.

"Sir Dashiel, Westhaven, St. Didier?"

Only Penelope joined Lucien in sampling Moreland's brandy. The vintage was excellent, but not on par with Sir Dashiel's stolen goods. This was fortunate, because one should not waste good brandy, and the look in Penelope's eye said that her serving was shortly to be tossed in Sir Dashiel's handsome face.

Which was the least he deserved.

St. Didier lurked by the window. Westhaven was ever so casually guarding the door on his pink-tufted throne.

"My lady," Lucien said, "you have the floor."

CHAPTER NINETEEN

"Firstly," Penelope said, marshaling logic, as she had for a thousand debates with Lucien, "I would not marry you, Dashiel Ingraham, if you were the sole legitimate heir to the crown, handsome, mannerly, and awash in wealth. Get that through your head. You have done me no honor whatsoever, and you will never get your hands on me or my money."

Dashiel produced a folded piece of paper from a breast pocket. "Be that as it may, my lady, I am yet responsible for—"

"I am not finished." Penelope spoke quietly, lest the footmen take a notion to join them long before she required their services. "Never interrupt a lady, especially when she's seeing justice done. If Purdy had taken the watch—*if*—then she would have done so solely because Dommie de Plessis left it out as a temptation. Dommie clearly sought an excuse to call on you at an unfashionable hour."

"Then you admit that your aunt stole the watch," Dashiel said, rolling up the warrant and brandishing it like some scepter of office. "You admit that you and your pet peer are abetting—"

"I admit that you are tiresome in the extreme, Dashiel, and nothing more. Turn out your pockets." Penelope's temper, which had been rumbling like an approaching storm, found expression in a complete lack of inflection.

"Turn out my pockets? Who are you to tell me what to do? If you think for one minute..."

St. Didier moved away from the window. Westhaven rose. Lucien gently set his drink on the mantel and plucked the warrant from Sir Dashiel's grasp.

"One does not argue with a lady," Lucien said. "Rather, a gentleman does not."

Sir Dashiel patted his pockets, went still, and then produced a gold watch. "I have no idea how that thing came to be in my possession."

Penelope knew exactly how that had come about, because it had been her idea. Amazing, the ingenuity one was capable of when sharing a kitchen picnic with the right inspiration.

"Open it," Lucien said. "Please."

When Sir Dashiel merely stared at him mutinously, St. Didier took the watch and flipped it open. "'To Roland de Plessis, from your loving father.' In possession of stolen goods, Sir Dashiel? Naughty, naughty, or perhaps a bad habit."

"I have never seen this watch before in my life." Dashiel regarded the watch on the desk as if it might bite him.

Penelope had the sense that the men in the room—the gentlemen—were enjoying themselves, despite their severe expressions. She was not precisely enjoying herself, but she was gratified to be holding Dashiel accountable. Very gratified.

"You have seen that watch on Dommie de Plessis's escritoire," Penelope said. "Lying will not serve you, and I care not one stale biscuit about the watch." Behind her, she heard the sound of paper being torn several times over.

"Lynnfield, when you tear up that warrant, you are interfering with the king's man in the pursuit of a lawful—"

"Tell us about the brandy," Penelope said as patiently as she could. "The exquisitely valuable brandy you stole in Spain, after you notified the French that you'd be willing to see the larger portion of it turned over to them in exchange for coin."

"I know nothing about any brandy." Dashiel's indignation would have been convincing, but for a flush nearly the color of his fake ruby rising over his countenance. "Nothing whatsoever."

"That's odd," Lucien murmured, dumping the torn-up bits of paper into the dustbin and taking the place on Penelope's right. "Malcolm clearly recalls the cases being unloaded at the Roost upon your return from Spain. Wellington had very, very strict orders regarding plundering, Sir Dashiel. Lethally strict. That brandy was in the possession of *nuns*."

"You stole from nuns?" St. Didier murmured. "One does not see you enjoying eternity in good company, Sir Dashiel."

"There was a war on," the baronet retorted, and never had he looked more contemptible to Penelope. "I was responsible for requisitioning that brandy, and my detail was ambushed by French snipers. Resistance would have cost lives pointlessly."

Lucien's posture subtly changed. "You bleating idiot, Lieutenant Lord Carweneth was scouting the area for potential bivouacs, and the French soldiers *you* had summoned behind British lines all but wiped out his patrol. They most assuredly put young Henry in his grave and his earldom with him."

Lucien had explained that part to Penelope, and she had cried and raged and cursed, but hearing the words again, with Henry's malefactor in the room, made her sick with grief.

"I didn't..." Sir Dashiel looked from Westhaven to St. Didier, anywhere but at Penelope. "I had no idea, none whatsoever, that any forces other than my quartermaster's escort were in that quadrant. The region was deserted, nothing but those old women and their skinny mules, and that..."

"You came home," Penelope said, "after having put into the enemy's hands the means to barter for their rations, and you commenced courting me. You *knew*, Dashiel. You knew that your actions had precipitated Henry's death, or you suspected strongly enough that you wanted to ensure I could never go looking for details or asking inconvenient questions. You wanted my fortune, but you needed to ensure my silence."

"I *did not* know for a certainty, but as a fellow soldier and Henry's lifelong friend, I suspected the French had disobeyed their orders. I thought, *as a gentleman*, that I owed you the protection of my—"

Penelope turned away lest she wallop him. "Shut your lying, whining mouth."

Sir Dashiel showed the instinct for self-preservation common to all furtive, slithering creatures and fell silent.

"Treason is a hanging felony," St. Didier observed. "As I understand the posture of the various warring factions at the time in question, the French would have been mad to retrieve that brandy unless some traitor to the crown had explained to them exactly when the lot was to be moved and assured Boney's men safe passage to that location."

"We needn't bother with treason." Lucien eyed Sir Dashiel as he would have regarded a dog's breakfast on the Axminster carpet. "Sir Dashiel traded in contraband and used the unsuspecting offices of a peer's widow to distribute the goods. He has taken bribes while serving as magistrate. He assaulted an old man, a neighbor of notably peaceful demeanor, on several occasions, beating the fellow mercilessly with his riding crop."

Dashiel stared at him. "I assaulted nobody."

The denials were as dishonest as they were tiresome.

"You assault my sense of decency just by drawing breath," Penelope said. "Malcolm is mute, also quite literate. He explained in a sworn affidavit that you accosted him when he was out walking alone, no weapons on his person, and you were on horseback. The last time it happened, some small boys climbing trees nearby saw the whole thing, but Malcolm asked them not to take you to task, lest *you* end up paying with your life. You repeatedly and viciously attacked a neighbor, hoping he would retaliate so you could claim that neighbor was a violent menace. If anybody's behavior shows inchoate madness, Sir Dashiel, yours does."

Though *arrogance* was the more accurate diagnosis, arrogance and the confidence of a petty despot.

Sir Dashiel smiled, all charm and innocence, and put period to any remaining shred of pity Penelope might have had for him.

"Very well, my lady, hang me. I've committed some bad acts, or so you claim, but you cannot prove any of it. Nobody will take the word of that old man when he can't even speak. Small boys lie all the time, and the war is over."

Penelope took one instant to consider her actions, and in that instant, she assayed the state of the three men in the room on hand to keep Sir Dashiel from leaping out the window. What she sensed from Lucien, St. Didier, and even Westhaven was a need for justice above all else.

"*I* speak for Malcolm," she said, "and for Purdy, Theo, the marchioness, outraged children, the sisters you stole from, and my brother gone too soon to his reward. *I* speak for them, and I say this..."

She drew back her hand in the expected preparatory maneuver, then let fly with her foot, striking Dashiel between the legs. Such a shame she hadn't worn hobnailed boots to the ball.

Dashiel dropped like a marionette whose strings had been cut and lay gasping and writhing on his side.

"Couldn't have said it better myself," St. Didier said. "But what's do be done with him?"

"He should be whipped at the cart's tail, pilloried, and hanged," Westhaven said coldly. "My brother Bartholomew *died* in that war, and St. Just is haunted by unspeakable memories. For all too many, the fighting will never be over."

"He cannot hang," Penelope said as Sir Dashiel's moans quieted to whimpers. "Tabitha's life would be ruined by the scandal."

"Banishment," Lucien said with cheerful malice. "Ingraham will grasp at that offer, thinking to live a life of ease in sunny climes, but banishment isn't like that at all. Banishment eats at the soul and the reason. Thoughts of home become an obsession, and all of life is a purgatory. To be cut off from the connections that nourished us in youth and sustain us in later life... Sunny climes are notorious for fleas and biting flies. Banishment might well suffice."

"Sir Dashiel's real property can be sold to cover his debts," West-haven observed, "which I understand are sufficient to land him in Marshalsea for the rest of his miserable life should he return to Albion's shores. His creditors deserve recompense for their patience."

Sir Dashiel struggled to sit, propping his back against the huge carved desk.

"Sell the Roost, then," Penelope said, "but keep the largest tenant holding as Tabitha's dower property, held in trust for her to dispose of as she pleases. She and Tommie deserve a decent start in life."

St. Didier regarded the slumped heap of baronet sniffling on the floor. "Banishment then, and we will wish him rough seas and sour rum on the way."

Westhaven shot his cuffs. "Let the footmen see him to the docks. They deserve their little diversions, and Martin and Jones are quite the pugilists. I'll be in the cardroom should your ladyship have further need of me."

He clasped Lucien on the shoulder in a gesture that put Penelope in mind of Uncle Malcolm, bowed graciously over Penelope's hand, nodded to St. Didier, and spared Dashiel not so much as a disgusted glance.

"I'd put him on the leakiest vessel you can find," Westhaven said. "My thanks for an interesting diversion. Mind the punch and have a pleasant evening." He sauntered out, and Penelope silently saluted an exquisitely choreographed exit.

"I will specifically inquire into seaworthiness when I'm about my next errand," St. Didier said, "and don't worry. I'll see Sir Disgraceful equipped with enough of the ready and some decent clothing. He will survive to suffer for some time yet. Come along, Ingraham, or shall I have those two liveried pugilists carry you?"

Neither Lucien nor St. Didier made any move to help the

baronet rise. He got to his hands and knees and then, leaning heavily on the desk, struggled to his feet.

"Don't even look at my marchioness," Lucien said. "We'll tell Tabitha where to write to you, if she's so inclined. Begone."

Dashiel shuffled toward the door, the two footmen flanking him from his first step into the corridor.

"I bid you both good evening," St. Didier said, sounding as close to jaunty as Penelope had ever heard him. "You will let Their Graces make the announcement?"

"After the supper waltz," Penelope said. "Thank you, Leopold, and you must come visit us at Lynnfield whenever you need some fresh air and good company."

Lucien wrapped an arm around Penelope's waist. "We mean it. You have good friends at Lynnfield whether you want them or not, but I suspect you do want them, being the prudent sort."

St. Didier, looking bashful and pleased, bowed. "I will make a full report once you return from your wedding journey."

He marched off before Penelope could threaten him with a hug and closed the door in his wake.

"Not here," Penelope said. "Not in this room, where that walking pile of offal tried to excuse the next thing to murder along with treason, malfeasance, extortion, bribery... I know why Malcolm never raised a hand to him."

She headed out the door and turned back in the direction of the ballroom.

"Because Malcolm would have done him lethal injury," Lucien said, "then buried the body in some forgotten ravine where nobody would ever find it, but Malcolm was too honorable for that. Where are we going?"

"The nearest alcove, because I need your arms around me, sir. I have never been so angry, and now I am so relieved. To think of all whom that miserable varlet threatened, and he nearly got away with it." She would ponder how close Sir Dashiel had come to succeeding in his varied schemes on another, braver, calmer day.

Penelope found an alcove lit by only one sconce and without occupants, unless a bust of some philosopher qualified.

"I'm so glad we used that special license." She slipped her arms around Lucien's waist and tucked in close.

He held her in a secure, warm hug, a *husbandly* hug. "I am too. St. Didier made a wonderful witness, Tommie and Tabitha were charming, and Phoebe and Wren will dine out on the memory for years. Discreet and romantic, they said."

"And our wedding breakfast a stop at Gunter's. Perhaps we should suggest that to Tabitha and Tommie."

Penelope was chattering, and for no reason. Her temper had calmed, her battle nerves were settling, but just for good measure, she kissed her marquess, and for reasons best known to him and grateful husbands the world over, he kissed her back just as fervently.

The wedding journey would take them to Wales. Lucien had already sorted that much out with his new bride. They'd have two weeks to themselves and then be joined by the elders and Tommie and Tabitha, if they weren't on their own wedding journey. Malcolm might even be inspired to speak, if he could once again be surrounded by the music of his native tongue.

Much remained to be done first, starting with a wedding announcement at some point in the next hour. First, though, Lucien needed to kiss his bride.

Penelope seized the initiative and treated him to a drubbing worthy of their wedding night. "I was so worried," she said. "What if Dashiel had had a warrant for my arrest or yours? What if he'd managed to pay off his debts with the last of the brandy? What if the marchioness hadn't been willing to explain her part in the whole business?"

Her part had been minor, thank heavens. She'd overseen the transport of the first round of cases as a favor to a neighbor, and only then had Dashiel told her that she'd trafficked in contraband. His innuendos had been subtle and hardly threatening at all—at first.

"The dowager marchioness," Lucien said, hugging Penelope a little tighter. "How do you like being Lady Lynnfield?"

Penelope eased back. "Some of it I like quite well. Particularly the parts that involve privacy and imagination. I wish we could go home, Lucien, just slip away right now."

"Comfort yourself with the knowledge that Dashiel will wish he could go home, too, wish he could simply ride by the Roost and lay eyes on the manor house's front door, but even that comfort will be denied him. The ache gets worse with each season, and every time he hears somebody speaking with a Kentish accent, every Yuletide when he can't find a good plum pudding for love nor money, he will die a little more."

Penelope straightened. "He will face exactly what you and I and all the elders faced when we were plucked up from Wales, and he will have a lot more in the way of education and experience than we did, but we had each other. We all had each other, and what a difference that made. Dashiel will have nobody. For Tabitha's sake, I hope he grows up."

Interesting way to put it, and apt. "Your knack for accurate insights is showing again. Are you ready to face the madding crowd?"

"I'm ready to face polite society, provided you are with me through the ordeal."

Lucien kissed her again, for luck and courage. "Through every ordeal. I do believe that's the supper waltz tuning up, and I beg the favor of a dance with my new wife."

Penelope granted him that favor, and Lucien stood beside her through His Grace of Moreland's long-winded and slightly ribald announcement of their nuptials.

He sat and rode beside her on lovely and leisurely journeys to Wales and back and kept her company through all of her lying-ins. St. Didier was honored to stand as godfather to their firstborn—a redheaded girl who quieted best when her papa sang to her—and every child of the union was blessed with robust good health, a full complement of brains, and an abundance of both curiosity and logic.

That St. Didier was to eventually encounter the full-grown version of a lady of keen wits and independent spirit might explain why he was such a devoted godpapa, though that is a tale for another time!

Printed in Great Britain
by Amazon

55587179R00149